To Love Free

Companion Publications

A COMPANION PUBLICATIONS BOOK

To my Little Phyllis Valentine… I love you with every fiber of my being.

And in memory of those we lost to cancer—my father, Morris, my Aunt Sadie, our cousins, Marina and Anthony, and our dear friend, Barbara "Tutu" Bennett. You will forever live on in our hearts.

**ALSO WRITTEN BY CHRIS PAYNTER AND
AVAILABLE NOW FROM COMPANION
PUBLICATIONS:**

Playing for First

Come Back to Me

Two for the Show (Book 2 in the *Playing for First* series)

Survived by Her Longtime Companion

And a Time to Dance

COMING SPRING 2015:

From Third to Home (Book 3 in the *Playing for First* series)

To Love Free

Companion Publications

A COMPANION PUBLICATIONS BOOK

by
Chris Paynter

To Love Free

Copyright © 2014 by Chris Paynter

Cover design by Chris Paynter and Ann Phillips
Editor: Julie Harthill Clayton
Line Editor: Nann Dunne

Published by Companion Publications

www.ckpaynter.com

ISBN: 978-1-942204-00-8

First edition: September, 2014

Printed in the United States of America and in the United Kingdom.

Acknowledgements

I began my career as a published author with Blue Feather Books in 2009. In each acknowledgements page of every book I published with Blue Feather, I thanked Emily Reed and Jane Vollbrecht for having faith in me as a writer—enough faith to publish five of my novels. Em, you are a blessing in my life. As you said to me, we will always keep in contact. Thank you for all you've done for me in my writing career and for being such a supportive friend.

Jane, I can't thank you enough for your guidance and mentorship in polishing my writing skills. You're with me with each book I write. "Jane would smack me for that" is a thought that frequently pops into my head when writing my first drafts. So thank you. More importantly, thank you, too, for being such a dear, dear friend.

Em and Jane, I can only hope to be as successful as you were in running such an outstanding publishing house for nine years. Although Blue Feather closed its doors, it lives on through each of your authors.

Thank you to my editor, Julie Harthill Clayton, for your invaluable suggestions and advice in making *To Love Free* a better book than it was when I first sent it to you. I look forward to working with you on future books. Thank *again* to the best damn line editor in the business, Nann Dunne. As I always do with each acknowledgement, I forgive you for being a Philadelphia Phillies fan… I guess.

A huge thank-you to my indie author friends who helped me navigate the self-publishing waters for my first book as an indie author—R. E. Bradshaw, Cindy Rizzo, Amy Dawson Robinson, Clare "Tig" Ashton, Caren J. Werlinger, and Lori L. Lake. Not only are you amazing authors whose work I greatly admire, you're selfless enough to help a newbie learn the ropes. Thank you, Patty Schramm, for your patience in answering my questions, not just about the typesetting of my book, but about the publishing business and how things work. You're a true friend. And a big thank-you to Toni Whitaker, e-book formatter extraordinaire. You're the best!

A special thank-you to Mary Buchanan who bid in the Golden Crown Literary Society character auction on the right to name a character in my next book. Well, *To Love Free* is the book! I didn't see Madison Lorraine's sister, Cyndra, having such a significant role in the story. But her personality couldn't be tamed. I hope I did the name justice, Mary.

Meli Lussier, thank you for allowing me to borrow the name of your daughter, Montanna ("Mo"). Every word that I wrote about the character Mo was infused with the spirit of your beautiful daughter. Thank you, too, for being such a good friend—especially during the months of Phyllis's cancer treatment. Your mom will always be with you, Meli. Remember that with each sighting of your dolphin.

As always, I save the best for last. Thank you to my heartbeat, the love of my life, my wife, Phyllis Manfredi. Phyllis, we lived this book. It was a difficult journey, but we walked together every step of the way. When we stumbled, we helped each other to our feet and marched on to each trip to the infusion center and each drive to your twenty-five radiation treatments. We even managed some laughs during those long hours of chemotherapy. I'll never forget you serenading everyone with Jefferson Airplane's "White Rabbit." You are my hero and you always will be. I love you, sweetheart.

Cancer sucks. Plain and simple. In the course of two years, Phyllis and I lost my father, my aunt, two cousins, and a dear friend to the disease. But even when facing death, all of our loved ones did so with humor and with a quiet resolve. Their courage was, and still is, an inspiration. Phyllis's courage in trudging through six months of difficult treatment will be ingrained in my heart and mind for the rest of my life.

The idea for *To Love Free* came to me as Phyllis was undergoing chemotherapy in 2012. I had started writing *From*

Third to Home and got about 25,000 words into it when I stopped. Then I started writing my last release, *And a Time to Dance*, and wrote 45,000 words before stopping and writing 25,000 words of this book. I went back to *And a Time to Dance* and released the book in June 2013. When my father died in April 2013, I struggled with my writing for months. My hiatus from the craft matches Madison Lorraine's hiatus from painting in this story. Eventually, after my heart began to heal, I was able to finish *To Love Free*.

Yes, this story is about cancer. But at its heart, *To Love Free* is about the human spirit's ability to push through the darkness of despair and reach the sunshine that awaits us on the other side. Sometimes, though, it helps if you have a good friend—or dolphin—to guide you along the way.

Prologue

Cool. He sliced through the cool water and swam up, up, up. Up to the light above. Up with his brethren beside him. Up until the rush of air hit his nose. Then back down, the water a calming sting against his skin.

Never a destination. Or so it seemed. They followed the One, wherever she led them. Today, they drew nearer to the shore. He had ventured this close before, always curious about the creatures there. He and his brethren had encountered these same creatures in their search for fish in the great deep they called home.

He sensed today was different. He felt it in his body with each leap out of the water. His skin tingled with anticipation.

Suddenly, the One veered back and circled him, emitting a series of clicks and whistles. She tossed her head toward the shore. Was it time to discover his Quest? He was younger than the others. He knew this because when he entered the world, the others were there, present from his day of birth. He was among the last to await the One's call. None of them knew when their time would come, only that she would summon them for a greater purpose.

She circled him once, twice, and darted even closer to the shore. He followed until she swam up to the surface. She didn't leap. She remained stationary, waiting for him to join her. They had arrived at a cove, not visible unless you swam this near. The One chattered at him and flipped her nose toward the cove.

He saw the structures where the creatures lived. And there on the shore, a small creature sat in the sand. He turned back to the One. She chattered at him again, but before he could react, she leapt from the water and swam away, with his brethren following her back to the deep.

He now knew where he'd meet his destiny. It wasn't with the safety of the others. It was there, ahead of him, to the unknown.

It was time. His time.

Chapter 1

"Mom! Wake up!"

Madison Lorraine, with her cheek buried in a pillow, popped one eye open and attempted to focus on her nine-year-old daughter's face within an inch of her own.

"It's Saturday, Mo. Cartoons, remember?" She closed her eye and tried to reenter her interrupted dream.

"But, Mom, there's a shark in the cove. Come on!" Mo tugged once on Madison's arm and ran out of the room.

Madison bolted upright. She scrambled to disentangle her legs from the sheet and blanket.

"Mo! Mo, wait. Don't you dare go anywhere near the water!" Madison managed two steps forward before falling onto her knees, still entangled in the bedding. "Damn it." She threw everything aside and sprinted out onto the deck. The hard wood reverberated through the soles of her feet. "Shit." She debated for a couple of seconds about going back for her shoes. Seeing Mo racing to the shore convinced her. She rushed down the steps. "Mo, what did I say?"

Mo pointed to the middle of the cove. Madison cupped her hand over her eyes and spotted the gray-skinned form swimming about twenty yards offshore. He was right at the drop-off into deeper waters. He swam parallel to them and turned to swim back, his dorsal fin barely visible.

Madison stepped nearer to the water. Mo edged even closer. Madison reached out and grabbed her hand to pull her back.

"Didn't I say not to go near the water?"

Mo looked up at her. Her blonde hair, bleached almost white from her days in the Florida heat, reflected the sun. Madison's breath caught in her throat as she met her daughter's bright blue eyes. The same blue as Callie's. Mo was Madison's life, but sometimes it hurt to look at her. The image of Madison's dead partner bombarded her.

"Mom? You okay?"

Before Madison answered, a splash brought her attention back to the water. Sharks didn't jump and splash in the water unless they were going after a seal. At least according to those *National Geographic* specials. Madison wondered if she'd mistaken the sound. Then the fish flew out of the water in front of them, performed a perfect pirouette, and landed back in the water with another resounding splash.

"It's a dolphin!" Mo jumped up and down. "Can I go in and swim with him?"

"No, you most certainly cannot. You don't know where he's been."

Madison cringed. *Did I actually just say that?*

"That's silly, Mom. He's been in the *water.*"

"Hey, don't get smart with me."

The dolphin leapt in the air again, this time barely causing a ripple as he dove back in. "He's wild, Mo. It's not safe."

The dolphin danced across the water on his tail. If Madison didn't know any better, she'd think he was showing off, as if to say, "See? I'm harmless."

Mo giggled. "Isn't he cute? He doesn't look like he'd hurt us." She broke free of Madison's grasp and sprinted toward their dock.

Madison hurried after her. "Montanna Marie, don't you *dare* get in that water."

Mo slowed to a stop at the full use of her name. Then she gave Madison her best "sad puppy" imitation, complete with cocked head to the side.

"Please, Mom? We don't have to go into the water. Maybe we can see if he'll come up to us." She stuck out her bottom lip in an adorable pout.

Since Callie's death a little over three years ago, Madison found she gave in to Mo's whims far too frequently. But this was a little much. Despite how friendly the dolphin seemed, it wasn't like they were dealing with Flipper here.

The dolphin stuck his nose out of the water, making a sound very much like Flipper communicating with the boy in the old television show. *Okay, now that's too weird.* She followed Mo to the end of the dock. Mo knelt down on her knees and held her hand over the water.

"Damn it, Mo." All of Madison's good thoughts about Flipper vanished as her mind flashed on an image of the dolphin latching onto Mo and yanking her down with him. She knelt, pulled Mo back, and hugged her tight to her body. She didn't realize she was trembling until Mo's excited expression turned to one of worry.

"I'm okay, Mom."

"I know you are, and we're going to keep it that way."

The dolphin dipped back under the water. Madison leaned forward with Mo to try to get a glimpse of him. He resurfaced, pushed his nose into the water, and flipped it out, spraying water toward them.

They skittered back from the edge but not before they were both drenched.

The dolphin made the laughing noise again, and Madison thought, I'll be damned if he doesn't look like he's smiling at us.

"That wasn't funny," she called out to him.

Mo held her sides as she giggled and pointed at Madison.

"You don't look much better, Montanna."

Madison thought the dolphin had left them, but he resurfaced in front of the dock. He jabbered for a few seconds, nodded, and did the oddest thing. He captured Madison's gaze and held it.

Madison stared, mesmerized. *What the—*

Mo said something that Madison didn't catch at first.

"What did you say?" Madison asked.

"Can we keep him?" Mo tugged on her hand. "Please?"

She shook free from her trance. "No. He's not a puppy, Montanna."

The dolphin whistled at them before he turned toward the area that led back to the Gulf. Madison wasn't sure he'd headed that way until he leapt into sight right before he entered open water.

"Ah, shoot. He's leaving." Mo crossed her arms and stomped her foot. She looked exactly like her biological mother when Callie and Madison would have an argument. Madison bit her lip to keep from laughing.

"There's proof he's not a pet." Madison motioned toward the water. "He's free to come and go as he pleases." She doubted he'd be back, though she didn't want to share that with Mo. She was already on the verge of tears.

Madison took her by the shoulders and aimed her toward the house. "Come on. I'll fix you some pancakes." As they walked down the dock, she turned back one last time to catch another glimpse of the dolphin. He was nowhere in sight.

Madison scooped two pancakes onto Mo's plate. She didn't know where she put the food, but Mo had always had a voracious appetite. She'd shot up in height in the past year, outdistancing her classmates at five-two. She enjoyed being only four inches shorter than Madison. Callie had been five-ten. Madison thought Mo might catch up to that height.

Callie. Some days, Madison thought about her constantly. This was one of them. And the dolphin? When he stared at her, it was as if he knew what she was thinking.

"Mom?"

"Hmm?"

"Do you think he'll come back?"

Madison didn't need to ask who. Mo had talked about the dolphin nonstop for the past thirty minutes.

"I don't know, honey. Probably not."

Mo shoved a forkful of pancake into her mouth and mumbled something.

"What?"

Mo grabbed her glass of milk and chugged down half of it. She wiped her mouth with the back of her hand.

Madison pointed at her napkin. "Remember what those are for?"

Mo rolled her eyes, picked up the napkin, and made a show of dabbing the sides of her mouth.

"Funny, Mo."

"I said"—Mo emphasized the word as if Madison were the child and she the adult—"it would be cool if he came back and stayed."

"Like I told you, I doubt it. This isn't Sea World. Dolphins are meant to swim out in the ocean with their dolphin brothers and sisters."

God, Madison thought, I sound like Jacque Cousteau. *The dolphin is such a misunderstood creature.*

Madison heard the front door open. A few seconds later, Beverly Carlson, Callie's mother, walked in and dropped her purse on the kitchen table.

"Good morning, you two," she said before pulling down a mug and pouring herself coffee. Madison turned back to making pancakes. Beverly was yet another reminder of Callie—of whom Callie would've become in another twenty years. Tall, with fashionably cut blonde hair that just reached her collar, Beverly also passed on her piercing blue eyes to her daughter. But Madison would never see Callie at fifty-five. Stage IV uterine cancer had seen to that. Callie had valiantly fought the disease for two years before succumbing.

Madison blinked away her tears, hoping Beverly didn't see

them, but especially hoping she'd kept her sadness from Mo. Mo had witnessed the deep lows that Madison had struggled through, days when she couldn't get out of bed. Beverly had been there every step of the way. She'd cared for Mo as much as possible. Finally, there was a day when she sat Madison down and told her she needed to go on with her life. Callie wouldn't have wanted her to give up and would've expected Madison to raise Mo into adulthood.

Getting on with her life didn't equate to picking up a paintbrush, though. Madison, world-renowned for her seascapes, hadn't painted since Callie's death. She lost her creative voice when Callie died. She tried to give back by teaching at the local community college. Despite the frequent calls from her agent, Madison couldn't recapture that spark. Her Muse had died. She wasn't coming back.

Beverly walked past Madison and squeezed her shoulder before sitting down at the kitchen island with Mo. "Thank you for indulging me and allowing me my jolt of java." Beverly briefly tipped her mug toward Madison and took another sip. "Hey, kiddo," she said to Mo. "What are those? Your sixth and seventh pancakes?"

"Nuh-uh, Grandma. I can't eat that much."

"Oh, I don't know. I've seen you polish off half a pizza before. And your mom is a mean pancake maker." Beverly smiled at her. Her smile quickly faded as she met Madison's eyes. "You okay?" she mouthed so Mo wouldn't hear.

But Mo, as always, was too perceptive. She jerked her head toward Madison.

"I'm fine. Really."

Mo narrowed her eyes. "You said you'd be honest with me. I'm old enough now."

God, my nine-year-old daughter thinks she's old enough to understand how it feels to have my whole world turned upside down. But it wasn't just her world. Her therapist, Dr. Baker, reminded Madison of that during her monthly visits.

"All right. I was thinking about your mom. It's one of those days." Madison slid the rest of the pancakes onto a plate and set them in front of Beverly. She walked around the counter and sat on the stool on the other side of Mo.

"What are you going to eat?" Beverly asked.

"I'm not hungry."

"Madison—"

"Like I said, it's one of those days. I haven't had a bad day in a while." Madison hated the looks she was getting from both of them, so she changed the subject. "Hey, tell your grandma about all the excitement this morning."

The change in Mo's demeanor was immediate. "Oh, Grandma. We had a dolphin in our cove! Right in front of our house. And he was funny. He kept doing tricks for us."

"I don't know if he was doing them for us, Mo. Dolphins like to play."

Mo continued, clearly undeterred. "I think he was doing them for us. And then"—Mo giggled—"he sprayed us with water. You should've seen us. We were so wet we had to change our clothes. He laughed at us, too."

"That's odd," Beverly said. "Dolphins don't venture this far inland unless they're sick or they beach themselves, but it doesn't sound like he's sick from the way you described him."

"Yeah, I thought it was odd, too." Madison brushed her fingers through Mo's soft hair. "This one asked if we could keep him."

"It would've been cool. Don't you think, Grandma?" Mo finished off her last bite of pancake.

"Dolphins are meant to be free. Of course, don't try telling that to Sea World or any of the other facilities around here who hold them captive."

"Oh, I don't know, Bev. I read that they only breed the ones they already have."

"Humph. It's what they want you to believe."

Madison shook her head. They'd had this argument before.

Mo talked incessantly for another fifteen minutes about the dolphin while Madison cleaned up. Beverly made an attempt to help, but Madison waved her off.

After Mo wound down, Beverly said, "So, what do you want to do today?" Every other Saturday, Beverly took Mo on an excursion, even if it was only to her house less than ten minutes away.

"Can we go shopping?" Mo asked as she spun her stool.

"We sure can. How about the outlet mall in Key Largo?"

"Yes!" Mo hopped off her stool. "Let me get my purse."

Beverly watched her sprint down the hall to her room. "To have that much energy again."

"Maybe we need to douse our pancakes in five gallons of syrup. That should do it."

Beverly laughed but quickly sobered. "Will you be okay today while we're out? If you need Mo to be here with you, I understand."

Madison couldn't have asked for a more supportive

mother-in-law. Beverly, a single mom who'd raised Callie on her own, had accepted Madison with open arms when Callie brought her home. She'd been thrilled when Callie and Madison announced they were trying to have a baby. She'd also been behind them one-hundred percent when Madison adopted Montanna as soon as Florida ended its ban on gay adoption. Her own mother was an entirely different matter.

"I want her to have fun. I have some things I can do around the house."

"Like paint?" Beverly asked with a hopeful tone.

"You won't give up, will you?"

"You're too talented to waste your gift." Beverly stood and moved around the counter to hug Madison. "It'll come back to you. You wait and see. It'll sneak up on you, and you won't be able to stop."

Madison relished the comfort of Beverly's arms. "We'll see."

Beverly pulled back and caressed her cheek. "I know."

Mo ran up to them with her purse hung on one shoulder and her sunglasses perched on top of her head. The trendy look reminded Madison of how old Mo was getting.

"Have fun with your grandma, and don't ask her to buy you anything. You still have your allowance money."

"Yes, ma'am."

Beverly paused at the door. "We'll be back in a few hours. Enjoy your freedom while you can."

"Thanks, Bev. Love you, Mo!"

"Love you, too, Mom," she shouted back.

After they'd gone, the silent house settled around Madison. Montanna's energy seemed to bounce off the walls when she was there. But in her absence, loneliness would sometimes hit Madison so hard, it took her breath away. Today was one of those days.

She wandered to the back deck and sat in one of the chaise lounges. She hugged her knees to her chest. Staring out at the cove, she found she was searching for the dolphin. "Their" dolphin. Although she'd told Mo she doubted he'd come back, she wished for his return as much as her daughter.

Madison remembered the uncanny look the dolphin had given her. Almost like he was challenging her. But why?

Chapter 2

"I don't understand why you can't finish up your treatment here, Gabrielle."

Gabrielle Valenci watched her girlfriend put on her makeup. She couldn't and wouldn't refer to Eva DuPree as her partner, although they'd been together for two years. She didn't feel the depth of love of a committed relationship. In fact, she'd yet to experience that feeling once in her thirty years.

Eva continued to apply eyeliner but turned to Gabrielle when she hadn't responded.

"I want to stay down at the house in Islamorada in the Keys. Dr. Karl already scheduled an appointment for me at the University of Miami on Tuesday. I plan to get down there on Sunday afternoon to rest before driving back up to Miami."

"Yes, but you have excellent oncologists here in Manhattan." Eva furrowed her brow, but it didn't take away from her beauty. Eva and Gabrielle were among the highest-paid models in fashion, and Eva had the "look." Tall and thin, almost too thin, as were most of them. Eva's highlighted, long blonde hair framed an angular face and aqua eyes.

Today, no one would take Gabrielle for a model. The first round of three chemo treatments had stolen most of her hair. After suffering through twenty-five radiation treatments, she was about to embark on the last round of chemotherapy. Her hair had started to grow back during radiation, but she knew the growth was short-lived.

She wore a wig during her rare public appearances. Along with her hair, she'd also lost twenty pounds. She'd never been bone-thin. Tall, with raven-black hair to her shoulders, she was proud she hadn't succumbed to the eating disorders some of her colleagues suffered from. Gabrielle's curvaceous body was her calling card.

At least it had been. Not now. Not after the diagnosis of uterine cancer. She was blessed, though, and she knew it. Stage IA was a far cry from Stage IV, but the oncologist had warned her that her cancer cells could be aggressive. After her radical hysterectomy, he'd advised the full treatment regimen as a preventative. She didn't argue.

"I know my doctors are excellent, Eva. But with these last three treatments, I want to be somewhere I can regain my strength and spirit."

"Are you saying I'm incapable of helping you do that here?"

Yes, that's exactly what I'm saying. She decided not to bruise Eva's ego, though.

"No. You're about to start a rigorous shoot that will last weeks. You don't need to be worried about me and my treatments."

Eva sat beside her on the couch. "Okay, I can see your point." Her face lit up. "Why don't we go to Elaine's tonight?"

Elaine's was one of the "in" lesbian nightclubs in Manhattan. Since her treatment, Eva unsuccessfully encouraged Gabrielle to accompany her. Both were "out" to those in the business. But they were savvy enough to wait until they were two of the most-highly-sought-after models in the world before coming out of the closet. By then, the fashion magazines and photographers didn't care.

"You go ahead, Eva. I think I'll stay in and pack."

Eva leaned forward and kissed her. She stroked Gabrielle's closely cropped hair. "You're sure you'll lose this again?"

A lump formed in Gabrielle's throat at the thought and at knowing this woman beside her didn't get it. She probably never would.

"The nurse told me I would."

"That's a shame." Eva stood up. "I think I'll call some of the girls. I feel like partying."

Gabrielle managed a weak smile. "Have fun."

After Eva left, Gabrielle poured a glass of white wine and moved to the loveseat overlooking the Manhattan skyline from their thirty-second-floor loft's floor-to-ceiling windows. Afraid of heights when she was a child, she recalled that her father, a first generation Italian immigrant, cured her of the phobia by taking her to his sky-rise office in the city where he was an investment broker. He hadn't sat her in front of the window, but the more he took her there, the more curious she got. Something she was sure he knew about her. Eventually, she'd stand with her nose pressed against the window and stare down at the traffic below.

She missed her dad and the love they shared, especially on nights like tonight when she felt so alone and vulnerable. Her mother had died when she was in high school, leaving her dad to raise a daughter on his own. But he'd never made her feel like she was an afterthought. Their strong bond lasted until his death three years ago.

Gabrielle took a sip of her wine and held the glass against her chest as she watched the city lights twinkle. Others would kill for this view. Gabrielle didn't take it for granted, but it also wasn't her life, as it was for Eva.

A tear trickled down Gabrielle's cheek. She flipped it away with her finger. "Enough of this." She set her glass on the end table and walked down the hall to the master bedroom. She paused at the painting that hung above the bed. It was her favorite Madison Lorraine. Lorraine portrayed the joy of a young girl building sand castles. Seated nearby on a beach towel was a beautiful woman. Lorraine had captured the woman in a full laugh, head tossed back with one hand on her sunhat. Gabrielle loved the painting. It brought back memories of the happy times she'd spent with her parents in Florida.

She turned away from the painting and strode into the walk-in closet. She caught her reflection in the full-length mirror. Brushing her fingers across her head and down her body, she took in her gaunt appearance. She raised her shirt and traced the vertical scar that rose from her pubic hair up to mid-stomach.

The scar wasn't just a reminder of the surgery that had removed the tumor. It was a reminder she'd never give birth to a child of her own. That possibility ended four months ago with her diagnosis.

Gabrielle dropped her shirt into place and began grabbing clothes off hangers, tossing them on the bed as tears streamed down her cheeks. She needed to get out of the city. Miami and Islamorada may not give her any more peace than she'd found here in Manhattan. But something was calling her to the family vacation home. Her father had taught her to follow her heart.

That's exactly what she'd do.

* * *

"I told you, Noah, I'm not painting, and I have no idea if I ever will again. If this guy is so interested, he can buy one of my prints." Madison frantically waved at Mo to get a move on so she could drive her to school on time.

"It's $20,000, Madison. God knows you don't need the money, but it's $20,000 to paint something you could do in your sleep."

"You know I don't work that way. I have to feel it while I'm painting, and I've not felt it since…" She let her voice trail off.

"Since Callie died."

Madison sighed. "Yeah." She couldn't be too upset with her agent. Noah Preston hadn't pressured her into painting during her three-and-a-half-year absence from the art. One reason was he still earned a commission on her sales in New York, Los Angeles, and some of the other cities that displayed her work. But he also didn't pressure her because he was a good friend—to her and to Callie.

"Look, I didn't mean to call you bright and early on a Monday morning to ruin your week."

"Speaking of which, what time is it there? Four-thirty? What does Marcus think of you making these early phone calls?"

"Marcus is sleeping like a baby in our bed. Don't you worry about him. We've been together long enough that he accepts my quirky hours."

"Give him my love when he wakes from his beauty sleep. Not that he needs it."

"No, he most certainly does not."

She hung up in a better mood.

"Montanna, it's seven-thirty," she shouted. "You know it takes me fifteen minutes to get there. We're cutting it close."

"I'm here, I'm here," Mo muttered as she came down the hall.

"Grumpy. That's one thing you inherited from your mother. She definitely wasn't a morning person." Madison smiled at the memory. She caught Mo staring at her with a curious expression. "What's that look for?"

"It's good to see you smile when you're thinking about Mama."

Sometimes it surprised Madison how much Mo paid attention. "Come on, missy. Let's get you to school. I don't want to incur the wrath of Mrs. Breckinridge again." Madison wouldn't forget the last lecture she'd received from Mo's assistant principal about Mo being tardy two weeks ago.

They piled into the Mazda CX-5. "Buckle up," Madison said before she pulled out of their drive. As they drove past the only other house in their cove, Madison noticed a Chrysler 300 parked in the drive.

Mo saw it, too. "Look, Mom. Someone's at the Valenci place."

In their nine years of living in the secluded cove, Mr. Valenci had visited his house only a few weeks in the spring and winter. The other months of the year, he had a service clean and landscape the place. Since his death three years ago, the house sat empty. Until now.

Madison drove slowly past the sleek, black car, knowing she was being incredibly nosy.

"Do you want to stop?" Mo asked.

"No, let's get you to school." Madison looked one last time before passing the drive.

"I wonder who moved in. I wonder if they have kids. Maybe that dolphin will come back, and we can play with him this time."

Just like that, Mo was off on a tangent about the dolphin for the remainder of the drive. They pulled into the school parking lot. The students were streaming into the building. Mrs. Breckinridge watched over them like a hawk. When Mo opened her door, Mrs. Breckinridge pointedly stared at her wristwatch and then at Madison.

Madison got out of the car and walked around the front to stand beside Mo. "My fault," she yelled to Mrs. Breckinridge. "I didn't set the alarm last night."

Mo hugged her. "Thanks for covering for me, Mom. Don't forget to pick me up at eleven. It's a teacher's workday."

Madison thought it was more like a "teacher's mental health day."

"See you at eleven." She watched as Mo hiked her backpack higher on her shoulder and walked toward the school. Mo waved one last time.

Madison left the school parking lot and drove to the mall. She needed to purchase some supplies at the arts and craft store for her evening class. When she arrived at the store, she walked down an aisle in the back and perused the brushes. She picked one up and was running her finger through the soft hairs when someone spoke to her from behind.

"Madison? Is that you?"

Madison turned her head to find Rachelle Thompson, the only woman she'd attempted to date since Callie's death, standing behind her.

"It's good to see you out," Rachelle said with a wide smile. "And here. I'm hoping that means you're back at work." She motioned at the paintbrush.

Madison set the brush back into its slot on the shelf like it was a hand grenade and she didn't want to chance pulling the pin. "No. Checking out their sales for my evening class."

"I hope you'll get back to it sometime soon, though?"

"Maybe."

"I'm sorry. You probably have enough people asking when you're going to paint again. More importantly, how are you?"

"I've been well. You?"

"Fine. I'm here to have some pictures framed."

Madison shifted in place. They'd dated for four months, but it hadn't worked out.

"Well, I'll let you get back to shopping," Rachelle said. "You look great, Madison."

Liar. Madison had lost more weight since they'd quit dating. She wasn't gaunt, but she knew she didn't look healthy. She brushed a lock of her short, dark hair behind her ear.

"Thank you, Rachelle. You look great, too."

Rachelle backed away. "Tell Montanna I said hi, all right?"

"Sure." Madison knew she wouldn't, though. Mo hadn't cared for Rachelle. She wasn't sure Mo would like anyone she dated.

"Take care of yourself," Rachelle said.

She walked away. At the end of the aisle, a blonde woman joined her. Rachelle met Madison's eyes briefly before she left with the woman.

"Well, that was fun," Madison said under her breath. She didn't debate any longer about the brushes. She picked up a handful of different sizes and made her way to the checkout. The store suddenly seemed stifling.

The humid September air that hit her when she left the store didn't help rid her of the closed-in feeling. She immediately cranked up the Mazda's air conditioning. Madison sat there for a moment, lost in thought about Callie and the realization she might never move on. She pulled out her cell phone and speed-dialed her sister, Cyndra.

"Hey, big sis, how's it going?" Cyndra's cheerful voice greeted her.

"Okay."

"That did not sound convincing. What's wrong?"

God, if she had a dollar for every time someone asked her that… "Feeling a little out of it these past couple of days."

There was a pause on the other end. "Why don't we meet for coffee at Buddy's Pancake House?"

"I'll see you there in ten minutes."

Madison spotted Cyndra's Prius when she pulled into the lot. She pushed through the door of the restaurant and saw Cyndra seated in the corner booth. Where Madison had dark hair and easily tanned, her sister, four years her junior, was blonde and had to apply sunscreen with an SPF of at least 50 to avoid burning in the sun. Cyndra's hazel eyes were a stark contrast to Madison's golden brown. The differences didn't stop there. Despite the weight loss, Madison was five-six and built solid as an athlete. Cyndra was five-two and petite. Madison had heard a few friends refer to Cyndra as "dainty," and the description fit. The "dainty" tag didn't apply to Cyndra's personality, though, which was as strong as a day-old pot of coffee.

"Hey, Madison. I already ordered your jolt of java. Did you want breakfast, too?"

Madison slid into the booth across from her. "Coffee's fine."

The waitress appeared and set their mugs down.

"I'll have two pancakes and a side of bacon, please," Cyndra said. "You sure you don't want anything?"

"Positive."

After the waitress walked away, Cyndra leaned her elbows on the table and stared at Madison. "You need to eat."

"I do eat."

"It doesn't look like it. How much weight have you lost?"

Madison tore the top off of two sugar packets and dumped them into her coffee. She stirred the coffee in earnest, trying to buy more time.

"Madison?"

She finally met Cyndra's gaze. "Five pounds."

"You've lost more weight than that. How much weight have you lost since Callie passed?"

"I don't know," Madison snapped. "Fifteen maybe?"

Cyndra reached across the table and touched her hand. "You know how much I love you, don't you?"

Madison sighed. "I love you, too, Cyn. I'm sorry. It's been a rough couple of days. It started Saturday when Mo gave me this look, and I saw so much of Callie in her eyes." Her voice cracked.

Cyndra gripped her hand.

"I know this is horrible, but sometimes I wish I'd been the one to carry Mo. Then I wouldn't have to be reminded of Callie so much." Madison swiped at the tears running down her cheeks. "I mean, how screwed up is that?"

"It's not screwed up. It's human, and you're allowed to feel that way. I know you, Maddie. You're not taking it out on Mo."

"She's a perceptive kid, though, and she notices things. Like on Saturday. She knew I was sad, and she called me on it when I told her

I was fine."

"Good for her." Cyndra sat back while the waitress placed her plate in front of her. "You need someone to call you on this stuff." She took a bite of pancake and downed it with a sip of coffee. "When's the last time you had a date?"

"Why do we always get to this topic?"

Cyndra set down her fork.

"Uh-oh," Madison said. "Now I'm in trouble."

"I'm not joking. You may not like to hear this, but Callie loved you." Cyndra softened her tone. "She wouldn't have wanted you to stop living, honey."

Madison sucked in a breath.

Cyndra picked up a piece of bacon. "She wouldn't have, and I think deep down, you know it." She took a bite of the bacon. "Hey, what happened with that Rachelle woman?"

"Funny you should ask. I saw her at Hobby World right before I called you. There was another woman with her."

Cyndra stabbed at another piece of pancake and waved her fork at Madison. "Just as well. You can do better. I didn't get good vibes from her anyway."

Madison chuckled.

"What are you laughing at?"

"Montanna never liked her, either."

"See? Mo thinks like her aunt. She has smarts."

Madison crossed her arms. "So, I need to date, but you're particular about with whom."

"Well, yeah. You can't hook up with just anyone."

"Couple of interesting things happened these past couple of days."

"I see. We're changing the subject."

"Yeah, we are. We had a dolphin visit our cove."

"Was it sick?"

"Beverly thought they only ventured in so close when they're sick, too. But, no, he wasn't sick. He was having fun, actually. Even managed to drench us, the sneak."

"Is he still there?"

"No, he swam back out to open water. Mo was disappointed." Madison realized she was, too.

"Okay, what's the other interesting thing?" Cyndra wiped her mouth with her napkin.

"The Valenci place. Looks like someone's moving in or at least renting the house."

"Didn't Mr. Valenci die a few years ago?"

"Yes, and we haven't had anyone in there since."

"Do you know who his daughter is?"

Madison shook her head.

"The supermodel, Gabrielle Valenci."

Madison tried to jog her memory to recall if she'd seen her next door but thought she'd surely remember a supermodel. "I don't remember seeing her."

Cyndra waved at her. "You wouldn't. You only had eyes for Callie."

"You act like that's a bad thing."

"It's not. But you only saw her, Madison. God, I wish I'd find a love like you two shared."

"Speaking of dating, what about you?"

"I'm still seeing Chuck."

Madison made a face.

"I know, I know. We can't all have the perfect love."

"Which is what I've been trying to tell you. Callie was my one and only."

"I disagree. I think we love differently. God didn't intend for us to live alone. I still think there's someone out there for you. You only need to give her a chance. Open up that big heart of yours." Cyndra held her gaze. "And paint."

"You've been talking to Mom, haven't you?"

"It doesn't matter. I feel the same way."

Madison picked at her napkin. "She doesn't care for my 'lifestyle,' but she worries if I'll ever paint again. Figures."

"Mom is Mom. She won't change."

"The fact that she's such a successful artist has a lot to do with wanting me to get back to it. I'm sure she doesn't want me to be an embarrassment."

"I don't think that's it," Cyndra said. "She knows you come alive when you paint. She's seen it in action."

"No, I came alive with Callie, *then* I came alive with my painting." Madison balled up her napkin and tossed it on the table.

"Hey, I'm sorry. I know Mom's a touchy subject. Let's concentrate on what I think. *I* care about your painting. I care because you're too damn good to waste your talent. Callie wouldn't want that, either."

"You know, I love how everyone seems to be so sure that

Callie would've wanted me to do and who she would've wanted me to be with."

"I think if you were completely honest with yourself," Cyndra said softly, "you'd know we're right."

The waitress stepped up to their table and asked if they needed anything else. Cyndra insisted on taking the bill. After she paid, they stood and walked out to the parking lot.

"Come here, you." Cyndra grabbed Madison and hugged her tight. "I only tell you these things because I love you. You know that, right?"

Madison swallowed hard. "Yeah, I know. Love you, too." She opened her car door. "Why don't you come over Saturday night and have pizza with us?"

"You mean, why don't I come over Saturday night and try to fight off Montanna for a couple of slices."

"Yeah, that."

"Sounds fantastic." Cyndra walked to her car. "Call me later in the week."

"Will do." Madison shut her door and keyed the ignition. She waved at Cyndra as she pulled out. On her drive home, she replayed their conversation. Madison didn't doubt how much her sister loved her. But it was still hard to hear the truth, no matter who it came from.

Chapter 3

Gabrielle opened the last of the windows to air out the house. The cleaning staff her father had hired had done an adequate job of maintaining the place. She took a slow stroll through all the rooms.

She passed photographs of happy times spent here as a child with her parents. In all of them, she sported a huge smile. Her older brother, Alberto, was always so serious, as if it were his place to maintain the dignity in the family. Gabrielle picked up one frame and ran her fingers over the faces captured in another time. A time when her parents were still alive, and the future was unknown but stretched out in front of her with hope and promise.

She thought of her life in terms of "BC" and "AD": "Before Cancer" and "After the Diagnosis." She was ready to move on and reclaim her career. Her agent assured her the agency was anxious for her to return when her health permitted it. She was sure that meant when she had a full head of hair.

After seeing the empty pantry, Gabrielle decided to take a trip into town. Before leaving New York, she'd reserved a monthly rental on the Chrysler 300 for the time she'd be in Florida. It was an extravagance, but if she'd be taking several trips to Miami, she'd rather do so in comfort.

She grabbed her purse and headed outside. She was about to get into the Chrysler, when an SUV edged down the private drive. The dark-haired woman at the wheel glanced over and immediately stared straight ahead again. Odd, Gabrielle thought. She watched the car head in the direction of the only other house in the cove. Well, one of them would have to break the ice, and it appeared they were both shy.

Two hours later, Gabrielle pulled into her drive. It had been a long time since she'd done any extensive shopping. Exhaustion settled into her bones like cement pouring out of a cement mixer. She sat in the car and tried to gather her strength before tackling the unloading. She finally decided sitting there wouldn't make her feel any better. She popped the trunk and reached inside for the first bag. After a couple of trips back and forth, she set a particularly heavy bag on the deck and slumped into a lounge chair to catch her breath. Sweat poured down her forehead and stung her eyes. She'd already removed the stifling wig on her first trip inside.

With her eyes closed, she didn't hear anyone approach.

"Are you all right?" a small voice called from below.

Gabrielle peered down at a blonde girl standing on the beach in front of her house. Even at this distance, Gabrielle saw the deep frown lines furrowing the girl's brow.

"I'm fine. Thank you for asking, though."

The girl pointed at the bag beside Gabrielle. "Do you have more?"

"Yes, but—"

The girl was already bounding up the deck stairs and in a flash stood in front of her.

"I can help." She didn't wait for Gabrielle's response but hefted the bag sitting beside Gabrielle and carried it into the house. As she passed on her way to the car, the girl said, "You stay there, and I'll do the rest."

In no time, the girl had carried the rest of the groceries inside. She was a little out of breath when she reappeared at Gabrielle's side. She held out her hand. "My name's Montanna, but everyone calls me Mo. Pleased to meet you."

Impressed with Mo's manners, Gabrielle shook her hand. "It's a pleasure to meet you, too. I'm Gabrielle."

"Are you living here now?"

"At least for a few months."

Mo sat down in the other chair and motioned at Gabrielle's hair. "Do you have cancer?"

Gabrielle tried to keep her expression neutral and not snap at the blunt question. "I had cancer. I'm finishing up my treatment."

Mo nodded once. "I thought so. My mama looked like you when she had her treatment."

"Your mom had cancer?"

"Yes. Mama Callie." Mo stared down at her feet. "But she died."

"I'm so sorry, Mo."

"She was really sick, though. She was in the last stage. I think that's what it's called. I was six when she died. I still miss her." Mo chewed on her lower lip. "My other mom misses her, too."

Now, this is interesting. "You have another mom?"

Mo jutted out her chin. "There's nothing wrong with it."

"No, there's not."

"Montanna!"

Mo jerked toward the sound. "That's my mom now." She ran to the railing and waved. "Mom! I'm up here."

Gabrielle tried to get a good look at the woman. She heard her stomping up the stairs. When she reached the deck, Gabrielle recognized her as the driver of the SUV earlier in the day.

"I'm sorry if my daughter's disturbing you."

"Not at all." Gabrielle pushed herself up, trying her best not to grimace at the aching in her joints. "I'm Gabrielle Valenci."

"Madison Lorraine." She grasped Gabrielle's outstretched hand.

"Madison Lorraine? The artist?"

Madison's smile slipped from her face. "Yes."

"I love your work." Gabrielle was about to pepper her with questions about her painting.

"Gabrielle had cancer, too, Mom."

"Montanna," Madison said sharply.

Gabrielle touched her arm and smiled. "It's all right. I think it's fairly obvious." She motioned at her hair… what there was left of it.

"Still, Mo has better manners than this. Usually."

"I'm sorry," Mo mumbled.

"Honestly, it's okay." Gabrielle was beginning to get uncomfortable. "Besides, your daughter came to my rescue and carried in the last of my groceries. There's no way I can be upset with her." She felt like she would fall over if she stood there much longer.

"It's the fatigue, isn't it?" Madison asked gently.

Gabrielle nodded. "I'm hoping to get some strength back this week. I start the last of my chemotherapy a week from tomorrow." She felt uneasy about going to the treatment alone, but she didn't have much choice.

"Last round then?"

"Yes, thank God. This has been hell." Gabrielle shook her head slightly. "You know that, though. Mo told me about your partner. I'm sorry for your loss."

"Thank you," Madison said softly.

Gabrielle was drawn to the sadness in Madison's light brown eyes. They were a unique shade—brown with a touch of gold. As if the sun had kissed the irises and blended the colors. They stood staring at each other for a few seconds before Madison blinked.

"We should be going so you can rest. It's very nice to meet you, Gabrielle."

"Nice to meet you, too. And you, Mo. Thanks again for all your help."

Mo grinned at her. "You're welcome."

They headed toward the stairs, but Madison turned to face her. "Please let us know if you need anything. Can I give you my cell number? It'd be so much easier than you walking over to our place if something were to come up."

"Sure." Gabrielle stepped inside and grabbed a tablet and pen. Madison gave her the number. Gabrielle wrote it down and scribbled her own number at the bottom of the page. She ripped it off and handed it to Madison. "That's mine. The same offer goes to you. Call if you need anything."

Madison waved the paper. "Thanks. Well, we'll leave you so you can unpack your groceries."

Gabrielle walked over to the railing as they made their way home. They'd gone about half way when Mo turned and waved and then Madison. She returned the wave and continued watching until they were closer to home. As she entered the house, she tried to shake the melancholy she'd seen in Madison's eyes.

After she waved at Gabrielle, Madison took Mo's hand.

"She was nice, wasn't she, Mom?"

"Yes, she was."

"You're not mad at me are you?"

Madison looked down at her daughter. She let go of her hand and ruffled Mo's hair. "Absolutely not."

"When I told you she had cancer, you seemed mad."

"I know, and I'm sorry. It kind of caught me by surprise, that's all."

"Because of Mama."

"Right. Because of your mama."

"I like Gabrielle, don't you?"

What's going through that little head of yours, Mo, and why is it I really don't want to know?

"I like her fine. I just met her, but she seems nice."

"Maybe we can have her over sometime."

Madison pulled Montanna to a stop. "Mo, she probably won't feel like visiting with us while she's here. Remember how tired and how sick Mama felt while she was undergoing treatment?"

Mo's face fell for a moment, but then she brightened. "Yeah, but, we can help her. We're right here." She pointed at their house. "And she's only there." She gestured back at Gabrielle's. "It's not that far, and she's alone. I think she'll need someone to look after her."

"Maybe she wants to do this alone."

Mo appeared to contemplate the idea, but very briefly. "But we can still ask her."

Madison wasn't going to win this argument. The logic of her precocious daughter was hard to beat. She took hold of her hand again and started for home.

"Let's wait and see. We don't want to scare her off. She just got here."

"Okay." Montanna swung their hands between them. "Love you."

"Love you, too, pal."

Chapter 4

"No, Eva, you don't need to fly down, especially with your shoot starting Wednesday. Remember, I know how crazy it can get. I'm fine. I can handle this myself." Gabrielle checked her rearview mirror and glanced over her shoulder before passing the car in front of her. Traffic was heavier than she expected on US 1, what locals called the Overseas Highway.

"Are you sure? I'm still not crazy about you doing this on your own."

"I'm positive. Listen, I'm on the interstate, and this isn't a good time to talk."

"I'll call you later this week."

"Talk to you then." Gabrielle disconnected the Blue Tooth.

Large raindrops plopped against the windshield. She flipped on the wipers as the rain quickly turned into a deluge. She debated about pulling over until it lightened up a little, but one look at the dashboard time told her she needed to stay on the road.

She switched on the radio and settled on the classical station to try to ease the tension between her shoulder blades. She quickly got lost in Barber's "Adagio for Strings." Listening to the haunting music, she thought back to meeting Madison yesterday. How difficult that must have been to lose a partner, especially one so young. And the mother of your daughter.

She smiled thinking about the impish Montanna. Maybe losing a mother at such a young age had made her brave enough to ask questions adults seldom asked. No one had ever been so bold to ask her if she had cancer. Granted, when she did venture out, she wore her wig. But it was obvious she wasn't well.

The classical music wafted over her and gave her peace as she drove the remaining miles to the University of Miami Medical Center's oncology office.

Gabrielle perused a magazine in the waiting area, not really reading any of the articles. She could easily compare the pages she flipped through to the blurring of her days of treatment, one photo bleeding into the next like one day bleeding into the next twenty-four hours. One step at a time, her oncologist in New York had told her.

"Gabrielle Valenci?"

She glanced up at the attendant who stood in the doorway and held the door open with her hip. Gabrielle set her magazine aside and stood. After getting Gabrielle's weight and blood pressure, the woman led her to an exam room.

"If you'd have a seat, Dr. Alvarez, a resident, will be with you soon, then you'll see Dr. Corrigan."

She sat in the silence of the room for approximately fifteen minutes, trying not to worry that she'd lost even more weight. The door opened, and a young Latina with a white lab coat entered. She introduced herself to Gabrielle and shook her hand. Dr. Alvarez sat down on the stool in front of Gabrielle and quietly flipped through her chart.

"So, you're here for your final round of chemotherapy treatments. Dr. Karl in New York referred you, I believe?"

"I told him I'd be in Islamorada, and he said Dr. Corrigan and the University of Miami would be a good fit."

Dr. Alvarez nodded. "Your blood work has been pretty consistent. You had a one-week delay in treatment"—she ran her finger down the page—"in June when your white blood cells were low."

"That's right. The third week, I believe." Gabrielle still remembered how frustrated she was when she'd gotten the call from Dr. Karl's nurse that she'd have to wait for chemo. She'd burst into tears.

"How did you tolerate the radiation?"

"I was okay until about halfway through. Then I had severe diarrhea, but I kept my electrolytes up as much as possible." She tried to banish the memories of the accidents she'd had. Having no idea when the diarrhea would hit had been mortifying. In those last weeks, she'd never ventured out for fear she'd be unable to control her bowels. She learned early on that her cancer journey was a humbling one.

She realized Dr. Alvarez had said something. "I'm sorry?"

"If you don't mind, could you take a seat on the exam table? I'd like to listen to your heart and your lungs."

Gabrielle complied and took deep breaths when asked.

"All right. Dr. Corrigan should be in here in a few minutes. Nice meeting you, Ms. Valenci."

About five more minutes passed before Dr. Corrigan and a young woman entered the exam room.

"Ms. Valenci?" Dr. Corrigan asked.

"Gabrielle, please."

He shook her hand and gave her a warm smile. "I'm Dr. Corrigan. This is my nurse, Allison."

Dr. Corrigan was a tall, bulky man, who looked like he could bench-press a building. She instantly liked him. His eyes held kindness.

"Hello, Allison." Gabrielle shook the tall redhead's hand.

Dr. Corrigan sat down on the stool and opened her chart. "I spoke with Dr. Karl. He filled me in on how you're doing. I also spoke with Dr. Porter, your radiation oncologist. He informed me you made it through the treatments just fine. It says here you did have trouble with diarrhea about midway through treatment?"

Gabrielle felt her cheeks flush. "That's correct."

"You've lost twenty pounds since your first treatment." He met her gaze. "And you don't need to lose weight."

"I understand. It was hard for me to keep anything down those last few weeks of radiation treatment. I've not intentionally lost the weight, believe me." Gabrielle wanted to add she wasn't like some of the other models who obsessed about their weight, but she refrained.

"Good. We need you to keep your strength up. I'm sure Dr. Karl told you that chemo is stacked—it's cumulative. You'll be getting a lower dose of the Taxol and Carboplatin, but it will still affect your stamina and your joints."

"He did tell me, yes."

"Let's have a listen to your heart and lungs." Dr. Corrigan went through the same routine as Dr. Alvarez. "Now, let's take a look at that incision." With Allison's assistance, she lay back on the table. Dr. Corrigan poked and prodded her abdomen. "Looks good." They helped her to a seated position. "We're doing the treatment as a preventative. I know it hasn't been easy, but as Dr. Karl told you, the cancer cells we're dealing with can be aggressive. A few years ago, we might've only performed the surgery. But we've found this treatment works best."

Gabrielle had heard the speech before. It had shocked her when the doctor told her she'd be undergoing not only radiation treatment but also chemo. The regimen had been every bit the hell she'd imagined.

"I understand, Dr. Corrigan."

He held out his hand again. "It's a pleasure meeting you, Gabrielle. We'll take good care of you here." He left, but Allison remained behind.

"I'm sure you remember the drill. We'll need you to get blood work by Friday to make sure you can start treatment next Tuesday. I have orders for you, but you can have this done at any lab that's nearer to you than Miami." Allison handed her the order. "Let me know where you have it done, and we'll get the results faxed to us the same day. This next part is important. You need to eat as much protein as you can in the coming weeks. Meat, yes, but also fruit and nuts. Keep your electrolytes up. Lots of water and Gatorade or something similar."

"I'll do my best."

"Here's my card with my email address and cell number." Allison handed her a business card. "And here's a prescription for your blood work and one for the steroids to prevent any allergic reaction to the drugs. If you'll email me when you get home, I'll send the schedule to you as an attachment. Please don't hesitate to contact me if you have any questions or if you're not feeling well. Anything you think I need to know, all right?"

"I'll email you today."

Allison gave her a gentle smile. "I realize how difficult this is, but you're nearing the end."

"The day can't get here soon enough." Gabrielle stepped down from the exam table and followed Allison to the checkout.

"Gabrielle needs to see Dr. Corrigan again the Monday before her next treatment, so in about a month," Allison instructed the woman behind the checkout window.

After Gabrielle made the appointment, she left and walked toward her car in the parking garage. The heat slapped her in the face as soon as she exited the medical building. She got into her car and adjusted the air. As she drove the city streets to the interstate ramp, she thought about how her life had narrowed to these six months of treatment, as if the days had passed through a funnel. Nothing seemed to come before, and from where she was right now, she couldn't see far ahead.

Only God knew what the future would bring.

Chapter 5

"Is she as beautiful as she is in the magazines?" Cyndra grabbed another slice of pizza. "Ha! Faster than you this time, munchkin," she said to Mo.

Mo wasn't listening, intent on the Wii baseball game she was playing.

"Well, is she?" Cyndra asked Madison again.

"Yes, she's very beautiful. I mean, right now, she doesn't look well. But it doesn't take away from her beauty." Madison bit into her slice of pizza. "I still can't believe I never noticed her in the years we've lived here."

Cyndra put her slice down, leaned over the table, and gave Madison a look. "Hello? What did I tell you before? That woman could've knocked on your door and propositioned you," she glanced at Mo and said in a lower voice, "wearing nothing but a G-string and pasties, and you wouldn't have blinked an eye. Callie was your life." She picked up her slice of pizza again. "As she should've been."

"Mo's taken to her... of course." Madison smiled as she watched her daughter play her game.

"And you?"

"Oh, now, don't you start, too."

"What?"

Cyndra's innocent tone didn't fool Madison. "You know exactly what I'm saying." She mimicked Cyndra by lowering her voice. "Mo's already trying to play matchmaker."

"What's wrong with that?"

"Didn't we have this discussion at the pancake house?" Madison heard the edge in her voice but couldn't help it.

"I'm not backing down from this, Madison. I'm not asking you to marry the woman. Simply get to know her. You never know..."

"Did you miss the part where I said she wasn't well?"

"I thought you meant she had a cold or something," Cyndra said.

"She's undergoing her last cancer treatments here."

Cyndra paled. "God, I'm sorry."

They let that sit between them for a while.

"Do you know what type of cancer?" Cyndra finally asked.

"No."

"But you can be friends. She probably needs a friend right now."

Madison thought about Gabrielle's exhaustion-lined face and her struggle to even stand up. She remembered the same look from Callie, how she'd only wanted to take it all away from Callie. If she could have, she would've done it in a heartbeat. She'd told Callie that once, and Callie had instantly gotten upset. "No one deserves to go through this," Callie had said, the anguish strangling her words. "No one."

"Hey, you all right?" Cyndra asked. "I'm sorry if I upset you."

"You didn't upset me, it's just that…"

"She reminds you of Callie."

Madison nodded, afraid to speak for fear she'd break down.

Mo came back to the dinner table and grabbed another piece of pizza. "Aunt Cyndra, did Mom tell you about the nice lady next door?"

"Yes, she did, sweetie. Did you like her?"

"Mm hmm. She has cancer. But she's getting better, I think. I hope we can be friends." With that, Mo went back to the living room.

"It amazes me how resilient she is," Cyndra said as Montanna continued with her game.

"You? She's ahead of me in so many ways. I'm afraid she tries to take on too much sometimes. Like she tries to take the sadness from me." Madison thought Mo was so much older than her nine years, and she felt guilty.

As if reading her thoughts, Cyndra said, "Madison, you can't blame yourself. She's a good kid. She has a heart as big as the world. You're still seeing your therapist together, right?"

"We are."

"How's that going?"

"Pretty well. Montanna didn't want to talk at first, but now she likes Dr. Baker. He's so good with kids. We don't go as often. About once a month, unless it seems something's especially bothering her."

"Or you, right?"

"Or me."

Mo turned off the game and joined them at the table. "Did Mom tell you about the dolphin?"

"She did." Cyndra winked at Madison.

"I hope he comes back, but Mom said he probably won't."

"Let's hope your mom's wrong, because I think it'd be pretty darn cool to have a dolphin in your cove."

Madison thought so, too, but she didn't want Mo to be hopeful for something that most likely wouldn't happen.

Cyndra glanced at the wall clock. "I better get going. I have grocery shopping to do tonight. No food in the house." She stood up. "Come on. Give your aunt a hug." She opened her arms, and Mo embraced her.

Madison hugged Cyndra when she reached the door. "Thanks for coming. We love having you over."

"Yeah, I know I'm the best darn sister and best aunt in the whole wide world. I rock, don't I?"

Madison playfully shoved her. "Go on before your head gets so big, you can't fit through the door."

"Good night, you two."

"Night, Aunt Cyn."

"Good night, sis," Madison said. "I'll call you tomorrow."

Chapter 6

Gabrielle awakened to a room brightening with the first light of dawn. She wiped the sleep out her eyes. She'd left the windows open for fresh air and the morning birdsong, but another sound tickled her ears. She cocked her head. Was that splashing? She slipped on her robe and slid her feet into flip-flops. Maybe Montanna was swimming. But on a school day?

Gabrielle went outside, stood at the railing, and attempted to get a good view of the water below. She didn't see Mo. She headed down the steps to the sand. She thought she saw movement in the water but wasn't sure.

"Must have been hearing things." As the words left her mouth, a dolphin pierced the surface and leapt high in the air. Gabrielle jumped back and gasped, clutching her chest as she tried to catch her breath. "Shit." She watched in fascination as the dolphin broke through the water again farther away.

The water grew calm. Gabrielle walked along the shore to her dock. When she reached the end, she bent over to try to get another glimpse. For her curiosity, the dolphin awarded her with another appearance, this time dousing her in water with a flick of his tail fin.

"Oh, you little brat!" She stared down at her robe, plastered now onto her thin nightshirt. She'd gone from halfway decent to almost obscene in a matter of seconds.

The dolphin popped back out of the water and sounded every bit like he was laughing at her distress.

"It's not funny."

"I told him the same thing."

Gabrielle jerked at the sound of a husky voice behind her. She teetered for a second and flailed her arms out to keep from falling into the water. A strong hand grabbed her forearm and yanked her back. Gabrielle fell into Madison's tight embrace.

"I didn't mean to scare you." Madison held her from behind,

arms encircling Gabrielle's waist.

Gabrielle shivered when she felt the press of Madison's breasts against her back. She pulled out of Madison's arms and turned to face her.

Madison's gaze dropped to Gabrielle's chest. She quickly raised her eyes. A full blush worked its way up her neck to her cheeks.

Gabrielle felt her own face warm. She crossed her arms over her hardened nipples. "You startled me."

"I know. I'm sorry." Madison appeared uncomfortable as she looked anywhere but at Gabrielle.

"Thank you for saving me from a dunk in the water, though." Gabrielle ducked her head so Madison would meet her eyes.

"I—"

"Mom! It's so cool that he's back, isn't it?" Mo was sprinting down the dock. She moved around Madison and took a step toward the end of the dock.

"Whoa." Madison grabbed her before she got closer to the water.

"Hi, Gabrielle. We thought we heard something and came down to see."

"Hi, Mo. How are you this morning?"

But Mo was already focused on the dolphin. Gabrielle and Madison turned toward the water where he was again putting on a show. He rode his tail backwards halfway across the cove. Then he dove in the water and jumped high in the air before swimming toward them again. He popped his head to the surface and nodded at them. Gabrielle swore he winked at her.

"Hey there," Gabrielle said and knelt on the dock. She tentatively held her hand out over the water.

"Do you think that's such a good idea?" Madison asked as she gripped Gabrielle's shoulder.

"He seems friendly."

"So do polar bears."

The dolphin disappeared and resurfaced in front of them, leaping high enough to barely touch the palm of Gabrielle's hand.

"Wow, did you see that?" Mo knelt beside Gabrielle and held her hand out.

"No, Montanna." Madison pulled her back.

"But, Mom, he's friendly. He didn't hurt Gabrielle."

Gabrielle couldn't stop the grin from spreading across her face. When the dolphin's nose had brushed her hand, it had felt almost spiritual. She noticed Madison's worried expression.

"He seems harmless, Madison. I think it might be okay for—"

"She's not your daughter." Madison's jaw tightened.

"No, she's not," Gabrielle said. "Listen, I didn't mean to tell you what to do. I apologize." Suddenly, the excitement drained from Gabrielle's body. "I think I'll head back to the house."

She started past Madison, but Madison grasped her arm. "I'm sorry. That was totally inappropriate on my part."

Gabrielle freed herself from Madison's gentle grip. "Don't worry about it. I'm tired, and I need to eat something. I can't go without eating breakfast, and I need to get as much rest as I can today. I drive into Miami for chemo in the morning." She looked longingly at the dolphin who chattered nonstop.

"Please stay and join us at our house. I'll fix you breakfast."

"No, thank you. You and Montanna enjoy." As she walked away, she felt Madison's gaze on her. But she didn't look back.

You're such an idiot, Madison. She watched as Gabrielle walked along the shore toward her house. Madison wanted to go after her but wondered what more she could say. *After losing my partner, I'm overprotective of Montanna? And that at times, my overprotectiveness can come across as rudeness?*

"Mom, look at him," Mo said behind her.

Madison watched in fascination as the dolphin swam parallel to the shore, breaking the surface to dive below and pop up again a few feet later. She noticed the white tip of his dorsal fin with each resurfacing. He seemed to be shadowing Gabrielle's movements as he kept pace with her. Madison glanced at Gabrielle to see if she was aware of the attention, but Gabrielle kept her head down as she walked up the steps to her home.

As soon as Gabrielle was out of sight, the dolphin swam toward the clearing that led to open waters. Just as before, he leapt high in the air one last time. Then, he was gone.

"Darn it. Do you think he'll ever stay here with us?" Mo asked.

"No, Montanna. He's free."

Mo's eyes lit up. "That's a good name for him. Free. Can we name him, Mom? Please?"

Madison smiled at Mo's enthusiasm for something so simple. "Yes. But remember, like his name, he's free to come and go, which means he might not return."

"You mean Free. Free might not return. He has a name now."

"All right. We'll stick with it. How about I make you

some breakfast while you shower?"

"Pancakes again?"

"Is that what you want?"

"Yup."

"Then that's what you'll get."

As they walked up their stairs, Madison glanced toward Gabrielle's place one last time. She needed to apologize again. She'd visit Gabrielle later after Mo was in school.

Madison transferred the apple cobbler to her left hand and knocked on Gabrielle's door with her right. She heard the sound of approaching footsteps. The curtain pushed aside, and Madison caught a glimpse of Gabrielle.

The door opened. Madison was momentarily speechless as she took in Gabrielle's appearance. Although Gabrielle was dressed in a worn Georgia Bulldogs T-shirt and cut-off jeans, it did nothing to take away from her beauty. Madison gazed down at legs that seemed to go on forever. She realized she was staring and raised her eyes. Gabrielle was watching her with a wary expression.

"Um, hi. I don't know if you like apple cobbler, but it's really the only decent dessert I make." Madison thrust the dish forward. "I'm so sorry again about earlier this morning."

Gabrielle took the dish from her. "I told you that you didn't need to apologize, but thank you for this. You're very kind."

Madison stood there hoping Gabrielle would ask her in. After a few seconds passed, she turned to leave, but Gabrielle's voice stopped her.

"Would you like to come inside? We could have some cobbler with coffee."

"If you don't mind sharing."

Gabrielle moved aside for Madison to step in.

"Let me get the coffee going. Go ahead and have a seat," she said as she motioned at the table in the dining room.

Madison started that way but stuttered to a standstill when she caught a glimpse of a painting over the couch in the living room. A sailboat was the focal point of the painting, one of the last pieces she'd done. Whitecaps rose in the ocean, a direct contrast to the sun reflecting off the sailboat. Madison always incorporated light into her work, and this piece was no exception.

"That's probably my second-most favorite of yours," Gabrielle said with a hushed voice from behind her. "It was my father's favorite. He always tried to purchase work from local artists, especially seascapes."

Madison turned to find Gabrielle staring at the painting.

"It's such a paradox. You have the crashing waves, yet the sky is clear and the sun shines bright. It's like life, wouldn't you say?" She met Madison's eyes. "Outwardly, things may appear fine, but below the surface, turmoil rages. We know this about ourselves, yet others are oblivious." Gabrielle focused on the painting again. "And the title, *The Storm Within*, even speaks to this. Am I right?"

Madison swallowed so she could answer. "I painted it not too long after the doctors gave us Callie's prognosis."

"Oh, I'm sorry, Madison." Gabrielle edged closer and reached out as if to touch Madison's cheek.

Her hand hovered so near that Madison swore she felt the warmth radiating from her fingertips.

Gabrielle let her hand drop and took a step back. "She must have been a special woman."

Madison let out a breath. A pang of disappointment rushed through her body that Gabrielle hadn't touched her. She tried to push the thought from her mind.

"She was my world."

"Do you mind me asking what type of cancer she had?"

"Stage IV uterine."

"Mine was also uterine, but I was blessed they caught it early. Stage IA. I'm sorry that Callie's was diagnosed so late." Gabrielle turned back to the painting. "Your work shows your passion for her." An awkward silence filled the room until she said, "How about that apple cobbler?"

Madison followed her to the kitchen and helped with the plates and coffee. They sat down and dug into the cobbler.

Gabrielle took her first bite and moaned. "Delicious."

Madison smiled. "Glad you like it."

They quietly ate until Gabrielle spoke again. "Did you stop painting when Callie passed?"

Madison jerked her head up, ready to bite off a "that's none of your business" retort. But then she saw the kindness in Gabrielle's eyes.

"I haven't painted a piece since then, no. I do work as an adjunct at the local community college. I teach beginning painting, mainly to older students. We touch on watercolor and oil mediums in a semester." She shrugged her shoulders slightly. "It's not the same, of course. But I still work with the paints."

"Do you think you'll return to it?"

Madison wondered why Gabrielle's probing questions weren't bothering her. But everything about Gabrielle was kind and delicate. Despite knowing her for only a few days, Madison already had a strong belief that Gabrielle wouldn't intentionally hurt her.

"I'm not sure. I have enough people asking, from my agent to my mother-in-law and sister." Madison frowned. "And my mother."

"Ah, I take it you don't get along?"

"No, not really. She doesn't agree with my lifestyle. She's never had that much contact with Mo, although she'll send her gifts at Christmas and on her birthday. Even though Mo's her only grandchild. She does, however, call to pester me about my painting. Or she goes through Cyndra, my sister."

"Wait. Is your mother the artist Louisa Lorraine?"

"The one and only."

"Wow. Your techniques and work differ so much. She's so, so..."

"Out there?" Madison said with a quirk of her lips.

"No, I don't mean that." Gabrielle laughed. "Well, I guess I do. Her work is so abstract, and yours is so grounded."

"True. Yet she still doesn't want me to embarrass her by not working. I'm not sure how it's an embarrassment, but she sees it that way and somehow takes it personally."

"I don't know you that well, Madison, but I think you'll return to your painting when you're ready and not a day or an hour or a minute sooner. It won't work any other way. It can't. It has to come from here." Gabrielle held her hand over her heart.

Madison sat back in her chair, surprised at how much Gabrielle understood her. "Yeah. That's how I feel." She took another bite of cobbler. "How about you? You're planning to work again, aren't you?"

"You know what my job is?"

"I didn't until Cyn pointed it out to me. You're so beautiful, I don't see how I..." Madison felt her face flush. "I'm sorry."

"For saying I'm beautiful? No woman would complain about that." Gabrielle stared down at her plate. "I don't feel beautiful, though."

Madison waited until she looked up to meet her gaze. "You are. Even now."

"Thank you," she said quietly. "As for working

again, yes, someday."

Madison changed the subject as she stabbed at her last bite. "What did you think of our friend this morning?"

"The dolphin? From what you said, I take it he's been here before?"

"Last weekend. Mo wanted to keep him. I had to break it to her that wasn't possible."

"I can imagine it's hard to disappoint her on anything with those big baby blues of hers."

"Just like her mother's."

"Isn't it unusual for dolphins to venture this far inland?"

"That's what I thought. I'm tempted to go to Marine World up the road to ask them about it, but I don't want to give away there's a friendly dolphin visiting us." Madison remembered Beverly's comment about aquatic shows. She didn't want there to be any chance of him being captured.

"He was cute."

"Did you see him following you along the shore this morning when you headed back here?"

"No."

"It was so strange. In fact, it's almost like he's watching over us or something." Madison shook her head. "That's crazy." Suddenly, the dolphin's image popped into her head as if an outside force had planted it there. Almost as though someone or something was speaking for her, she blurted out, "I know you may not want this, but I was wondering if you'd like me to go with you tomorrow to your treatment. I remember how it was for Callie. I can't imagine going through it alone." She still couldn't believe she was asking something so incredibly personal.

Gabrielle seemed surprised. "You'd go to the infusion center with me? Are you sure it's not too much?"

"I just need to check with Beverly, my mother-in-law, to see if she wouldn't mind taking Montanna into school and picking her up. Mo could stay with her until I got back."

Gabrielle's surprised expression turned to one of relief. Her lips slowly creased into a smile. "I'd like that very much."

Chapter 7

"You'll be okay going back there, Madison?" Beverly asked.

"I think so." Madison searched for her keys. She never put them on the key hook where they belonged.

Beverly held them up. "Looking for these?"

"Thanks. Callie always made fun of me for misplacing my keys."

"Do me a favor. Call me if you need to talk. I know it'll be a long day if it was anything like Callie's treatment."

Madison touched her hand. "I will, but I think I'll be fine."

Mo bounded into the dining room. Lord, the kid doesn't have a slow speed, Madison thought. She checked the time.

"I'm late. I told Gabrielle I'd be there by seven."

"Go." Beverly pushed her toward the door.

Madison stopped to give Mo a hug. "You mind your grandmother."

"I always do, Mom."

Madison gave Mo one more squeeze before hugging Beverly.

"This won't be easy," she whispered in Beverly's ear. "But it feels right."

Beverly hugged her tighter. "That's what matters."

Gabrielle looked at the clock again. She yanked her T-shirt on over her head and rushed to tug on her sweatpants. Although it was still quite warm out, she wanted to be comfortable for treatment. She was tying the laces on her sneakers when she heard the knock at the door.

"Coming!"

She opened the door and did a quick scan of Madison's clothing. God, she looks good in those cargo shorts. Gabrielle quickly raised her eyes when she realized she was staring at Madison's tan, muscled legs.

"Ready? Sorry I'm late."

"No problem. I just finished dressing." Gabrielle was about to follow Madison out the door when she put her hand on her head and remembered her wig. She turned toward her bedroom to retrieve it.

"Don't," Madison said as she touched her arm.

Gabrielle stopped. "Don't what?"

Madison motioned at Gabrielle's head. "You're beautiful without it."

"I don't think so."

Madison gently brushed her fingers through the little hair Gabrielle had. "You are."

Gabrielle's breath hitched, and warmth spread through her body at Madison's touch. She met Madison's gaze and saw only honesty there. She nodded slightly. "Okay. Let's go then."

Madison kept her attention on the road, almost afraid to look at Gabrielle. She wasn't sure what she was feeling. Why had she brushed her fingers through Gabrielle's hair? And why had it felt so right? She took her eyes off the road briefly and caught Gabrielle staring at her.

"I'm glad you're coming with me."

"I'm glad I am, too." Madison only hoped she'd feel the same way when they got to the infusion center.

Gabrielle glanced at Madison as they stood in the elevator. Madison had been very quiet on the drive, and now, her tan face was slightly pale. Gabrielle decided to leave her to her thoughts.

They walked down the hall toward the infusion center. As they neared the door, Madison's steps faltered.

Gabrielle reached for Madison's hand. "If you can't do this, I completely understand. I was afraid it might be too much for you. Why don't you go to the cafeteria? Or stay in the lounge here while I get treatment?"

Madison, who seemed almost panic-stricken, looked at their joined hands and met Gabrielle's gaze. "I can do this. I want to be here for you."

"All right. Let's walk in together." She didn't let go of Madison's hand until they entered the infusion center.

One of the nurses at the nurses' station spoke to her. "Gabrielle Valenci?"

"Yes."

"I'm Trish. I'll take your vitals first. Then we can get started with the treatment."

Madison hung back while Gabrielle stepped up to the scales. Trish checked the digital readout and hit a button to translate it from kilograms into pounds. Damn, Gabrielle thought. I've lost another two pounds.

"You've shown a steady decrease in weight since the first treatment in your initial round of chemo. How have you been feeling?"

"Tired mainly. And I have joint pain, which I understand may get worse with these next three treatments."

"You've finished your radiation?"

"About three weeks ago."

"Between the two, yes, your joint pain can get worse. Did you take your steroids last night and this morning?"

"Yes, I did." Gabrielle noticed Madison fidgeting in place nearby.

After Trish took her blood pressure and temperature, she led them toward the cordoned-off infusion cubicles.

"You have your pick this morning." Trish motioned to the individual units. Each had an open area facing the nurses' station.

"Six is fine, I guess."

"Can you pick another one?" Madison asked.

Gabrielle caught her pained expression. "How about eight, Trish?"

"Eight it is."

Gabrielle sat down on the cot, while Madison took a seat in the lounge chair next to her. Trish readied the fluids and IV.

Trish glanced at Madison. "You seem familiar. Have you been in here before?"

"My partner, Callie, was a patient here," Madison answered. "She passed a little over three years ago."

A look of sympathy crossed Trish's face. "I'm sorry for your loss." She addressed Gabrielle. "You don't have a port, correct?"

"No."

"Which hand do you prefer?"

"Probably my right since it's closest to the IV drip."

Trish held the needle in place over the top of Gabrielle's hand. "You'll feel a stick." She poked the needle in and tried to hit the vein. After a few wiggles and a lot of pain for Gabrielle, she pulled it back out and pressed a piece of gauze over the spot. "Did you stay hydrated?

"I think so." Gabrielle pointed to the bag she'd brought in. "Madison, can you grab a Gatorade for me?" Madison lifted out a bottle and handed it over. Gabrielle took a long drink.

"How about we try the other hand?" Trish asked as she prepped her left hand.

Gabrielle watched her work and was surprised when Madison took hold of her other hand.

"Try to relax," Madison said.

She was so mesmerized with Madison's gentle smile, she barely noticed the stick of the needle.

"Got it." Trish taped the needle in place and set up the IV drip of fluids. "I'm sure you know the drill. We'll get you halfway through this and then the Benadryl and anti-nausea meds." She gathered up the detritus from the IV insertion, tossed it in the nearby wastebasket, and went back to the nurses' station.

Gabrielle turned toward Madison. "You can crack open that book you brought, if you like."

When Madison released her hand, Gabrielle immediately missed her touch.

"I'd rather talk with you."

"What do you want to talk about?"

"How about how you got started in modeling?"

Gabrielle made a face. "It's not an exciting story."

"And I'm sure you're being modest."

"I wasn't anything special growing up. Braces. Gawky teenager. The whole bit. I graduated in the top ten percent of my high school class and attended the University of Georgia on scholarship."

"In?"

"Business. My dad wanted me to go to NYU, but I wanted to spread my wings a little. I was there for two years, and I guess you could say I blossomed during that time. I began filling out more. On a dare from my roommate, I went to a modeling fair. A headhunter was looking for the All-American Southern Belle for his agency. Little did he know I was from New York. After a long, heated discussion with my father, I signed with the agency and never looked back."

"I take it your dad wanted you to graduate?" Madison asked.

"And join him at his investment firm. But once he saw how happy I was modeling, he was behind it one hundred percent." Gabrielle smiled sadly.

"He passed a few years ago, didn't he?"

"Massive heart attack. I was devastated. He took care of me after my mom died when I was in high school. We were very close."

Trish interrupted them, bringing over a syringe full of medicine. "Ready for your Benadryl?"

Gabrielle sighed. She hated this part of the treatment. It wiped her out for several hours. Again, she wasn't sure what she'd been thinking when she thought she could do this alone. Eva hadn't accompanied her to her treatments in Manhattan, but she had a limo drive her to the hospital and back to her apartment.

"Not really," Gabrielle said, "but I know it has to be done."

"Right. Can't chance an allergic reaction to the Taxol." Trish pushed the syringe into her IV. Within minutes, Gabrielle felt loopy.

Madison gave her a sympathetic look. "Callie hated this, too."

"Now, you can really go somewhere to relax and read that book. I'll be out in another fifteen minutes."

"Just like Callie, you're trying to get rid of me."

Gabrielle laid her head back on her pillow. She didn't know she'd dozed off until Trish awakened her, asking her to repeat her name and birth date. Trish had donned the "hazmat" garb that went along with the dispensing of these drugs—goggles, gown, mask, and gloves.

After Trish had finished, Madison leaned over and said, "You know, Callie and I always joked about the hazmat suit. It isn't very comforting, is it?"

Gabrielle laughed. "No, it isn't." She reached her hand out, and Madison gripped it. "Thanks for coming."

"You don't need to thank me." Madison squeezed her hand. "But you're welcome."

Eventually, Gabrielle drifted off to the sound of the IV dispenser's steady clicking. Occasionally, she'd awaken and find Madison engrossed in her book, oblivious to Gabrielle's attention. Even in the fuzziness of her mind, she knew these hours spent together were somehow special. Something to build upon in the infancy of their friendship.

Chapter 8

"So?"

Madison glared at Cyndra. "So?"

"Are you going to make me ask?"

They'd driven up to spend Saturday on the gulf-side beach in Key Largo, and they sat there now in canvas chairs. The temperature wasn't as unbearable as it had been in the previous weeks. The water was still warm enough for Montanna to wade in, and Madison kept an eye on her as she searched for seashells.

"If you're asking about Gabrielle, I'm glad I went with her Tuesday."

"What made you go with her, by the way?"

"It kind of came to me out of the blue." Madison thought back to how the idea popped into her head after picturing the dolphin. "I didn't want her to be alone, you know?"

"And…" Cyndra made a motion with her hand.

"And she's very nice." Madison kept her head down as she plucked the material of her one-piece swimsuit. "And I like her." She peeked up to find Cyndra grinning at her. "It doesn't mean we're dating or anything, Cyn."

"No, it doesn't. But it doesn't negate that possibility, right?"

"Look, I don't even know if she has a girlfriend back in New York."

"Does she talk about anyone?" Cyndra asked.

"So far, no. I can't imagine her without someone, though. She's beautiful and kind and has a good sense of humor and…" Madison tried to grasp what she was feeling. She hadn't felt like this about any woman since Callie. *Callie.*

"Hey," Cyndra said gently. "Where'd you just go?"

"Nowhere."

"Maddie, you're talking to me, remember?"

"Montanna, what did I say about not going in past your knees?"

Madison shouted. Mo had waded into water up to her waist.

Mo's shoulders slumped. Madison could almost hear her heavy sigh. "Okay, Mom." Mo sloshed back into shallower waters.

"Madison." Cyndra raised her sunglasses.

"I was thinking about Callie."

Cyndra looked toward Mo and didn't say anything for a long moment. "I imagine it was hard for you going back to the same place that Callie had her treatment."

"It was at first. I almost had a panic attack when we walked into the infusion center. But then..."

"Yes?"

"Then I only thought of Gabrielle and being there for her."

"There's nothing wrong with feeling that way."

"I guess."

Cyndra grasped her forearm. "Gabrielle needed you, and you were there for her. Because that's the kind of friend you are."

"I just met her, but already I feel like I know her. How can that be?"

"I think you have a connection because of Callie and the cancer."

Madison didn't say anything, but Cyndra was probably right.

"Have you talked to her since Tuesday?"

"I've called her a few times to check on her and ask if she needs anything, but she says she's fine. She reminds me of Callie that way. So, I'm sure you're right about the connection. By tomorrow and Monday, though, she should feel the exhaustion when the steroids wear off."

A loud splash distracted Madison from the conversation. She jumped to her feet when she saw the dolphin leap into the air again. She ran to Mo.

"Get out of the water, Mo. Now!"

Mo, entranced with the dolphin, wasn't listening. Madison grabbed hold of her hand and pulled her to the shore. The dolphin couldn't have reached Mo where she'd been standing, but it still frightened Madison to think of Mo in any kind of danger, imagined or real.

"Is that him?" Cyndra appeared at her side and cupped her hand over her eyes to watch the dolphin's antics.

"It can't be. It has to be another one." But with each jump, Madison was pretty sure it was their cove visitor.

"Mom, it's Free! I can tell."

"How?"

"He has that white spot on the tip of his fin. See?" Mo pointed.

Madison remembered back to when she'd first noticed it—almost like a birthmark.

"It's him?" Cyndra smiled as she watched the dolphin.

"Sure looks like him." Madison laughed when he spun high in the air and smacked down on the water.

"He's kind of a showoff, isn't he?"

"Oh, he sure is." Free dipped in and out of the water. He faced them and nodded, making the laughter-sounding noise. Then he leapt once more before disappearing from view. They stood there anticipating a repeat performance, but he'd left them again.

"That's just too weird," Madison muttered. "How'd he know to come here? It's not like we told him our plans or anything."

"Um, Madison, you realize you're talking about a dolphin, right?"

"Yes, I know, you dope. But he's so… odd." Madison motioned at the water. "It's almost like he has a connection to us."

They stared at the water a little longer, though Madison sensed he was gone.

* * *

Gabrielle awakened from the fog of sleep to the sound of knocking on the door that led to the back deck. Struggling to her feet, she pulled on her robe and shuffled from the bedroom. She grabbed onto furniture along the way to stay upright. Pushing the curtain aside, she saw Madison begin to walk away and she pulled the door open.

"Madison?"

Madison had her hand on the railing but turned around when Gabrielle spoke her name. "Hey."

Gabrielle shivered at the sound of her husky voice.

"I'm sorry. You're cold and here I have you standing with the door open."

Gabrielle didn't tell Madison the real reason for her reaction. She wasn't exactly sure what was going on with her. She didn't know if it was her emotional state, the chemo drugs, or the comedown from the steroid high. It was a mixture of excitement and calm, a heady combination that left her a little confused.

"Would you like to come in?" Gabrielle stepped aside as Madison moved past her.

"I have a feeling I woke you up."

"I was asleep, but it's okay."

"I was worried about you. I hadn't heard from you since Friday. I remember from Callie how the exhaustion usually hits about now, and I wanted to make sure you're all right."

Gabrielle walked into the living room and almost flung herself on the couch. Madison hurried in and sat beside her. She reached out to touch Gabrielle but quickly withdrew her hand.

"Is there anything you need? Juice? Gatorade? Any food you like? I'm not the best of cooks, but I can make do. Or I can go out and get you anything you'd like to eat. Or—" Madison stopped. "I'm babbling."

Gabrielle patted her knee. "You're not babbling." Madison tensed under her fingertips. "I have juice and Gatorade, but thank you for your offer."

"Food?"

"I've not felt much like eating. I've slept most of the day." Gabrielle craned her neck to try to see the clock. "What time is it?"

"Seven."

"Oh my God. I've been in bed since ten this morning. I did manage to eat a little breakfast earlier."

"That settles it. You need to eat, Gabrielle. I have some homemade vegetable soup on the kitchen stove. Why don't you let me bring you some?"

Gabrielle's cell phone vibrated on the table beside the couch. "Excuse me for a minute." She stared down at the caller ID. *Eva.* Did she really want to take the call? She stifled a sigh as she picked up. "Hello?"

"I was getting worried. You've not answered any of my calls since Thursday."

"I'm fine, Eva. Tired, but fine."

Madison mouthed, "I'll go."

Gabrielle shook her head and motioned at her to stay on the couch.

"I thought I'd come down to see you this week," Eva said.

"This week isn't good."

"Next week?"

"Aren't you busy with the shoot?"

"I can still take some time away to fly down. How about the week before your next treatment? And I won't take 'no' for an answer."

Gabrielle heard someone yell Eva's name in the background.

"Coming!" Eva shouted. "Listen, I need to go. Frederick's being a bitch on this shoot. I'll call you when I firm up my flight plans."

"You don't—"

The line went dead. Gabrielle stared at the phone in frustration, half-tempted to toss it across the room. Madison shifted again on the couch, appearing very uncomfortable.

"A friend of mine," she told Madison.

"A girlfriend?" Madison winced as soon as the words left her mouth. "Sorry. It's none of my business."

She gave Madison an honest answer. "I'm not sure what to call her. I mean we've been together for two years, but—"

Madison stood up abruptly. "Like I said, it's really none of my business, Gabrielle. I'm sorry I asked. The vegetable soup?"

"That would be nice."

Madison rushed out the back door. Gabrielle tried to figure out what she had seen in Madison's eyes when she told her about Eva.

Madison kept her head lowered as she walked back to her house. *She has a girlfriend.* She let the words sink in. She'd told Cyndra that she would be surprised if Gabrielle was unattached, but to hear her talk on the phone with Eva was upsetting.

Going up the steps to her deck, she wondered at the disappointment that churned through her body. The feeling was an even bigger shock to her than Gabrielle's revelation.

Chapter 9

"You're doing fine, Esther. Just add a little more white to your palette to lighten the sky and punch up the vivid landscape colors." Madison moved on to her next student. "Nice, Deidra. Are you sure you've never worked with oils before?"

Deidra, a middle-aged woman who, like most of her students, was taking the art class for fun, beamed at her. "No."

"Well, you have a natural talent for it." Madison meant the words. Sometimes, she gave extra encouragement to some who struggled, but Deidra had a way with the brush. She went from student to student, offering suggestions or a verbal pat on the back when needed.

The time rapidly slipped away as it always seemed to when she taught. No, it wasn't the same as painting, but it was the best Madison could do. Hell, it might always be the best she could do.

After class, she locked the room and headed down the hallway to the outer doors. She'd just reached her car when she heard someone call her name. She turned, surprised when she saw Gabrielle walking toward her.

"Gabrielle? What are you doing here?" Madison flinched. She didn't mean that quite like it sounded. Or maybe she did. She'd been avoiding Gabrielle since the night she'd brought over vegetable soup. Yes, she'd still called to check up on her, but she hadn't made any special trips over to Gabrielle's house.

"I walked over to see you this evening. Your sister was there babysitting Montanna. She said I'd find you here and gave me directions." Under the glare of the parking lot lights, Gabrielle appeared almost ethereal, her skin pale and drawn.

She's not getting enough rest. Madison remembered something else. Wasn't this the week for Eva to make an appearance? Madison tried to push the unpleasant thought from her mind. It was good to see Gabrielle. "This was a bit of a drive for you, too." The course she taught for the northern branch of Florida Keys Community College was located about ten miles from Islamorada.

Gabrielle leaned her hip against Madison's SUV. "It was no trouble. I've missed seeing you. You've not been avoiding me, have you?"

Madison delayed answering by putting her paint-supply case and easel in the back of the SUV. When she returned to the driver's side, Gabrielle still stood there waiting for her response.

"I... well... I..."

Gabrielle cocked an eyebrow.

"I didn't come over this week because I didn't want to interfere with your time with Eva."

Gabrielle gave her a knowing smile. "I thought that might be it. She didn't come down."

Madison didn't know what to say, so she kept quiet.

Gabrielle waved her hand dismissively. "She had to stay. The photographer wasn't happy with some of the shots."

Madison tried to determine if Gabrielle was upset about Eva's absence. She didn't seem upset—more like resigned to the fact her girlfriend didn't make time for her. She wanted to ask about the nature of their relationship but decided to let it go... for now.

"Can I buy you some coffee or something?" Gabrielle asked.

Madison stared down at her keys. "I should get home. Cyndra's waiting."

"Actually," Gabrielle drew out the word, "your sister suggested we stop for some coffee. She's fine watching Mo a little longer. I passed a diner along the way. It looked busy, so I have a feeling it's decent."

"I think I know the place." A lot of her students would go there after class. "Rick's Coffee House?"

"Yeah, I think that was the name."

Madison fiddled with her keys some more.

"Remember I'm buying," Gabrielle teased.

"Okay. You talked me into it. Do you want to follow me over?"

"If you don't mind, could you drive? I'm lousy at following another car."

Madison keyed open her car. "Hop on in." After they settled into the SUV, Madison motioned to Gabrielle's hair. "I like that you're not wearing your wig."

Gabrielle fingered her hair. "It makes my head sweat, and you convinced me I don't need to hide that I'm going through treatment."

They were quiet on the drive over. Once they arrived, the hostess led them to a booth.

"Coffee, please," Gabrielle said.

"Same for me, except I think I want a slice of your apple pie."

Gabrielle's eyes widened. "Is it good?" she asked the waitress.

"Better than my mama's."

"Then I'll have one, too, please."

In no time at all, the waitress returned with two slices of pie and two cups of coffee. Madison grabbed her fork and dug in. She closed her eyes. "God, this is to die for." She looked over at Gabrielle who was staring at Madison's mouth. Madison cleared her throat and took another bite. She tried to ignore the jolt of electricity Gabrielle's gaze had shot through her body.

"Madison, I…" Gabrielle pushed a piece of the pie around on her plate. She raised her head. "I want us to be friends. I feel like we could be good friends, and I don't want anything to change that."

Madison stared at her plate. "I feel like we could be good friends, too." She wanted to say more, wanted to say she was attracted to Gabrielle. But she held back.

"I'm not sure about Eva and me. Like I told you the other day, I'm not even sure of my feelings toward her anymore. She's had a hard time with the cancer. She doesn't know how to handle it."

"You can't 'handle it.' You support your loved one who's fighting it with every ounce of their being." The words caught in Madison's throat. She took a breath before continuing. "You hope your support is enough."

"Callie was a lucky woman."

"I was the lucky one. I was able to love someone who brought so much light into the world. Sometimes I feel that light was snuffed out when she died."

"No, Madison." Gabrielle reached across the table and brushed her thumb against Madison's hand. "The light lives on through Montanna."

"What a kind thing to say," Madison said, blinking her tears away.

"Can you tell me how you and Callie met? If it's too personal, I understand."

Madison's mouth tugged into a smile as she thought back in time. "No, it's not too personal. We met in Providence my last year at the Rhode Island School of Design."

"Wow. I know how prestigious that school is."

"I received a full scholarship, or I never could've afforded the place. Callie was a graduate student at Brown. We attended the same LGBT party. I spotted her across the room talking with two other women. When she glanced my way, it was literally as if time stood still. You know how you always hear that expression and think it's a myth?"

"Love at first sight," Gabrielle said with a touch of wonder in her voice.

"I hadn't planned on staying in Providence after I graduated, but with Callie still working toward her master's in history, I stayed. Much to my mother's displeasure. She of course didn't accept me being gay. But she also wanted me home in Kansas City to begin my career there, as if it were the only place to paint." Madison shook her head as she thought about her mother's histrionics at the time.

"But you were in love, and you stayed."

"Yeah. There was no way I could leave Callie. She was my touchstone, you know?"

"You were both blessed, just like we said."

They stared at each other a long moment until Gabrielle broke the spell and went back to her pie.

"Hey. Remember the dolphin?" Madison asked.

"How could I forget him?"

"Cyn, Mo, and I went to the beach at Key Largo. I'll be damned if the dolphin didn't show up there."

"You're kidding. Wait, how did you know it was him?"

"He has this white spot on the tip of his dorsal fin. The thing I can't figure out is how he knew we were there."

"Coincidence?"

"I don't know. There's something about Free that's—"

"Free?"

"Yeah, Mo named him. Seems to fit."

Gabrielle smiled. "I like it." The waitress showed up to top off their coffee. Gabrielle held her hand over her cup. "No thank you. If I drink anymore, I won't be able to sleep tonight."

"I'm done, too," Madison said.

The waitress placed the bill on the table. Gabrielle snatched it up.

"You really don't have to buy," Madison told her.

"Nope. I said I would, and I always keep my word."

Gabrielle paid the bill, and they left for the SUV. On the drive back to the parking lot to pick up her car, Gabrielle turned to

Madison. "Back to Free. Do you think he's like an escapee from one of the marine parks?"

"No, he seems… almost magical. There were a couple of times he looked at me and I swear he knew what I was thinking." Madison glanced over at Gabrielle to gauge her reaction. "You're not laughing."

"No, I'm not. Dolphins are very intelligent. Frankly, I think they're more intelligent than we are. They're also intuitive. Many reports tell of them coming to the rescue of people out at sea." Gabrielle gazed out the side window and grew quiet.

"What are you thinking?" Madison asked when they pulled into the school parking lot.

"Maybe he came to us for a reason." Gabrielle shook her head. "Now, you probably think I've lost my mind."

"No, I don't. Free's special. I don't believe we've seen the last of him."

"Good." Gabrielle opened her door and got out but lingered.

"Good?"

"Yes. Because your face lights up when you talk about him, and I enjoy seeing that."

Madison responded on impulse. "Let me take you to treatment again on Tuesday."

"If it's not too much for you, I'd love for you to come with me again," Gabrielle said with a smile.

She walked to her car, and Madison waited until she was safely inside. The radiance of Gabrielle's smile lingered with her long after Madison got home. It was the last thing on her mind as she drifted off into a peaceful sleep.

* * *

The week following her second treatment, Gabrielle was feeling the effects of the chemo even more. Thank God she only had one more treatment. She stood in the shower and tried to wash off the bone-crunching fatigue, knowing it was impossible.

She shut her eyes to the sting of the shower spray, but then she felt the water pool at her feet. *Oh, no.* She looked down and saw the hair clogging the drain. Gabrielle pulled on her hair, and a big chunk came out in her hand. She leaned against the tiled wall and sobbed. Yes, she'd been told she'd lose her hair again, but it didn't make it any easier to take.

She finished her shower, dried off, and stared at her reflection in the mirror. Bald patches were noticeable. She opened the medicine cabinet and pulled out her dad's old clippers. She had a few things of his she couldn't part with. Something tangible to keep his memory alive.

But she needed help to do what she had in mind.

Gabrielle opened the door on the second knock. "Thank you for coming over, Madison."

"I was worried when I heard you on the phone. Do you need anything?"

"Hold on a sec." Gabrielle went to the bathroom and grabbed the clippers and a towel.

Madison glanced at the items in her hands and then met Gabrielle's gaze. "You're sure?"

Gabrielle was glad she didn't have to explain herself. She knew Madison would understand. Gabrielle handed her the clippers, sat down in one of the deck chairs, and draped the towel around her shoulders.

"Take it all off."

Madison hesitated.

"God, Madison, I didn't even think about how this would affect you." She started to stand.

"Wait." Madison touched her shoulder and managed a tremulous smile. "I understand why you want this. Callie was the same way, and even though it was hard, I wanted her to feel right about everything. I mean nothing is ever 'right' with cancer, but there are some things you just have to do. Shaving her head was one of them for Callie. So, I get this, and I'm honored and touched you'd ask me."

It was Gabrielle's turn to well up. She bit her lip and nodded once.

Madison switched on the clippers. She took a deep breath and let it out before she started. Gabrielle kept her eyes closed while Madison pushed the clippers over her scalp. Clumps of hair fell softly on her bare feet.

Finally, Madison turned off the clippers. Gabrielle ran her fingers over her head and felt only stubble. Her eyes stung, but she blinked a few times to keep the tears from falling. Madison was watching her with a worried expression on her face.

"Oh, Gabrielle, I—"

Gabrielle stood and placed her fingers over Madison's lips. "No.

This is what I wanted, remember? I'd rather do it this way than lose it in chunks over the next couple of weeks." She rubbed her scalp again. "I bet I look a sight, though, huh?"

"You're perfect," Madison whispered. She gently lifted Gabrielle's chin and pressed her lips to her cheek.

Gabrielle's breath hitched at the contact. She stared at Madison's mouth and leaned forward as if an invisible force was pushing her body toward Madison.

But then Madison backed up a step. "Uh, here." She thrust the clippers into Gabrielle's hand. "I should get back home. I have to pick Mo up in about an hour." She moved toward the steps.

"Madison?"

Madison paused at the top of the stairs.

"Thank you for doing this."

Madison gave her a small smile. "I'll check on you tomorrow, okay?"

Gabrielle nodded. She went to the railing and followed Madison with her gaze as she headed home.

I wanted to kiss her, she thought. She wondered at the mixture of emotions she was feeling. Was it because of her battle with cancer that everything seemed magnified? She touched her cheek, still feeling the brush of Madison's soft lips. Before stepping back inside, she glanced out at the cove, hoping to catch a glimpse of Free. But he was nowhere in sight.

Chapter 10

"What are you thinking about?"

Madison didn't answer right away. She kept her sight on the cove below as if an appearance of the dolphin would clear away the confusion cloaking her mind. Cyndra waited her out.

"I'm thinking I shouldn't have kissed her." Madison took a long pull of her Budweiser.

Cyndra whipped her head toward Madison. "You kissed her? Where?"

"On her back deck."

"That's not even funny, Madison. You know what I mean."

Madison tapped her cheek. "Here."

"And? I swear getting information from you is like picking a tick off a dog."

Madison laughed. "Where the hell did you come up with that expression?"

Cyndra clinked the ice in her glass of tea. "I don't know. Some movie about the South. You have to admit, though, it's quite a visual. Once a tick latches on, it's hard as hell to pull it off a dog. It's the same with you. You keep shit bottled up. You always have."

"Thank you, Oprah, for your astute observation."

Cyndra squinted at her. "You know, a couple of beers, and you lose your sense of humor. You're supposed to loosen up and tell your little sister all your secrets."

Madison stared down at her beer bottle and slowly peeled off the label as she thought about the look in Gabrielle's eyes. How she'd stared at Madison's mouth. How she would've kissed Madison if Madison hadn't stepped back. "She was going to kiss me."

Cyndra stilled Madison's fingers that were systematically tearing the label apart.

"What happened?"

Madison met her gaze. "Monday afternoon, she called me to

come over. I sensed something was up, like she wasn't doing well. So I went over to her place, and she asked me to clip off the rest of her hair. She'd already lost chunks of it from her last two treatments. Just like Callie, she didn't want to wait for it to slowly fall out. I did what she asked. When I was done, she was so vulnerable and… beautiful. Hell, she *is* beautiful. She doesn't have to work at it. She teared up, and I couldn't stand it. So, I kissed her cheek." Madison gazed out again at the water below. "She stared at my mouth and leaned forward. She would've kissed me, but I backed away."

"Why?"

Madison turned to her. "Because she has a girlfriend."

"Oh, poo." Cyndra took a sip of her iced tea.

"Poo? Where the hell are you coming up with this shit?"

"Madison, she obviously doesn't have deep feelings for this girlfriend of hers."

"And you know this because…"

"Let's see. Maybe because Gabrielle Valenci's here and her girlfriend's not."

"Her girlfriend's a model, too, and she works in New York."

"Ah, but said girlfriend has yet to show up in Islamorada."

"Doesn't mean she won't," Madison mumbled.

"Oh, I give up."

"You do?" Madison didn't attempt to hide her sarcasm.

"You wish. Have you thought about talking to her about your feelings?"

"I won't do it."

"Why not?" Cyndra asked, clearly exasperated. When Madison didn't answer, she leaned over and put a hand on her knee. "Madison, I know how hard it is for you to allow anyone to get close to you again."

"Do you? Do you really?" Madison didn't mean to sound angry, but she was. Or maybe she was frustrated. She caught Cyndra's hurt expression. "I know you love me, and you want to see me happy. But I have to think about Mo, too. I don't want Mo to get attached and then have it all fall apart. I can't do it to Mo. It wouldn't be fair to her."

Cyndra stood up and walked to the railing. With her back to Madison, she said, "Do me a favor."

"It depends."

Cyndra faced her. "If this feeling gets any stronger, don't push it aside. Callie would want you to love again."

Madison started to speak, but Cyndra held up her hand.

"You can't talk me out of that one. Callie told me she was afraid you'd push everyone away." Cyndra started crying. "And you did a damn fine job of it. Slowly, you came back to us—to Mo, to me, to Beverly—but the last part is the hardest. You pushed your heart and happiness away the day Callie died. You have to stop."

Madison wiped at the tears streaming down her cheeks. "I'm afraid, Cyn."

Cyndra went to her, pulled her out of her chair, and gave her a tight hug. "That's what we're here for, sis."

* * *

Gabrielle sat with her feet dangling off the dock, the encounter with Madison fresh in her mind. It was Thursday now. With the way Madison fled after clipping Gabrielle's hair, she wondered if Madison would take her to her final treatment next week. Sometimes she still couldn't comprehend she had cancer. She saw the proof every day in the mirror, but it was as if she were looking at another person. Someone else going through the treatment.

She leaned back on her hands and raised her face to the warm November sun. She drifted back to days spent with her parents here at the Islamorada house. Her father would grill burgers and bratwursts, her mother would fix her "famous" potato salad. They'd sit on the deck, discussing nothing and everything.

But then life moved on. The days drifted by like the flipping of a calendar in an old movie to denote the passage of time. There was Gabrielle at four, holding up her sore finger to her mother for inspection as Gabrielle tried her best not to cry. There she was at fourteen, talking to her parents about her feelings about girls. Then the first trip down to Islamorada with her father after her mother had died; the sadness seemed to follow them from New York and drift over them like a raincloud.

Almost on cue, a cloud passed over and darkened the back of Gabrielle's eyelids. She opened her eyes and sighed when she saw the gathering storm on the horizon. A metaphor for her life.

She thought she spotted movement in the water. Instinctively, she brought her legs up onto the dock and rose to her feet. Then she saw the dorsal fin of the dolphin above the surface.

"You're back," she said with a smile. "Why does that not surprise me?"

In answer, the dolphin poked his nose out of the water in front of her and started a one-sided conversation with her.

"Did you know you have a name now?"

He nodded.

Gabrielle laughed. "Oh, you do, do you? What do you think about being named 'Free'? You have to like it, by the way. Mo named you, and you don't want to disappoint her." *She's had enough disappointment and sadness in her life.*

Free became more animated as if to voice his stamp of approval on the name. He flipped his nose back. He dipped under the surface, splashed a little farther out in the cove, and came back to repeat the same backward flip of his nose. He seemed to be beckoning her into the water.

"You want me in there with you?"

This time, he whistled and nodded vigorously.

"I don't know, Free. The water's usually not as warm in November."

He stared at her, and she became mesmerized. She'd never noticed his eye color before. Blue. He held her gaze. A memory from her childhood returned. As a teenager, she and her father swam in wetsuits in November.

Gabrielle mentally shook herself free of the vision. When she became aware of her surroundings again, Free was still staring at her. He repeated the backward flip of his nose.

"You want me to get my old wetsuit and join you in there? Free, I don't even know if I'll have the strength." *Okay, I'm losing it. I'm talking to him like he understands me.* The scary thing was, maybe he did.

He dove below the surface and leapt high in the air in front of her, pirouetting and slapping his body sideways into the water to create a huge splash. He swam around the cove a few times. On one last pass of the dock, he swam near enough for him to make eye contact. Then he was gone until he performed his final acrobatic leap at the mouth of the cove.

Gabrielle stood there, stunned. What had just happened? As she walked back to the house, she tried to dismiss the thought. Every time she convinced herself it was a silly notion, Free's antics replayed in her mind. She climbed the steps and tried to concentrate on what to have for dinner. When she neared the top, her knees almost gave out. She cried out in pain and sank down on a step to gather enough strength to make it to the deck. After five minutes, she chanced it again, struggling with each lifting of her foot.

Dinner was an afterthought as Gabrielle entered the house. Her bed and sleep beckoned to her. She stripped, not even bothering to dress in her nightclothes. She pulled the covers up to her chin. As she drifted off, the image of Free appeared as if summoned. And blue. The color enveloped Gabrielle in a warm and comforting embrace.

* * *

Monday night, Madison picked up the phone and started to dial Gabrielle's number. She quickly hit "Off."

"Come on, Madison, you can do this."

"Did you say something, Mom?"

Madison was in the studio she'd converted into a makeshift den since she'd stopped painting. Apparently, she'd spoken loud enough for Mo to hear her from her bedroom.

"No, Montanna. Go back to studying." Madison heard a muffled "… all I ever do." She stared up at the skylight she and Callie had installed when they'd purchased the house. Madison strained to see any visible stars, but the full moon hampered the starlight from shining through.

"Screw it." She punched in Gabrielle's number without another thought about backing out.

"Hello?"

"Um, hi, um, Gabrielle?" *You* called *her*, idiot. Of course it's Gabrielle.

"Madison?"

"Listen, um…" Suddenly, Madison became incapable of stringing together a meaningful sentence. "I was wondering if you'd still like me to drive you to Miami tomorrow morning," Madison said in a rush. Silence greeted her words. She hurried to fill it. "I mean, that is unless you had someone else taking you. I mean—"

"I wasn't sure if you'd still want to drive me," Gabrielle said in a hushed tone.

"Why wouldn't I?" Madison had a pretty good idea why Gabrielle felt that way, but she asked anyway.

"Well, I didn't know after…" Gabrielle seemed to flounder.

Madison didn't want to address the non-kiss. Not now. Maybe never. She decided to sidestep it completely.

"Do you want me to swing by at seven again?"

There was a slight hesitation before Gabrielle said, "That's fine."

"I'll see you bright and early then. Try to get some rest."

"See you in the morning, Madison."

* * *

Gabrielle was looking out the passenger window, lost in thought. She realized Madison had asked her something. "Hmm?"

"How do you feel about your last treatment?" Madison flashed her a bright smile.

Gabrielle's heart fluttered. It was the second heart-stopping smile of the day from Madison. When she'd picked Gabrielle up about an hour ago, Madison had greeted her the same way.

"A little surreal. It's hard to describe."

A few minutes passed before Madison spoke again.

"Callie… she didn't really have a last treatment, at least not like you're having today. She chose to stop treatment. I argued with her. But she told me she was tired. Tired of fighting. Tired of feeling so horrible. She wanted some 'quality days,' she called them." Madison's voice broke. "They didn't seem like quality days to me. I knew it meant the cancer would claim her life."

Gabrielle reached across the console and squeezed Madison's shoulder. She wanted to say again she was sorry for Madison's pain, but this morning, it sounded so trite. She didn't say anything.

Madison swiped her cheeks with her left hand. "The thing I hate the most? That Mo will grow up without that beautiful woman as her mother. I try to keep Callie's memory alive, but sometimes it hurts so damn much to even think about her."

"Madison, you're too hard on yourself. Remember you're a wonderful mother to Mo."

"I don't know…"

"Oh, honey. She worships you. You only need to be around the two of you once to see that, to feel it."

A slight blush colored Madison's cheeks. Gabrielle wasn't sure if it was the result of her compliment or the endearment that seemed so natural passing her lips.

They arrived at the hospital and took the elevator to the infusion center. They didn't speak as they walked to the entrance.

"You ready to ring the bell?" Madison asked when they reached the double doors.

"The bell?"

"They didn't tell you? After your final treatment, you

ring the 'last chemo' bell."

"You're kidding."

"Nope." Madison's expression saddened. "With Callie, it was bittersweet. She was glad to be done, but I knew what it meant."

On impulse, Gabrielle grabbed Madison and hugged her. Madison briefly tensed in her arms, then she relaxed and returned the embrace. Gabrielle let the hug convey her unspoken words.

After Trish took Gabrielle's vitals and asked the pertinent questions, they settled in cubicle Number Five. With quiet proficiency, Trish started an IV line and administered the fluids.

Gabrielle talked with Madison before Trish returned to infuse the Benadryl and anti-nausea medication. She was unexpectedly nervous. Thoughts bounced through her mind like bumper cars at an amusement park. *What if this doesn't work? What if the cancer comes back? What if she has to endure this horrible treatment regimen yet again?*

"Hey, you all right? You're a little pale."

"I'm fine."

Madison reached for her hand. "I would hope by now you'd know you can talk to me about anything."

"What if it comes back?" Gabrielle said in a rush, startled when tears trickled down her cheeks.

"You need to hope for the best, Gabrielle. You have some of the most skilled doctors here at the University of Miami. They'll stay on top of everything. You have to believe that."

"Yeah?" Gabrielle felt like a little child needing reassurance after falling from a bike and scraping her knee.

Madison gave her a comforting smile. "Yeah."

Trish returned to start the Taxol drip. She glanced at Gabrielle when she switched on the machine. "Ready for your last treatment?"

"As ready as I'll ever be."

After Trish walked away, Madison said, "I'm still thinking we're in some kind of sci-fi flick with all the hazmat gear."

They both giggled. Gabrielle stopped laughing when she heard a familiar voice at the nurses' station.

"Is Gabrielle Valenci here?"

She listened as Trish directed Eva to their cubicle.

"Gabrielle? God, it's good to see you." Eva leaned over the cot and gave her a quick kiss. She then noticed Madison who was looking like a deer caught in headlights. "Oh, hello."

"Hi." Madison stood up and held out her hand. "Madison

Lorraine."

"Eva DuPree," Eva replied, coolly. "Gabrielle's girlfriend."

Why is Eva suddenly so possessive? She hadn't been before. At all.

"Listen, Gabrielle. I should leave. I'm sure Eva would be happy to drive you back to Islamorada."

Gabrielle grabbed Madison's hand. "Please don't go."

"I can drive you back," Eva said, staring at their clasped hands.

"Madison can stay, Eva."

Anger flashed in Eva's eyes, but she seemed to quickly recover. "All right."

Madison sat back down, and Eva settled into the other seat in the cubicle, crossing her long legs in front of her. "So, how do you two know each other? And where's your wig, Gabrielle?"

"Madison's my neighbor. We've become friends. Well, after her daughter gallantly rescued me one day from carrying in groceries." Gabrielle shared a look with Madison. "In answer to your second question, I decided to clip the rest of my hair and go without the wig. It's too hot, and honestly, I don't care anymore about my appearance."

Eva looked like she was going to say something but must've thought better of it.

"Madison Lorraine, Madison Lorraine. Why does that name sound familiar?" Eva snapped her fingers. "The artist."

Madison remained silent.

"We have one of your paintings in our bedroom." Eva emphasized "we" and "our." If Gabrielle had been sitting any closer, she would've kicked her.

"You do?" Madison turned to Gabrielle. "You never told me."

"Remember I told you the painting in the house here was my second favorite. The one in my bedroom in Manhattan is the one I love most."

Eva continued as if Gabrielle hadn't spoken. "Entitled *A Good Day*, I believe. A beach scene with a woman and a small child. It's much different from your other work. It seems very personal."

Gabrielle watched Madison's pained reaction.

"Yes. It was very personal."

It suddenly dawned on her the painting was of Callie and Montanna. Why hadn't she seen it before?

"You're not painting now, are you? I thought I read that

somewhere."

"No," Madison said in an even tone. "I do teach."

"Why aren't you painting?" Eva asked.

Now, Gabrielle really wanted to throttle her. "Eva, it's none of—"

Madison interrupted her. "It's okay." She turned back to Eva. "I've not painted since my partner died."

Eva at least had enough sense to look apologetic. "I didn't know."

"It's all right." Madison stood up. "Listen, I think I'll run downstairs and grab a cup of coffee."

"They have that here." Gabrielle motioned at the menu beside her. "I can order it for you."

"I need to stretch my legs and get some fresh air. I'll be back later."

"You'll be here when I ring the bell, though?"

Madison relaxed her tense posture. "I wouldn't miss it for the world."

"Ring the bell?" Eva asked Gabrielle.

"For my last treatment."

"I'll leave you two alone," Madison murmured. "You probably have some catching up to do. Nice to meet you, Eva." She hastened out of the infusion center.

Gabrielle turned toward Eva. "What is with you?"

"I don't know what you're talking about."

"Oh, cut the innocent act. You've been extremely rude."

"You seemed pretty chummy with her."

"She's a friend, Eva." As Gabrielle spoke the words, the realization hit her that she wished it was more than a friendship.

"You might want to tell her."

"What do you mean?"

"Sometimes you're clueless to a woman's attention. She's very attracted to you." Eva paused. "As she should be. And maybe I'm wrong, but the way you look at her... I don't know." When Gabrielle didn't respond, she said, "Listen. Let's not argue. I wanted to surprise you. I flew in from New York after I remembered your last treatment was today at the University of Miami. I called to find out where their infusion floor was. I thought I'd stay the week."

Gabrielle blanched. "That's very sweet. But don't you remember how my treatments hit me before? Your stay would consist of you watching me sleep."

"Maybe we can celebrate later?"

Gabrielle's temper spiked. "You don't get it, do you? It's not like I can turn back into healthy Gabrielle Valenci overnight. It'll probably take several months before I'm feeling even fifty percent better, let alone one hundred percent."

"That long?"

Instantly, Gabrielle's anger fizzled and died. Eva had no clue and probably would never understand. Not like Madison, she thought. Eva was Eva DuPree, a coddled supermodel used to everything being perfect. Gabrielle was anything but perfect.

"Yes, that long."

Eva smoothed her linen capris. "Maybe share a glass of wine later? At least?" She actually pouted.

Gabrielle stared up at the ceiling and took a calming breath. "We can share a glass of wine, but don't expect me to last any longer. I'll be asleep by eight, if not sooner." She met Eva's gaze. "But we need to talk."

Eva frowned. "Those are some of the most dreaded words in a relationship."

Gabrielle had to stop from saying, "We don't *have* a relationship."

"Why don't we hold off on that conversation until you're feeling better?"

"Eva—"

"Please?"

Gabrielle sighed. "Fine. We'll wait."

Eva visibly relaxed and began talking about her photo shoot. As she droned on about how much of a queen the photographer was, Gabrielle thought about Madison and how comfortable she was with her. How much she enjoyed talking to her. Unlike now with Eva. If Gabrielle didn't have an IV line pumping into her veins, she would've sought out Madison.

Gabrielle's eyes drooped shut, and Eva's voice faded. Gabrielle gradually drifted off and dreamed of a mother and her daughter and the dolphin that had brought them all together.

* * *

Madison sat on a bench outside of the hospital and sipped her coffee. *Of course she's freaking gorgeous.* Eva was possessive, too, which was a bit of a surprise since Gabrielle didn't talk about her that much. If Madison needed confirmation to back off on her attraction to Gabrielle, Eva's appearance sealed it.

Madison watched the visitors come and go. She tried to guess their stories by their body language. Two women laughed together as they headed to the parking lot. *Good news.* A middle-aged man walked hunched over, his jacket bunched up around his neck. His expression held a deep sadness, his eyes vacant as he stared straight ahead. Madison didn't need to guess his story.

She thought back to when she sat in this very spot a few years go with tears streaming down her cheeks. Callie was still upstairs in the infusion center, finishing up what she'd decided would be her last treatment. She'd wanted Madison to stay with her while she rang the bell to signify her final chemo. But Madison couldn't do it. Because she knew what it meant and what the coming months would bring. Callie would die. She'd enter hospice, and they'd prepare her for her passing.

The hospice staff had been so kind. They were there for her, as well as Callie. But no one could prepare Madison for that last moment when Callie had turned to her and said so much without speaking. It was the look of goodbye. Madison cradled Callie in her arms. She sobbed until there were no more tears. At least she thought she'd finished crying. But more tears came at the memorial service when she attempted to struggle through Callie's eulogy. She finally gave up, folded up the paper with her prepared words, and spoke from the heart. She said what a good wife Callie had been, that she'd been an amazing daughter to Beverly. What a wonderful mother she'd been to Montanna. Madison met Mo's blue eyes shining with tears. She watched from the podium while Mo buried her face into Beverly's shoulder.

At that moment, Madison stopped speaking. She wanted to curse God, to yell at Callie for leaving them. To tell everyone to go home; this was such a private grief. But she choked out, "I love you, Callie," and stumbled back to sit next to Beverly. She still felt Beverly's protective arm around her.

Madison returned to the present. She hadn't felt the tears dribbling down her chin, hadn't even known she was crying until a woman asked if she was okay. Embarrassed, Madison assured her she was fine.

She glanced at her watch. She needed to head back upstairs.

* * *

Gabrielle smiled at Madison when she rounded the cubicle partition, but her smile slipped from her face and her brow creased. Madison tried to give her a reassuring smile but wasn't sure if she'd pulled it off. Then Gabrielle's expression turned to one of understanding. God, Madison, thought, we've not known each other that long, and already she can read me.

Eva was still sitting in the lounge chair beside the bed, but she was staring at Gabrielle's IV. She glanced up and nodded slightly at Madison.

"You made it in time," Gabrielle said. "I was beginning to get worried."

"I said I'd be here, and I always keep my word."

Trish moved in front of Madison to detach the IV from Gabrielle's hand. "This is it, Ms. Valenci. No more treatment after today."

Gabrielle's shoulders relaxed and a peaceful expression replaced the worried one from earlier in the day. Good, Madison thought. This is a positive day, and she doesn't need to have any "what if?" thoughts. Gabrielle rose to her feet and teetered. Madison rushed to her and held onto her elbow.

"You okay?"

Gabrielle gave her a sheepish smile. "A little lightheaded for a moment. I'm fine now, though."

Eva stood up and grabbed Gabrielle's other elbow. Madison backed away once she was sure Eva had steadied her.

"All right, Trish. Where's this bell you keep talking about?"

"Right this way." Trish led her to the nurses' station and handed the bell to Gabrielle. "Ring away!"

Gabrielle rang the bell for all it was worth. Madison clapped when she was done. The nurses and some of the patients joined in. Eva hugged her and kissed her on the cheek.

Gabrielle wiped at her eyes. "I can't believe I'm done. Can you, Madison?"

Seeing Gabrielle overcome with emotion, Madison embraced her, not caring that her girlfriend was standing two feet away. This transcended Madison's attraction. This was about new beginnings. A new life.

"I'm so proud of you," Madison whispered in her ear. When Madison let her go, her arms ached to again feel the warmth of Garielle's skin.

Madison stepped aside as Trish and a couple of the other nurses hugged Gabrielle.

"Even though you weren't with us for your full six treatments, we still got attached to you," Trish said. "This is what I say to all my patients. No offense, but I don't want to see you in here again."

Gabrielle laughed. "I'll try my best."

Madison walked behind Eva and Gabrielle as they left the infusion center. She hung back and listened to Eva talk about her plans for that week. Madison wanted to strangle the woman who obviously was clueless about the effects of chemotherapy. When they stepped into the elevator, Madison decided to tell Gabrielle she was heading home.

"I'll drive back on my own. I'm sure Eva's anxious to take you to Islamorada."

Gabrielle frowned. "But—"

"Thank you, Madison," Eva said. "We need some alone time to catch up on things." Eva slid her arm around Gabrielle's waist. "Right, honey?"

Madison faced the elevator doors. She couldn't watch anymore. When they got off the elevator, Madison walked ahead of them. Not so far ahead as to be rude, but far enough where she didn't have to overhear their conversation. She slid on her sunglasses when they stepped outside.

"I'm in the first row, here." Eva motioned at a Mercedes coupe.

"I'm parked in the back of the lot," Madison said. "Thank you for allowing me to take part in your journey, Gabrielle."

"I'm the one who should be thanking you. I couldn't have finished this without you."

Eva stiffened beside Gabrielle and folded her arms across her chest.

"I'll see you back home." Madison hugged her one last time before she walked away.

"See you there," Gabrielle called out.

Madison waved. She fought the urge to run back to Gabrielle and whisk her away. Away from the hospital and any dark thoughts of chemo treatment… and away from Eva DuPree.

Chapter 11

"How'd it go today?" Beverly asked as Madison entered the house.

Madison tossed her keys on the dining room table, pulled out a chair, and slumped into it.

"That bad, huh?" Beverly sat down across from her.

Madison ran her fingers through her hair. "The treatment went fine. It was rewarding to see her ring that bell." She hesitated. "I still feel bad I wasn't there for Callie."

"Callie understood, honey. She knew how hard it was for you to accept she no longer wanted to undergo treatment."

"First Cyndra, now you."

"What do you mean?"

"Letting me in on private conversations you shared with Callie. Cyndra told me Callie confided in her that she hoped I could move on after she died."

"Yes. She told me the same thing."

"Every time she tried to talk to me about it, I'd stop her and tell her I didn't want to hear it and we needed for her to stay positive." Madison shook her head. "God, I lost time with her by being stubborn."

Beverly's expression turned pensive. "But you're not telling me something. What else happened today?"

"I swear, Bev. I know where Callie got her insight. Nothing slips past you."

"You act as if it's a bad thing."

"Not at all." Madison debated how much to tell her, but she'd never held anything back from Beverly before. "We had a surprise visitor at the hospital."

"Oh?"

"Eva DuPree."

"That name sounds familiar. Wait, isn't she a fashion model

as well?"

"And Gabrielle's girlfriend."

"How was Gabrielle about the surprise?"

Madison thought back to her reaction. "To be honest, she didn't seem overly excited to see Eva there." She snorted. "Eva isn't the most sensitive soul in the world, either. She wanted to spend the week celebrating."

"Doesn't she know how much chemo drains you?"

"Apparently she didn't get the memo." Madison stood up and went to the refrigerator for bottled water. She popped it open, took a long drink, and rejoined Beverly at the table.

Beverly rested her chin in her hand and didn't say anything.

Madison took another sip of her water. "What?"

"You're not telling me something and yet, by not telling me, you're saying everything. You like her, don't you?"

"Have you been talking to my sister?"

"I don't have to. It's very obvious."

Madison squirmed in her chair. "Like I told Cyndra, it doesn't really matter. She has a girlfriend. I was aware of this before, but now I've actually met the bi... woman."

"That bad?"

"They don't seem to fit together, Bev. They're both gorgeous, but Gabrielle is so kind and bighearted."

"What are you going to do about it?"

Madison squinted at Beverly. "Okay, 'fess up. You did talk to my sister, didn't you?"

"Maybe."

Before Madison answered, Mo trounced past them and into the kitchen. She grabbed a Coke from the refrigerator.

"How many does that make for you today, Mo?" Madison glanced at the clock. "It's seven-thirty. You're pushing it. You have trouble sleeping if you have caffeine too close to bedtime."

Mo was about to twist open the cap. "Grandma, please tell Mom this is only my first Coke."

"I don't know, Montanna," Beverly said. "She has you on the drinking caffeine when you're going to bed in an hour. I'd listen to her."

"Oh, man."

"No, it's Grandma. Drink water." Beverly had a slight edge to her voice. Her "Don't Mess with Grandma" tone—that's what Callie and Madison used to call it. Madison was always thankful for that tone. Too often, she gave into Mo's whims, especially right after Callie died.

Mo sighed and stomped back to the refrigerator. She switched out the Coke for water, opened the bottle, and took a drink. "Oh my God. This is sooo good!"

"Montanna Marie," Madison warned.

"Sorry, Mom."

"Did you finish your homework?"

"Yes, ma'am. I'm going to listen to Taylor Swift for a little bit on my iPod."

"And then?" Madison said.

"Shower and bed."

Madison opened her arms. "Come here."

Mo fell into her embrace. "Missed you at dinner."

"Missed you, too, kiddo." Madison squeezed her one last time. "Get in your music fix and then your shower. Holler when you're done, and I'll come in for our prayers."

"Okay." Mo kissed her cheek and went to Beverly to do the same. "Love you, Grandma."

Beverly hugged her and returned the kiss. "Love you, too, Montanna." When Beverly faced Madison again, her eyes were moist. "Callie would be so proud of you."

"I like to think she's looking down on Mo from heaven with a big grin on her face."

Beverly smiled wistfully. "Yes. That would be Callie." She pointed at Madison. "If this Gabrielle gives you an opening, take it."

Madison studied her. "You'd be okay with that?"

"Yes, I would be. As would my daughter. This is the first time I've seen you light up when you talk about someone since Callie passed. I don't think this Eva woman will stay in the picture."

"How can you be so sure?"

"Call it intuition. Or maybe it's because of how clueless Eva is to the effects of chemo. Obviously, she's not been attentive in the past. I'd say Gabrielle isn't as enamored with Eva as you think she might be." Beverly stood up and grabbed her purse. "On that note, I bid you goodnight."

Madison followed her to the front door. "Thanks again for picking Mo up after school and watching her."

"You know how much I love to be with her. It's never a hardship. You call me anytime."

"Can we take you out to dinner Friday night?"

"Sure. My choice?"

"Of course," Madison answered.

"The new Mexican restaurant on Old Highway."

"Perfect. Let's try it out."

Madison watched Beverly pull out of the drive. She shut the door and went to the kitchen. As she lifted clean dishes out of the dishwasher and placed them in the cabinets, she thought about Gabrielle. Did she get home okay? What was she doing? As soon as Madison's thoughts drifted that way, she shut them down.

She headed down the hall to Mo's room, but Mo was already in the shower. Madison sat on her bed and looked around the room. Her gaze landed on a framed photo of Callie, Madison, and Mo taken in happier times before any doctor had uttered the dreaded word "cancer."

Madison didn't hear Mo come into the room, but she felt the mattress shift beside her. Mo held her hand.

"I miss her, too."

Madison didn't try to speak, only gripped Mo's hand a little tighter.

"Can we say our prayers now?" Mo asked.

Mo climbed under the covers, and Madison tucked them around her chin even knowing that in less than an hour, Mo would toss them aside. She still performed the act if only to think Mo was just a little safer.

Mo began with, "Dear God, thank you for all my blessings, especially for my mom and Grandma Beverly. Thank you for our home and all the good you do for us. Thank you for Free. Please, God, please have him come back to visit us. Please say hi to Mama and let her know we love her and miss her."

Madison shut her eyes tight against the tears that always came when Mo said those words.

"If it's not too much to ask, don't let Gabrielle ever have cancer again. Please look over her and let her know that we'd love for her to visit us." At those words, Mo popped one eye open and peeked at Madison. "Right, Mom?"

"Finish your prayers, Mo."

"And, God, please let Mom smile more, which by the way, she seems to do when Gabrielle's around. Amen."

Madison didn't know what else to say but, "Amen."

"Why don't you ask Gabrielle to come over for lunch or something, Mom?"

"Not this week, kiddo, she has a friend over."

"What kind of friend?"

"A good friend from New York." Madison leaned over and kissed Mo's forehead. "Go to sleep. I'll see you in the morning."

Madison started for the door.

"Mom?"

"Yeah?"

"Can she come over for lunch next week?"

"We'll see. Now, get some rest. I love you, Montanna."

"Love you more." Already Mo's voice sounded sleepy.

Mo rolled onto her side and pulled the covers with her. Madison cracked the door so only a slit of light would leak into the bedroom.

She was about to settle on the living room couch when a visit to the deck sounded like a better idea. Leaving the sliding glass doors cracked open so she could hear if Mo needed her, she sat in a deck chair and leaned her head back. The lapping of the water against the shore helped soothe her mind a little. She glanced over at the lights of Gabrielle's home. Voices carried toward her, but Madison didn't strain to hear the words. She didn't want to. She gazed up at the night sky and took in the expanse of stars.

"Tell Callie I said hi, too, Lord," she whispered. A star twinkled as the words left her mouth. Madison smiled. "Thank you."

* * *

"I'm taking a shower and going to bed, Eva."

"What about that glass of wine?"

Gabrielle pulled her T-shirt over her head on her way to the bathroom. "No, thank you. There's an open bottle in the fridge." She turned on the water, finished stripping, and stepped under the spray.

"On second thought, I think I'll skip the wine, too. Tell me more about Madison Lorraine."

Gabrielle could see Eva's outline through the steamed glass of the shower door. "What do you want to know?"

"I know she's a hell of an artist who unfortunately isn't painting. But what else?"

"She has an adorable daughter. That's probably the most important thing I can tell you about her."

"You've met the daughter, too?"

"Remember, I told you she helped me bring in groceries. Mo's a great kid."

"How did her partner die?"

"Uterine cancer, only hers was Stage IV by the time they diagnosed it."

Eva grew quiet. Gabrielle finished her shower and grabbed her towel. Eva's eyes traveled over Gabrielle's body. Gabrielle watched for her reaction to the scar, but Eva's gaze didn't linger.

Feeling vulnerable, Gabrielle pulled the towel in front of her. "We need to—"

Eva's cell phone rang. She held up her index finger and left the bathroom. "Frederick, I told you I'd be in Florida this week. What's the problem?"

Gabrielle quickly dried off and threw on her nightshirt. She heard Eva's raised voice as she tossed out a few obscenities. Eva was hanging up when Gabrielle entered the living room.

"I'm sorry. I have to fly back to New York. There was some trouble with the prints. We have to redo some of the shoot, and he can't wait."

Relief flowed through Gabrielle's body like a balm. "When?"

Eva flipped her wrist to check her watch. "Unfortunately, I need to be there first thing in the morning, so I'll take the next flight to New York tonight." Eva gave her a quick kiss. "I'll try to come back in a couple of weeks. Didn't you tell me you have a scan coming up?"

"In about three weeks."

"I'll make it a point to be here for what I'm sure will be good news." Eva picked up her bag where she'd left it at the door. "I'll call you when I get to New York."

"We still need to talk."

Eva came to her and held her index finger against Gabrielle's lips. "Let's at least wait until then," she said, meeting Gabrielle's eyes.

She knows.

Gabrielle walked her to the Mercedes. Eva slid into the driver's seat and powered down the window. "I'll talk to you soon, Gabrielle."

Eva drove away into the night. A chill ran through Gabrielle, and she rubbed her arms. As she was heading back inside, she gazed toward Madison's house. She thought she saw a shadow of someone standing on the deck but wasn't sure. For a moment, she considered throwing on some clothes and walking over to see Madison. Another wave of fatigue hit her. *No, I need to rest.* She went back inside and turned off the lights.

* * *

"No!"

Madison jerked awake, disoriented. She was still on the deck, slouched down in the lounge chair where she'd fallen asleep. She scrubbed her hand over her face in an effort to rouse herself from her slumber.

"Mama, don't go!"

With Mo's second cry into the night, Madison yanked the sliding glass door open and sprinted down the hall toward Mo's bedroom. Mo was tossing and turning, the covers thrown off and pooled on the floor.

Madison sat down on the edge of the bed and gently gripped Mo's shoulder, trying not to startle her as she thrashed in her sleep. Mo bolted upright, her cheeks wet from tears. At first, she looked right through Madison. Then she started sobbing.

Madison pulled her tight to her chest and patted her soft hair. "Shh, honey. I'm here now."

Mo's sobs eventually trickled down to hiccups. "It was Mama when she died. I asked her not to go, but she left us anyway. Why? Why couldn't she stay?"

Madison held Mo tighter and rocked her in her arms. She knew Mo understood about how bleak the cancer diagnosis was. When they realized the inevitable outcome, she and Callie had sat her down and explained it to her. Even though she was only six at the time, they both felt the more information Mo had, the better prepared she'd be for when Callie passed. Madison mentally shook her head. Like anyone could prepare for such a loss.

Now, freshly awakened from a nightmare, none of that mattered to Mo. She just wanted her Mama.

"I don't know why Mama couldn't stay with us, sweetheart." Madison asked the same question almost every day. But right now, Mo needed her comfort. "She gave us a gift, though. She's one of God's angels watching over us."

Mo sniffed a few times and asked in a voice so soft that Madison strained to hear her. "Can you sing our song?"

Madison swallowed the lump in her throat before she began singing, "Sunshine on My Shoulders." She didn't know how she was making it through the song. She and Callie used to sing it to Mo each night. Even when Callie was weak from the treatments, she still managed to sit long enough to sing the song with Madison.

Madison imagined Callie sitting on the bed beside her. She could almost hear her humming along. They never sang all the lyrics, but Mo didn't seem to mind when they repeated verses, as Madison did tonight. Mo relaxed in her arms, and her breathing evened out. Madison eased her back on the pillow and brushed her light blonde hair from her face. She let her fingertips linger on Mo's cheek as she stroked the soft skin.

"You were our sunshine, Montanna," Madison whispered. "You still are."

She placed a kiss on Mo's forehead, curled up beside her, and closed her eyes. She recalled a day before cancer had so cruelly visited their lives. They were at the beach. The sky was the bluest she'd ever seen. If only the future were so bright...

Chapter 12

Madison woke up to the pale light of dawn slipping through the blinds. And the smell of something burning. Frantic, she sat up and reached for Mo to get them safely out of the house, but the bed was empty. She jumped to her feet and ran down the hall.

"Mo? Mo? Where are you?"

She rounded the corner into the kitchen and skidded to a halt. She discovered the source of the smell. Mo's "cooking."

"These don't look like yours," Mo said with a frown.

Madison hurried over and stared down at the charred remains of what was supposed to be pancakes. Gripping Mo's shoulders, she spun her around. "How many times have I told you that you can't turn on the stove when I'm not with you?"

Mo's lower lip trembled. "I'm sorry, Mom. I wanted to surprise you. That's all." She brushed her finger under her nose. "I wanted to thank you for singing to me last night."

Madison melted at the sight of her tears. She pulled Mo close. "It's okay. But you have to be careful, Mo. I don't want anything to happen to you." She cupped Mo's chin. "Don't you know how much you mean to me?"

Mo nodded.

Madison wiped at her wet cheeks. "Why don't you go get ready for school while I clean this up?"

Mo started down the hall and stopped. "Can I still have pancakes?"

"Aren't you tired of those? How about scrambled eggs and toast?"

Mo scrunched up her nose.

"I take that as a 'no.'"

"Just two pancakes, Mom," Mo said as she took off for her bedroom.

An hour later, they were pulling out of the drive on their way to Mo's school. They were passing by Gabrielle's house when Mo pointed. "Look, Mom."

Dressed in a pair of cut-off jeans and a worn T-shirt, Gabrielle was picking up trash strewn around her two garbage bins that sat behind her garage.

"I bet I know what caused this mess." Madison slowed to a stop. She powered down Mo's window and leaned across her to call out to Gabrielle. "Raccoons?"

Gabrielle rose up from her task. "Oh, hi." She gathered up a few more torn wrappers and tossed them in one of the cans. "I'm sure you're right. I forgot all about the little buggers and didn't seal my garbage cans like my dad used to when we'd come down. Obviously, they had a feast." She made a face as she looked at the mess.

"Listen, I need to take Mo to school. Leave it, and I'll stop by to help when I get back."

"You don't have to do that."

"It's no big deal, Gabrielle. Let me help, okay?"

Gabrielle gave her a grateful smile. "Thanks."

"Promise not to clean up any more?"

"Promise."

"Be back in a few." Madison powered the window up, waved, and pulled away.

It was quiet in the car as they continued on the drive to school. Too quiet. She glanced over at Mo who was sporting an adult-looking bemused expression on her young face.

"What?" Madison asked.

"Nothing."

"I'm simply helping her out. That's a huge mess, and I don't think she's feeling up to it."

"I'm glad, Mom."

"It doesn't mean anything other than one friend helping another." *God, why am I defending my actions to my nine-year-old daughter?* Madison answered her own question. *Because I care what she thinks.*

Madison slowed to a stop at the school entrance. Mo gave her a kiss on the cheek and bounded out of the car.

"Love you, Montanna," Madison said before she got too far.

Mo turned toward her. "Love you, too. Have fun with Miss Gabrielle." She winked and joined her friends as they walked toward the entrance.

"Did my daughter just wink at me?" Madison shook her head. Sometimes she wondered who was the parent and who was the kid.

* * *

When Madison returned, Gabrielle was sitting in a lounge chair with her face tilted toward the sun. She was glad to see Gabrielle had listened. Turning at the sound of the closing car door, Gabrielle motioned to the mound of garbage.

"Didn't touch anything, just as you asked." Gabrielle stood up to join her.

"Why don't you sit back down while I pick up the rest?" Madison bent over and grabbed an empty juice bottle.

"Madison, I'm not completely helpless. It's my fault there's a mess out here anyway. Let me help." She leaned over to retrieve an energy bar wrapper and staggered.

Madison quickly grabbed her elbow to steady her. She noticed Gabrielle's eyes had clouded over. "Let's take you upstairs for a rest." She led Gabrielle toward the stairs to the deck.

Gabrielle dug in and prevented Madison from moving any farther. "I hate that I can't do anything. It seems all I do is rest, and I'm sick of it." Her expression had darkened. Then she sighed. "I don't mean to take my frustrations out on you. It's not your fault I have cancer."

"You know, it's okay if you call it 'fucking cancer.' I think you've earned the right."

"It's definitely that, isn't it?"

"Yes, it is. And it sucks, I know." Madison guided her up the deck stairs and into her house, never letting go of Gabrielle's elbow. She looked around the living room. "Couch or bed?"

"Couch, please. I don't want to chance falling asleep for the rest of the day."

Madison grabbed a pillow and helped Gabrielle settle onto the couch. "Sleeping the rest of the day wouldn't be a bad thing." She pulled down a blanket from the back of the couch. With the move, her breasts brushed against Gabrielle's stomach. Gabrielle tensed. Madison kept her face averted as she laid the blanket across Gabrielle. When she finally got the nerve to meet her gaze, Gabrielle was staring at her.

"You're so kind to me. I feel like we've been friends for such a long time." She touched Madison's hand.

Madison's skin tingled with the brush of Gabrielle's fingertips. "It does feel that way, doesn't it?"

Gabrielle hesitated for a moment. Then she said, "Eva and I... well, I plan to break it off with her. I wanted to talk to her before she left, but I think she knows what's coming and asked me to wait until she returns in three weeks."

Madison's stomach fluttered. She wasn't sure what to say. Gabrielle didn't seem upset but rather resigned to something she must've felt was inevitable. But more than anything, the feeling nestling into her heart like a baby nestles into a bassinette was relief wrapped around a kernel of hope. Gabrielle seemed to be awaiting a response.

"I'm sorry it didn't work out for you and Eva."

Gabrielle broke eye contact. "I was always hoping for a closeness that never came. With the cancer, I began to see how shallow she was. But it really isn't entirely her fault. She's been told she was beautiful since she was a child. She's used to having others fawn over her. She didn't know what to do when I was diagnosed. She hadn't signed on for it."

"But if you're in a relationship, and you love the other person, you sign on for everything. Not just the happy days. That's the easy stuff."

Gabrielle's expression softened. "If anyone would know, it would be you." She tugged on the blanket to bring it up to her shoulders. "The thing is, I don't think I ever loved her. Maybe I hoped I'd eventually feel something other than attraction."

"You deserve to be happy. Everyone does." Madison gestured to the blanket. "Do you need anything warmer? I know Callie often felt cold when she was going through treatment."

"If you don't mind, I have a light sweater in my bedroom closet. My bedroom's at the end of the hall on the right."

"I don't mind at all." Madison walked down the hallway. She went to the closet and rifled through a couple of hangers before she found the sweater. As she turned to leave, she stopped dead in her tracks. There on the wall was another of her paintings—a view from their beach cabin in Key West of the moon shining on the midnight-blue Caribbean water. She'd painted the scene from her memory of a night of passionate lovemaking. She remembered Callie stealing up behind her as she painted and whispering in her ear, "I know where your head is." Madison had set her brush down, turned, and swept Callie into her arms in a passionate embrace, her painting all but forgotten.

Madison shook free from her thoughts. Gabrielle was probably wondering what was taking her so long. When she entered the living room, Gabrielle was fast asleep. Madison approached the couch. In her sleep, Gabrielle appeared much younger, the lines of fatigue faded away with the softening of her face in slumber. Rather than wake her, Madison draped the sweater over the blanket and across her shoulders. She stood for a moment as she watched the gentle rise and fall of her chest. Without thinking, she leaned over and brushed her fingertips against Gabrielle's cheek. Then she went to the refrigerator, retrieved a bottle of water, and set it on the coffee table next to the couch.

Madison walked to the back door. With one last look at Gabrielle, she left for the deck and climbed down the other set of steps to the garage to finish her task. As she cleaned up the rest of the garbage, she thought back to how she felt as she heard Gabrielle tell her that she was ending her relationship with Eva. In her mind's eye, she saw Mo winking at her.

Gabrielle stirred awake. From the long shadows enveloping the room, it had to be afternoon. She lay there and tried to get her bearings. The last remnants of her dream came to her. She'd been lying on a beach. The warmth of the sun had kissed her skin and caused her blood to throb with life. Then she felt the gentle caress of her lover's fingertips against her cheek. She'd opened her eyes and smiled at the woman leaning over her. Her lover's face was backlit by the sun, but Gabrielle was stirred by the familiar and comforting presence.

She sat up and stretched. She noticed the sweater pooled in her lap. The last thing she remembered before dozing off was asking Madison to bring it to her. She touched her cheek. Had Madison caressed her? She shook her head. No, it was only a dream.

Gabrielle shrugged off the sweater and blanket and headed toward the deck. She stepped out, walked to the railing, and looked down. The water was calm in the cove. No sign of their friend. A movement out of the corner of her eye caught her attention. It was Madison strolling down her dock. Unlike earlier, she was dressed in shorts and a tank top. She sat at the end and leaned back on her hands. It was a pensive pose. Gabrielle wondered if she'd mind company, even though she'd just seen her this morning. She descended the stairs to the sand.

She continued down the shore between their docks until she reached Madison's. Her gait faltered when Madison turned to give her a big smile.

"Hey. How was your rest?" Madison asked.

"Restful." Gabrielle sat down next to her.

Madison chuckled. "That's always a good sign if your rest was restful." She looked out at the water. "I didn't want to disturb you, so I draped your sweater on your shoulders and left." She turned back to Gabrielle. "Hope that was okay. You really *did* need the sleep, despite what you may have thought."

Gabrielle got lost in her eyes that sparkled in the afternoon sun.

Madison frowned when she didn't respond. "I didn't mean to tell you what to do."

"Oh, no. That's fine. You were right. I get stubborn sometimes. I had so much energy before the treatment. It gets frustrating having it sucked out of me by the chemo."

"But you're through it now. You should gradually regain your strength as the months go by."

"So I've been told."

They sat quietly for a while, neither seeming to want to break the silence. Gabrielle was the first to speak. She motioned at the dock behind them. "Why no boat?"

Madison stared back out at the water. "I didn't see the need to keep it once Callie passed. We only used it for family outings."

Gabrielle wondered what else Madison had given up in the time since Callie died. Things that reminded Madison of her late wife seemed to have fallen victim to Madison's grief.

"My dad had a boat. He sold it a few years before he died. Said he wasn't using it enough to maintain it."

"Makes sense." Madison picked at one of the dock's splinters. "I was wondering if you'd like to come over Saturday for a cookout. Cyndra will be there. And, of course, Mo."

Gabrielle didn't answer right away. She felt the attraction building between them but wondered if it would be a good idea to pursue anything if she'd ultimately leave for New York.

Enough time passed that Madison must've taken it for rejection. With her head still lowered, she said, "I understand if you can't make it."

Gabrielle was about to respond when, without warning, Free leapt from the water about twenty feet in front of them.

"Holy Christ," Gabrielle gasped as her hand flew to her chest.

Madison was about to stand up, but Gabrielle stopped her. "No, Madison. He's not going to hurt us."

Free performed a series of jumps and pirouettes and disappeared from view. They leaned over together to peer down into the water. He suddenly emerged a few feet in front of them and started chattering. His nonstop chatter seemed directed at Gabrielle. When he finished, he flipped his nose toward Madison. Then he turned back to Gabrielle and chattered some more. He repeated the nose flip, this time spraying a little water on Madison.

"Hey! Cut it out." Madison brushed the water from her face.

One of Free's blue eyes focused on Gabrielle. Once again, another vision came to her. Only this one was of her laughing as Madison flipped burgers on her outdoor grill. Mo was there, too, talking to Cyndra.

As if in a trance, she turned to Madison. "Yes."

Madison's was still staring at Free. "Yes what?"

"Yes, I'd love to come to the cookout next Saturday."

Madison beamed. "That's fantastic. Mo will be thrilled. I'm thrilled you'll be there, too."

Gabrielle looked back at Free who was nodding.

"I think he approves," Madison said.

Gabrielle had to bite her tongue to keep from blurting out, "I know he does. It was his idea."

Madison glanced at her watch. "Oh, wow. I didn't know it was almost time for me to pick up Mo." She stood and helped Gabrielle to her feet. They watched Free frolic some more before he disappeared.

They began walking down the dock. When they reached the end, Madison stopped. "I'm glad you told me about Eva."

"I wanted you to know. She'll be back in three weeks for my CT scan. I'll talk to her then. I hope she and I can remain friends."

"I have a feeling you will." Madison tilted her head toward her house. "I'd better go. Saturday night at five?"

"I'll be there. Can I bring anything?"

"Just yourself." Madison leaned forward and kissed Gabrielle's cheek. "Take care, and call if you need anything."

When she pulled back, Gabrielle's gaze drifted to Madison's mouth. She shook herself from her thoughts of kissing Madison fully on the lips. "I'll see you Saturday night."

"See you then." Madison turned and headed for the stairs to her deck.

Gabrielle stood and watched while she ascended, her gaze drawn to the muscles rippling in Madison's thighs and calves with each step. When Madison reached the deck, she gave Gabrielle a little wave.

Gabrielle turned for home, her sandals sinking into the sand with each step. She thought back to how Free had held her captive with his stare as if he were casting a spell. "What's happening to me?"

Chapter 13

"You should have heard Mo," Madison said as she stepped out onto the deck. She handed Cyndra a soda. It was Wednesday night, and Cyndra had stopped by to say hello. Madison had talked her into joining her under the stars. "She didn't want to go to school this morning. Tonight, she stayed at the dock and pouted when he didn't show again."

Cyndra took a sip of her drink. "You have to admit this dolphin is special."

Madison glanced at her and then down at her Coke.

"What is it?" Cyndra asked.

"He seems to show up right when he's supposed to. I asked Gabrielle to join us Saturday for the cookout. I'm pretty damn sure she was going to say no, but then he pops out of the water, does his little tricks, and starts chattering."

"Isn't that what dolphins do? Chatter?"

"That's just it. He wasn't chattering at me. He was totally focused on Gabrielle." Madison laid her head back on the lounge chair and sighed. "God, that's crazy, isn't it?"

"I dunno. Did he suddenly start speaking English?"

Madison jerked her head toward Cyndra. The citronella candles encircling the deck captured the smirk on her sister's face.

"You do think I'm losing it, don't you?"

"No. I don't. Like I said, the dolphin… what did Mo name him again?"

"Free."

"Right. I'd personally like to shake Free's little fin for talking Gabrielle into joining us Saturday night."

Madison stood up and went to the railing to gaze out at the cove where the moonlight shone on the water. "She's breaking up with her girlfriend."

"I'm assuming we're still talking about Gabrielle. That's

good, right?"

"Yeah. Yeah, it is." Madison searched the cove for any sign of Free, as if she and her insecurities needed a reassuring head-nod from the dolphin. "Sometimes I miss Dad at times like these." She turned around when Cyndra didn't say anything."

"I miss him, too, Maddie. A lot. Especially when something's going on in my life that only he'd understand, you know?"

Their father had passed away four years ago from pancreatic cancer, which had been swift and unyielding, another reminder of how deadly the disease could be. First her father and then Callie…

Madison returned to sit beside Cyndra. "Yeah," she said quietly. She grinned. "Remember when he'd take us fishing, and he'd tell us to keep quiet? That the fish wouldn't bite if we were talking?"

Cyndra laughed. "Later, I figured out it was to keep our big mouths shut so he could get some peace and quiet. Had nothing to do with catching fish. He needed to get away from Mom, but he didn't tell us that. She was starting to change even before she got to be the 'famous' Louisa Lorraine." Cyndra was gripping her Coke can so tightly, Madison was surprised the soda didn't shoot out the top.

Her sister was right, though. After their mother's paintings started selling, gone was the simple, carefree woman who raised them. Her replacement focused more on appearances and things that simply didn't matter to Madison or Cyndra—like insisting they move into an oversized mansion and hiring servants to cater to their every whim.

As if reading Madison's thoughts, Cyndra said, "Like her telling Daddy our house was too small and didn't suit her needs. Which is freaking ridiculous. She drove Daddy away."

"I'm sorry, Cyn. I know how much you missed Dad when they divorced. How hard it was on you." Madison was sixteen when their parents separated. It nearly broke twelve-year-old Cyndra's heart.

"I need to remember he was happy with Roxanne."

Madison silently agreed. Their father's second wife was like a breath of fresh air.

"She was so different from mom," Cyndra said. "Well, really she wasn't. Just the mom who became the snob after her paintings took off. I only wish he'd had more time with her."

Madison mentally shook off the sad thoughts. She raised her can of Coke in the air. "Here's to Free, who seems to know what's best even when I don't."

Cyndra laughed and clicked her Coke can against Madison's.

"Amen to that."

* * *

Saturday at four-thirty, as Madison tried to light the charcoal, she questioned why she hated gas grills... other than the sound they made when you lit them. The loud "whoosh" always scared the shit out of her.

"Finally," Madison muttered, as the charcoal stayed fired up.

The sliding glass door opened, and Cyndra poked her head out. "How's it going, he-woman? Are you one with the fire?"

"Very funny." She glanced back at Cyndra. "How's the Great Potato Salad Experiment coming along?"

"Look, I told you it's not exactly my specialty. But, no, you insisted there had to be potato salad."

Mo pushed past Cyndra and ran up to Madison.

"Do you want me to get Gabrielle, Mom?"

"No. She'll be here at five, and she doesn't need an escort. What you can do, though, is help your aunt with the potato salad."

Mo scrunched her face. "Is that what it's supposed to be, Aunt Cyndra? I couldn't tell."

Madison tried to stifle a laugh.

"It's all your fault, Madison."

"Hey, I'm sure it'll be quite tasty." Madison burst out laughing again.

"I'll drive down to the store and buy some at the deli. At least theirs is edible." Cyndra waved Mo over. "Come on, munchkin. You can go with me."

"But I want to be here when Gabrielle comes," Mo said with a pout.

"Pouting may work on your mom, but it doesn't on me. Come on. Maybe we'll get back before Gabrielle arrives."

"Mom?"

"Go on, Mo. It's only four-thirty and the store's five minutes down the road."

Mo sighed. "Fine." She stomped back into the house.

"I'm not such a horrible aunt, am I?" Cyndra called after her.

Mo mumbled something from inside the house.

"Be back in a few. Get those burgers fired up."

Gabrielle stood in front of the mirror and smoothed out her sun dress. With daytime temperatures still in the low eighties, she decided to wear one of her favorites. She'd picked it up on a trip to Italy with her father. She was thinner than when she'd bought it, but she thought the white cotton dress adorned with a colorful flower pattern still fit her fine.

Scrutinizing her appearance, she noticed her face was beginning to soften from the lines of fatigue put there by months of treatment. She hadn't paid attention to how she'd looked recently, instead concentrating on making it through each day. Today she cared, and she knew the reason why.

She was almost to the door when she remembered the lemon tart she'd made. She went back to the refrigerator and pulled it off the shelf. Gabrielle's mother had taught her never to return a borrowed dish empty to its owner. Smoothing her dress down one more time, she headed toward Madison's. Since she'd chosen to wear sandals with low heels to go with the sun dress, she decided to take the front door and not the beach route.

A few minutes before five, Gabrielle rang the doorbell and waited, suddenly feeling nervous. Cyndra opened the door. She smiled warmly at Gabrielle.

"Hi, Gabrielle." She held out her hand in greeting. "Please. Come inside."

Mo sprinted into the foyer and slid to a halt on the tile in front of Gabrielle. "I'm so glad you could make it. My mom is, too. She hasn't stopped talking about it."

Cyndra gave Mo a curious look, but Mo continued on, undaunted.

"She even got ground sirloin to fix on the grill. She said only the best for you. Me and Aunt Cyndra picked out the best potato salad for us to eat."

"Mo, why don't you take Gabrielle's dish into the kitchen."

"But—"

"Please."

"Okay. Will you sit next to me at the picnic table, Gabrielle?"

"I'd be delighted to."

Mo carried the dessert around to the entryway that led to the kitchen.

"Lord, her energy wears me out sometimes." Cyndra turned back to Gabrielle. "I know we met briefly the night I was babysitting, but I've heard so much about you from my sister. Let's go out on the deck where the grill master is hard at work."

Gabrielle, taking in her surroundings as they walked, followed Cyndra through the house. The furniture all looked lived-in and comfortable. She searched for Madison's artwork on the walls, but most of the prints hanging were large photographs of the ocean and sea life. There was one photograph of Madison and Mo with a woman with light blonde hair and vivid blue eyes. The woman had to be Callie—the resemblance to Mo was unmistakable.

All thought left her mind when she caught sight of Madison standing at the grill. She had her back to Cyndra and Gabrielle when they stepped out to the deck.

"Look who I found on your doorstep," Cyndra said. "I'll go back inside to get the drinks ready."

Madison turned around. She set down her spatula and came over to Gabrielle. "I'm so glad you could make it." She held Gabrielle's hands and leaned in to give her a kiss on the cheek. Gabrielle was growing to love this greeting of Madison's and found she yearned for more. The talk with Eva couldn't come soon enough.

"You look wonderful, Gabrielle. You have more color to your cheeks. Are you getting enough rest?"

"It feels like I get too much sometimes. It's so annoying to have my energy zap to nothing, with little or no warning."

Madison turned back to the grill and lifted off some of the burgers. "Callie would say she felt like a puppy."

Gabrielle moved to stand beside her so she could see Madison's face as she talked. "A puppy?"

"You know how when puppies play, they run around like crazy, chasing a ball or nipping on your hands to get you to play with them. Then all of a sudden, they just plop down in the middle of the room and zonk out. Like their fatigue came out of nowhere."

A look of pain skittered across Madison's face. "It was like that with Callie. We'd be talking, and suddenly, she'd tire like a deflated balloon." Madison blinked and cleared her throat. "It was hard to watch." She took the last of the burgers off the grill.

Gabrielle touched her arm. "I didn't mean to bring back bad memories. Sometimes, I think being around me might be too painful for you."

Madison's expression immediately changed. "Oh, no. It's just that…" Her voice trailed off as she stared out at the water below.

"It's just that you loved her."

Madison smiled sadly. "I did. With every fiber of my being."

The sliding glass door opened behind them, and Cyndra came

out with a pitcher of what looked like iced tea. Mo was juggling bottles of soda.

"Here, let me help you." Gabrielle quickly moved over to take two of the bottles from Mo. "Anything else in there I can bring out?"

"Glasses of ice, if you don't mind," Cyndra said. "Mo, why don't you join her and help out."

Mo grabbed Gabrielle's hand and led her into the kitchen. "Glasses are in there." She pointed to a cabinet next to the sink.

Gabrielle took down two glasses and another two and set them on the counter.

"The ice is the easy part." Mo grabbed two of the glasses and went to the refrigerator. She pushed one against the automatic ice bar and then filled the other glass. Gabrielle followed suit.

When they approached the sliding glass door, Gabrielle noticed Madison and Cyndra seemed to be in a serious discussion... at least from Madison's expression it seemed serious.

"She's a kid, Madison. You got to love her incentive," Cyndra was saying when Gabrielle and Mo rejoined them. Cyndra glanced at Gabrielle a little sheepishly as Madison glared at Mo.

Cyndra motioned to Mo to help her with the dishes, and soon they were all seated around the picnic table and enjoying a meal.

Gabrielle had just taken a bite of her burger when Cyndra spoke.

"Madison tells me you're staying in your father's house for the next several months. Do you plan to go back to New York or do you think you might live here permanently?"

Gabrielle didn't miss the look that Madison gave her sister. She swallowed before replying.

"I've finished with my treatment. I'll be here for a few more months. After I recuperate, I'll go back to modeling. At least those are my plans." Sometimes she wondered if she even wanted to return to that lifestyle, especially now with the way she was feeling. Perhaps when her full strength returned, she'd feel differently.

"Aw, man. We want you to stay. Don't we, Mom?"

"We want Gabrielle to be healthy more than anything and to do what makes her happy."

Gabrielle was a little disappointed Madison didn't show much enthusiasm about her staying. *Come on. It's not like you're dating.*

"Mo, I'm enjoying my time here with you and your mom." Gabrielle glanced at Madison who was staring down at her plate. To change the mood, she asked, "Cyndra, what do you do for a living?"

"I work as a paralegal at a small law firm across the highway."

"Sounds interesting."

"Trust me, it really isn't."

Mo, who was clearly not excited about the turn in conversation, suddenly blurted out, "Hey! Why don't you come over for Thanksgiving dinner? You'd have fun with us, wouldn't she, Mom?"

Gabrielle watched Madison's reaction which thankfully was one of pleasure.

"You're welcome to join us. Cyndra and Bev will be here, too."

"Well, only if you have enough food."

"Please," Cyndra said. "Enough food? This one here"—she hooked her thumb at Madison—"thinks a twenty-pound turkey is the only size bird that'll do."

"It's true. Especially with the way Mo loves turkey."

"Mommmm…"

They laughed.

"Seriously, Gabrielle, we'd love to have you over," Madison said.

"Then I'd love to join you. Thank you for the offer."

Mo bounced up and down on the picnic bench. "Maybe Free will show up on Thanksgiving, too."

As if summoned by the mention of his name, loud splashes erupted from the cove below. Mo was the first to jump to her feet and stand at the railing.

"It's him! It's him!" She raced down the deck stairs.

Madison bolted to her feet and followed close behind. "Montanna! Don't you get near the water!"

"Shall we join them?" Cyndra asked with an upraised eyebrow that looked so much like her sister's expression. "I hate to have our sandwiches get cold, but Free beckons."

They walked side-by-side down the wide deck stairs. Gabrielle kept her focus on Madison, who caught up to Mo at the end of their dock. Free was several feet away, performing a series of flips and spins.

"He looks so happy," Cyndra said as they reached Madison and Mo.

"Yeah, he does."

Madison still held Mo's hand, as if afraid she'd jump in the water.

"How long does he usually stay?" Cyndra followed his progress around the cove.

Madison looked over at Gabrielle. "Seems to have his own

agenda, don't you think?"

"I have to agree." *I still think he's smarter than we are.*

Cyndra edged her way to the end of the dock. She knelt down and held her hand out over the water.

"Whoa, Cyn. Do I have to worry about you, too?"

"I don't think he'll hurt me, Madison."

"But—"

Cyndra glanced over her shoulder. "Seriously. I'm thirty years old. I'm capable of making a judgment call."

Just as she finished speaking, Free popped his head out of the water and touched his nose to her hand. She yelped and fell back on her butt.

Madison helped Cyndra to her feet. "See, what'd I tell you?"

Free began chattering and motioning with his nose to the cove behind him as if telling them, "Come on in, the water's fine!"

"We're not coming in there with you, so you might as well stop," Madison yelled. Gabrielle didn't miss the set of Madison's jaw.

This time, Cyndra got down on her stomach and stretched her hand out. "I think you need to lighten up."

"Jesus, Cyn!"

Free nodded a couple of times and pressed his nose into Cyndra's palm before dipping back into the water and swimming swiftly to the middle of the cove.

Cyndra got to her feet. "See? He's friendly."

"Mom! Aunt Cyndra touched him. How come I can't?"

"Yeah, sis. How come? It's no different than when you took her to Sea World."

"I didn't let her get up close and personal with the dolphins there either, if you remember."

"Madison—"

"Let's drop it, okay?"

Cyndra sighed and turned her back on Madison to watch Free perform more leaps and spins. After several moments, he was gone.

"I'm going into the water the next time he comes." Gabrielle wasn't sure why she was sharing this with them, especially after seeing again how adamant Madison was that Free wasn't safe.

Madison jerked her head around to stare at Gabrielle, her mouth gaped open in shock. "You're what?"

"He came to me once, and I swear it was like he was telling me to grab my wetsuit and jump in the water with him."

"Gabrielle…"

"No, listen. I wasn't even thinking about the wetsuit, but when he stared at me, it was like I had a vision of getting in there with him. I've got my old wetsuit. I'm sure it'll still fit me, especially with the weight loss."

Madison's expression grew even more incredulous. "Surely you're not thinking it's safe for you to be in the water." She held up her hand to stop Gabrielle from interrupting. "I'm not talking about the safety issue of swimming with Free. I'm talking about how you've just gotten out of treatment. I don't think it's a good idea when your immune system is so weakened."

Cyndra grabbed Mo's hand and slowly led her down the dock. They stopped far enough away to be out of earshot.

"Madison, I think—"

"No, that's just it. You're *not* thinking." Madison sounded almost panicked, but it didn't keep Gabrielle from bristling with anger.

"Well, guess what? I'm not your daughter, and you can't tell me what to do."

"Gabrielle—"

Gabrielle slashed her hand in front of Madison's face to cut her off. "It's time for you to listen to me. I'm a big girl. I can make my own decisions. Yes, I've had a catastrophic illness. Yes, it's been hell going through treatment, but I'll be damned if I stop living. I'll be damned if I don't grab onto enjoyment when it's staring me in the face. And I'll be *damned* if you can tell me what to do." She fought hard to hold back the tears prickling her eyes.

"Hey, hey, I'm sorry." Madison laid her hand on Gabrielle's arm, but she shook her off.

"Listen, I've lost my appetite. I'm going to call it a day and head home. Thanksgiving isn't a good idea, either." Gabrielle turned on her heel to leave.

"Please, Gabrielle. I'm sorry." Madison tried to keep up with her long strides.

"Cyndra, Mo, I'm going home," Gabrielle said as she approached them. "I apologize about not finishing our picnic. Maybe another day."

"Don't you want to come back with us to eat your burger?" Mo asked.

Gabrielle almost gave in to the plaintive expression, but one glance over at Madison reminded her why she was so angry. "Like I said, Mo. We'll have to do it again some other day."

She slapped at her damp cheeks as she strode quickly toward the shore and the steps leading up to her home.

Cyndra wheeled around, thrust a fist on one hip, and glared at Madison. "What was that?"

Madison held her hands up to ward off Cyndra's anger. "I tried to apologize. I... I..." She ran her fingers through her hair in frustration. "Damn it. I had no intention of telling her what she should do."

"You didn't? Because you did just that. What came over you?"

Madison stared down at the worn slats of the dock as she tried to put into words exactly how she'd felt when Gabrielle had shared her plans to go into the water. "I guess I had a flashback to when Callie was undergoing treatment and how paranoid I was with anything that might affect her health."

Cyndra's expression softened. "Yes, I remember. I also remember how Callie would get frustrated with your overprotectiveness."

Madison opened her mouth to protest, but Callie's face suddenly came to mind. How she'd roll her eyes when Madison would launch into what Callie called, "Madison's Sermon from the Mount," about how careful she needed to be.

"Crap."

"Mom, that's the second bad word you've said."

"I know, kiddo. I'm sorry." Madison suppressed a sigh. It seemed lately, the only thing she was capable of doing was apologizing—and not very well.

Cyndra put her arm around Madison. "Sweetie, you had the best intentions, I'm sure, but you came across like a lawyer cross-examining a hostile witness."

Madison watched as Gabrielle entered her house and shut the door. She was surprised she didn't hear the echo of it slamming.

"Do you think I should go up there?"

"No, I think that's the last thing you should do. Allow her to let off some steam, which, by the way, she has every right to do in this case. Give her a little time." She squeezed Madison's shoulder. "But not too long. In the meantime, remember you can't keep Gabrielle from doing what she wants. She's not your daughter, Maddie."

Madison gazed out at the cove with a sudden craving to see their friend. He seemed to know what to do... much better than she did.

* * *

Gabrielle grabbed a juice out of the refrigerator and slammed the door so hard, the glass containers rattled on the shelves.

"How dare she try to tell me what I can and can't do." She twisted off the lid with so much force the apple juice sloshed onto her hand. "Shit." Gabrielle snatched up the paper towels and yanked off a couple of sheets. "If I want to jump into the cove naked, I'll do it, and she can't do a damn thing about it." That thought brought a flash of Madison shedding her clothes and joining her. Gabrielle flushed. She guzzled the apple juice and wiped her mouth with the back of her hand. "Christ, what is it about that woman? I don't know whether to slap her or kiss her."

Chapter 14

"Madison, please sit down. I need to talk to you."

Madison stopped mid-stroke with her paintbrush and met Callie's gaze, shaken again by her wan appearance. She was standing in the doorway of Madison's studio, the sun from the skylight catching the blue of her eyes. With one hand, Callie held her stomach. The other hand gripped the doorjamb. A tremulous smile graced her lips. She was still the woman Madison had fallen in love with ten years before, yet she was also all but a shadow of herself. Thin and pale, her beautiful blonde hair all gone from the many chemo treatments, she was obviously holding onto the doorjamb for support.

"What is it, sweetheart?"

Callie shuffled to the small couch by the floor-to-ceiling window that overlooked their cove. She slumped into the cushions. Often, she'd join Madison in her studio as she painted. Sometimes, Callie would read a book. Other times, she said she simply wanted to be near Madison as she worked. Madison would glance up from her painting to find Callie staring at her. Callie patted the cushion beside her. "Come here."

Madison set down her paintbrush and walked to the couch. She slowly settled onto the cushion and tried to prepare herself for whatever Callie was about to say. Madison knew from the expression on her drawn face this wasn't going to be good news.

Callie reached for Madison's hand and cradled it in her lap. She gently brushed her fingertips over the splashes of paint decorating it. "You have such graceful hands. They're like a work of art." She closed her eyes as if to steel herself and faced Madison. "I want to stop treatment."

Each word was like a punch to Madison's gut. "Oh, no, baby." She cupped Callie's face. "We can fight this thing. Don't give in now. There's more—"

Callie placed her fingers on Madison's lips. "No, sweetheart.

There's nothing more they can do." She dropped her hand in her lap as if the strength had suddenly left her. "I can't continue treatment and allow my last days to be consumed by a poison we both know isn't going to work."

Madison began to cry. She didn't even bother to wipe away her tears. "Callie, you can't do this."

"I want my remaining time with you and Mo to be as fulfilling as it possibly can be. Driving to Miami and coming home only to spend my time in bed and away from you both isn't what I want the end to be. My next treatment is in two weeks. I'll make an appointment with Dr. Gillespie to tell him I want to stop."

Madison was about to argue, to come up with reasons Callie should continue, but ultimately, it was Callie's decision. "Do you know how much we're going to miss you?" she choked out.

"Oh, Madison." Callie pulled her into her arms and whispered in her ear, "I'll always be watching over you and Mo. God will allow me that, I think."

Madison, unable to speak, only nodded into Callie's shoulder as Callie gently rocked her. In a few months, the feel of Callie's warm embrace would be but a memory…

* * *

"Mom! Mom, wake up!"

Madison jerked awake. Her face was still wet from the tears she'd shed in her dream, a dream that was once their reality.

Mo used the bottom of her nightshirt to wipe Madison's cheeks. "Please don't cry. It makes me sad."

Madison normally held it together for Mo's sake when thinking of Callie, despite her promise to Mo that she wouldn't hide her emotions. She'd always feared if she truly let go, Mo would think Madison was lost to her as a mother. But at this moment, in the darkness of her bedroom and in the emptiness of her bed, she couldn't hold back the sob that tore from the depths of her soul.

Mo climbed into bed, curled up next to Madison, and put her arm around Madison's waist. "Did you have a bad dream?"

Madison nodded.

"About Mama?"

Madison nodded again as she tried to rein in her jagged sobs.

"Do you want to sing our song?"

Oh, God, no. Madison thought she'd lose it completely if Mo

started singing, so she quickly shook her head.

"Can I say a prayer then?" Mo asked. Madison could make out Mo's shimmering eyes, questioning her with the open innocence only a child possesses.

Although Madison's sobs had trickled down to sniffles, she still couldn't speak. So, again, she nodded.

Mo took a deep breath and began, "Dear God, Mom had a bad dream and needs your help. She always tries to be strong for me. Please let her know that it's okay to cry and okay to miss Mama. Please give Mama a hug from both of us. And please let Gabrielle know Mom wasn't mad at her last Saturday. Tell her Mom was worried and it all came out wrong. Amen."

Madison brushed Mo's hair from her face. "Thank you, baby."

"Are you going to go over to Gabrielle's house?"

"No," Madison said quietly as she continued to sift her fingers through Mo's hair. "I think we need a little timeout."

"You won't wait too long, though, right? Because she's your friend, and I like her, too. What about Thanksgiving?"

"She doesn't want to come over." Mo was about to interrupt, but Madison stopped her. "I made a mistake with how I talked to her. We need to respect her wishes. Like I said, we need a little time away from each other. I'll talk to her soon. Don't worry."

Mo put her head on Madison's shoulder. "Can I sleep here with you the rest of the night?"

"Wouldn't want you anywhere else. Get under the covers, though."

Mo flipped the covers back and scrambled underneath. She pressed tight to Madison and patted her arm. "You wake me up if you have another bad dream."

Madison bit her lip to keep the tears at bay. "I will, sweetheart. Love you."

"Love you, too, Mom."

* * *

Gabrielle was in the bedroom dressing when the doorbell rang. At first, her heart skipped a beat, thinking it might be Madison. But she had a feeling Madison wouldn't be over anytime soon, especially since Gabrielle had chosen not to go over on Thanksgiving. Madison had left her alone, and it was probably for the best.

She opened the door and came face-to-face with Eva toting a

small suitcase. Eva's smile was tentative. "Can I come in?"

Gabrielle had never seen this side of Eva. She was used to the confident, almost cocky way that Eva carried herself. This Eva almost looked defeated. In answer, Gabrielle held the door open wider.

Eva set her suitcase by the couch and sat down. "I remembered your scan was this afternoon. I hope you don't mind if I go with you?"

"Of course," Gabrielle said as she sat down beside her. "I knew you were coming in, but I didn't know when. You hadn't called."

"To be honest, I was afraid you'd insist I stay away." Eva cocked her head with a sad smile.

Gabrielle opened her mouth to speak, but Eva reached for her hand. "I think I know what you're about to say, Gabrielle, so let me speak first. I have an opportunity for a photo shoot in Paris. It requires me to be gone for a month because I'll also be there for fashion week." She stared down at their clasped hands. "It's not fair to you to think you have an obligation to stay in this relationship." She raised her head, her eyes shimmering with moisture. "So, I think after your scan results, I'll go back to New York and find another apartment. I'll have everything moved out as soon as possible."

Gabrielle was speechless. She thought she'd prepared for this moment, even had a "let her down easy" talk ready. Yet, here was Eva doing it for her.

"Just know," Eva continued, her voice trembling slightly, "I love you. Please say we'll remain friends."

In answer, Gabrielle lifted Eva's hand to her lips and kissed it. "Yes, we'll always be friends. I love you for so many reasons, but right at this moment, I love you for having the courage to say what you've said."

They stared at each other before Eva spoke again. "Well, let me get freshened up a bit before we go to your test." She stood and picked up her suitcase. "Which bedroom is the guest room?"

Gabrielle was about to object, to tell her that she could sleep in the master bedroom, but Eva was right. They were beyond that now.

"Second door on the left down the hall." Eva was almost to the hallway when Gabrielle said, "Thank you, Eva."

Eva turned back to her. "You don't need to thank me. We both knew this is where we were headed."

* * *

They sat quietly in the waiting area of the Sylvester Comprehensive Cancer Center in Miami. Their drive to the university was a quiet one, with only occasional conversation about safe topics like Eva's shoot in Paris and places Eva might look for her next apartment.

Gabrielle had noticed once they'd entered the waiting area, Eva had gone quiet. She'd drawn a few glances from others in the room, mostly from the two men seated across from them. Although not dressed to the nines, she was still stunning in her designer jeans and thin, short-sleeved mock turtleneck.

Eva leaned closer to Gabrielle and asked in a lowered voice, "Does everyone in here have cancer?"

There were about ten people seated with them. For some, it was obvious; others were probably there for their first scan.

"Either they have the disease or are waiting for a loved one to return from their scan."

Eva didn't speak for several moments. "It's so sad," she finally said, her tone hushed and reverent.

Before Gabrielle could respond, she was called up to the window. She provided the pertinent insurance information.

"If you'll take a seat again, someone should be out soon with the preparation."

She barely restrained from making a face. She'd only had to drink the stuff once before when she'd first been diagnosed. The scan then was to find out if the cancer had spread outside the uterus. Now, it was to ensure she was cancer-free.

She returned to her seat. Eva was taking surreptitious peeks at a young woman with a colorful scarf wrapped around her head. She'd just sat down with another woman who appeared to be the girl's mother. The girl looked frightened. Gabrielle could tell by the way the woman sat straight in her chair that she was trying to put up a brave front, but the exhaustion lining her face was a giveaway to her concern.

"Oh, Gabi," Eva whispered.

Gabrielle gently patted Eva's arm. No words were necessary.

A few minutes passed before a young man named Steve asked for Gabrielle and carried over four large Styrofoam cups filled with a lime-colored liquid.

"I don't know if you remember the drill. Drink these slowly over the next hour. Each cup is marked with the times. Try to do the best you can at finishing them off."

Eva's eyes widened. "You have to drink all of *that*? You've always had trouble drinking the bottled water at our shoots. I remember arguing with you about it because you needed to stay hydrated in the sun."

Gabrielle picked up the first cup. "Cancer has a way of not giving you much of a choice." She began sipping the nasty concoction though she only barely detected a hint of the lime flavor.

After she'd finished, Steve called for her, and she walked with him back into another room resembling a vault with its thick, heavy door. He directed her to the table. Since she'd had the scan before, she knew what to expect. She lay perfectly still while the table first slid rather quickly through the slowly rotating donut-shaped scanner. Then, with a series of clicks and whirs, the table slowed as her body passed through the scanner again.

The test was quick, painless, and over in about fifteen minutes. She had to wait for another few minutes while the technician checked the images. In half an hour, she rejoined Eva in the waiting area.

"That's it?" Eva asked, obviously surprised at the quick time.

"Yes, that's it." Eva had been in Brazil on the *Sports Illustrated* swimsuit photo shoot during her last scan. Gabrielle remembered how she'd watched with a pang of envy as Eva packed. Gabrielle had adorned the magazine's cover just the year before. How quickly life could change.

They walked to the parking lot and Gabrielle's rental. "Do you mind driving back?" Gabrielle asked.

Eva took the keys. "Not at all. Remind me where to turn off."

On the drive to Islamorada, Eva kept the conversation light as if to ward off the somber images of the cancer patients they'd encountered. Gabrielle murmured a few words here or there, not really wanting to delve into any serious conversation. As she reclined in the passenger seat, she gave into the inevitable fatigue that always hit in its own time. And she thought of a dark-haired artist and her spirited daughter. *We need to talk, Madison.*

* * *

"So, when will you get the results? Monday?" Eva took a sip of wine as she waited for Gabrielle's response. They were enjoying a quiet evening out on Gabrielle's deck.

"Yes. Are you sure you don't mind staying the weekend?" Gabrielle tried to make out Eva's face in the shadows but could only see the outline of her body as the moonlight glinted on her blonde hair.

"I think it's the least I can do." Eva set her wineglass on the deck beside her chair, stood, and walked to the railing, keeping her back to Gabrielle. She was quiet for a long time.

"What's on your mind?" Gabrielle finally asked.

"I'm sorry for my insensitivity when you were diagnosed and then during treatment. I'm sure you thought I was being dismissive of your cancer, as if it were a cold to get over and then move on in your life as if nothing happened."

"You don't need to apologize."

"No, please let me finish. If I do anything right this weekend, I want it to be what I'm about to say." Eva turned around, folded her arms across her chest, and leaned her back against the railing. "You deserved so much more from me... so much more. I should've been there for your treatments, and I wasn't. You had the limo driver take you and pick you up as I begged off being too busy with another shoot. But that wasn't the case." She stared down at her feet. "I was at Elaine's for every one of your chemos, drowning myself in margaritas. I was afraid. Afraid to be with you. Afraid to see whatever pain you had to go through because I had no idea what a treatment entailed. I didn't know how involved it was until I came down for your last one."

She walked over to Gabrielle and knelt in front of her, placing her hands lightly on Gabrielle's bare knees. "I wanted everything to go back to the carefree time we shared before this dreaded disease swooped in like a vulture and picked at what I thought of as our perfect lives." Eva spoke with a brutal honesty Gabrielle hadn't heard from her before. "But then I realized what we had was never perfect, was it?"

Gabrielle placed her hands on top of Eva's. "No, it wasn't. I'm sorry it took me having cancer for us to face the fact it wasn't going to last between us."

"I'm sorry you've gone through this mostly alone. I'm sorry I wasn't brave enough to hold your hand on the day the doctor gave you the diagnosis. I'm sorry for so many things, but mostly I'm sorry that you ever got this cancer. You're such a kind-hearted soul, Gabi. If anyone deserves to be spared, it's you."

It didn't escape her that Eva was on her knees, essentially begging for forgiveness. "No one deserves this hell, Eva." Gabrielle looked over at Madison's house. "Especially the mother of a small child, who had so much more to live for."

Eva gripped Gabrielle's hands to bring her focus back. "You have everything to live for, too. We won't share our lives together, but it doesn't mean that you can't share it with someone else. Someone who, from what I've seen, needs your healing touch."

Gabrielle raised her eyebrows in question.

"I saw how she looked at you, remember? As she should. You're a beautiful woman, but you're even more beautiful here." She rested her palm over Gabrielle's heart.

This change in Eva was such a revelation, Gabrielle couldn't help but ask, "What happened in the weeks since I last saw you?"

Eva lifted one shoulder in a slight shrug. "I did a lot of soul-searching."

Gabrielle smiled. "Obviously."

Eva rose to her feet and bent to place a light kiss on Gabrielle's cheek. "Thank you for listening."

Gabrielle stood up and embraced her in a tight hug. She pulled away and brushed back a lock of Eva's hair. "Let's enjoy this time we have together."

Left unsaid was this weekend they would share their last intimate moments.

* * *

"How are you and Madison Lorraine doing?" Eva asked as they took the exit toward the University of Miami.

Gabrielle was a little surprised at the change in conversation since, again, they'd kept their interaction light for the drive to Miami Monday morning. She wondered if she should stay close-mouthed about her disagreement with Madison but thought maybe Eva could offer some advice.

"We had a disagreement a couple of weeks ago... well, an argument really." Gabrielle glanced over in time to see the surprise on Eva's face.

"What about?"

"She didn't want me to go into the cove in my wetsuit." Now, it seemed a little bit childish on her part, but at the time, Madison infuriated her with her insistence and overprotectiveness.

"Why would you need to get into the water? Isn't the water too cool anyway?"

"The surface temperature is warm enough, and the water is, too.

The high today is supposed to reach eighty-two. The water temperature is still in the seventies."

"Still, aren't you supposed to be cautious just a few weeks after chemo treatment?"

First, Gabrielle couldn't believe Eva remembered that tidbit of information, and, second, she felt her anger spike in hearing the same argument coming from Eva. She tamped down on her ire before speaking.

"The wetsuit will protect me, so I'm not worried." Besides, she added in her mind, Free won't let anything happen to me.

Eva must've sensed she touched a nerve. "Hey, you have every right to do what you want. I take it Madison thought the same thing about you getting in the water?"

"Yes, only a little more vehemently."

Eva waited a beat before saying, "It might be because her partner died, Gabrielle. I'm sure she's even more protective of something happening to you. That, and the fact she is totally smitten."

Gabrielle pulled into the parking garage into an empty spot. She turned off the engine. "Totally smitten?"

Eva's lips curled into a smile. "I'll not try to convince you of that fact again because you know deep down, it's true," she said as she unbuckled her seatbelt.

They were quiet as they walked into the building and got on the elevator. Gabrielle watched the floors register above them until they stopped on the seventh floor. *Okay, maybe I do hope it's true.*

They didn't have to wait long for Gabrielle to be called back after she checked in with the receptionist. Eva accompanied her to the exam room and sat through the visit with the resident. Then Dr. Corrigan and Allison entered. Each took turns shaking Gabrielle's and Eva's hands. Dr. Corrigan perched himself on a rolling stool while Allison stood behind him with a knowing smile. He flipped through her chart and raised his head.

Gabrielle's heart tripped in her chest as she awaited his verdict.

"Good news, Gabrielle. You're CT scan shows you're cancer-free and your CA-125 came back with a level of four."

Gabrielle exhaled a breath. Knowing her tumor marker was that low was a relief. But hearing the scan was clean made her light-headed. Eva grabbed her hand.

"That's such good news, Gabi," she said, her voice catching.

"Let's have you sit up here on the exam table so I can get a look at your incision."

Gabrielle complied as he pushed and prodded while Allison stood by like a watchful angel.

"It's healed nicely." He held out his hand to help Gabrielle sit up while Allison pressed her lower back to support her. Gabrielle stepped down to sit beside Eva again.

"Now we enter what we call 'stealth mode.' You'll have an exam every three months for the first two years, followed by an exam every six months for the next three years. Unless you have any unusual symptoms pop up or unless your CA-125 shows a sudden, high elevation, you won't need to have another CT scan." He studied her, his dark brown eyes locking onto hers. "How's your appetite now, by the way?" He opened her chart. "I see you've gained a few pounds."

"Yes, my appetite's improved."

"And the fatigue?"

"It's gotten a little better the farther we've gotten away from my last treatment."

"Good."

"I still have joint pain, though."

Dr. Corrigan nodded. "Unfortunately, that can be one of the aftereffects of the chemo. Try to stay moderately active and if you need us to, we can refer you to a physical therapist to help improve your motion and loosen your muscles." He stood and held out his hand again to both of them. "I'm glad to see you've recovered so nicely, Gabrielle. Are you planning on remaining in Miami long enough for your three-month follow-up?"

Gabrielle didn't even hesitate. "Yes."

"All right. I'll see you then."

Allison stayed behind. "I'll get you the script for your next set of labs and bring it to you at the desk. Remember, you'll need to have the blood test done a few days before your next exam. That will give us enough time to go over the results."

After setting Gabrielle's appointment and retrieving the script from Allison, they left for the car. Before they got in, Eva enveloped Gabrielle in a warm hug. "I'm so happy for you, honey."

Gabrielle blinked back her tears. "Me, too." Maybe her life would become normal again.

Eva drove up the ramp and merged into freeway traffic. "So, you're staying in Florida longer than you first thought?"

"I could use the warm weather."

"Just the warm weather, huh?" Eva's mouth curled up on one side.

Gabrielle laughed, a lighthearted laugh coming from a place in her heart that left her feeling as carefree as she'd felt in some time. "Maybe for a couple of other reasons."

Madison and Montanna...

Chapter 15

Madison stood on Gabrielle's deck, raised her hand to knock, stopped, raised it again, and stopped. She let out a disgusted sigh. Since when had she become so indecisive or insecure? She'd noticed the Mercedes parked in Gabrielle's drive after passing her house over the weekend. If she recalled, Eva drove a Mercedes rental when she'd last visited.

She raised her hand again and had to keep from jumping back when the door swung open before she knocked.

"Hello," Eva said with a smile. "I saw you through the window and thought I'd save you the trouble of knocking."

Feeling a little foolish with her hand still in the air, Madison quickly dropped it to her side. "Uh... hi. I was hoping to see Gabrielle."

"Who are you talking to?" Gabrielle appeared behind Eva. Her face lit up when she saw Madison.

At least she doesn't seem mad at me. "Hi, Gabrielle."

"Madison. It's good to see you."

"Good to see you, too." It was especially good to see her so rested. Madison wondered if Eva had helped with that. The thought wasn't a pleasant one as she imagined just *how* Eva had helped Gabrielle relax.

"Please come in," Eva said.

Madison stepped past her into the dining area that led off the back door.

Eva stood there but must have noticed Gabrielle and Madison weren't talking.

"I need to finish packing, so please excuse me."

Eva walked away and Gabrielle turned back to Madison. "She's leaving in thirty minutes for the airport."

"Listen, Gabrielle—"

"Madison, I wanted to—"

They laughed as they tripped over each other's words.

"Please. Let me go first," Madison said.

"Before you say anything, how about we take a quick walk down by the cove?"

"All right."

"Just a sec." Gabrielle went around the corner to the hall leading to the bedrooms. Madison heard quiet murmuring before Gabrielle returned. "Okay, let's head down." When they reached the water, Gabrielle slipped off her sandals. The only sound made was the quiet lapping of the water against the shore until Madison spoke.

"I'm sorry for my overreaction about you swimming with Free. I'm also sorry it's taken me this long to come over to apologize." Madison had been staring down at her sandals but now ventured a glimpse at Gabrielle's reaction.

Gabrielle was sporting a small smile. "Thank you for that. It's my turn to apologize for blowing up like I did. I haven't felt in control since I was diagnosed, and when I decided to take back some control and do something fun, I didn't want to hear 'no.'"

Madison stopped walking. Gabrielle took a couple of extra steps then also stopped and slowly approached Madison. Madison took a chance and reached for Gabrielle's hand. "I realize that now. Since I saw you last, I thought about Callie and how overprotective I was of her. Believe me, we had some heated discussions." Madison shook her head. "Make that fights. She convinced me she needed freedom to do what she wanted. Then later, when the doctor told us she didn't have much time left, I didn't care what it was she wanted to do. We were going to do it." Madison gazed out at the cove. "As for not apologizing sooner, I was being a chickenshit." She met Gabrielle's eyes, which now twinkled in amusement.

"That's definitely one word I wouldn't use to describe you."

"Oh yeah?" Their lighthearted banter made Madison feel like a load had been lifted from her shoulders.

"In fact, I would say you're brave." Madison was about to object, but Gabrielle stopped her with a slight raising of her hand. "You're brave for not giving into what I can only imagine was unbearable grief when Callie died. Brave for raising a beautiful daughter on your own."

Madison's throat tightened. "I couldn't let Callie down."

"No, you couldn't," Gabrielle said. "And you didn't." She gave a sly grin. "You're also brave for coming over when Eva was still here because I'm sure her rental didn't go unnoticed in my driveway."

Madison scratched the back of her neck. "Um… no."

Gabrielle intertwined their fingers, making Madison's pulse pick up. "Eva and I had a good talk this weekend. She was more understanding and sensitive than she'd ever been before in our relationship. We're parting as good friends, which is all I want. What we both want."

"How do you feel about all of that?"

Gabrielle stared up at the sky and blew out her breath. "Relieved, more than anything." She started walking again, and much to Madison's delight, didn't drop Madison's hand. "I have some good news. My CT scan came back clean, and my CA-125 is at four. I don't go back to see Dr. Corrigan again for three months."

Madison stopped and embraced her. "This is wonderful news." She heard the catch in her voice. "We should celebrate." She pulled back and gripped Gabrielle's hands. "Let me take you to dinner."

"You don't need to take me to dinner."

Madison's smile slid off her face.

"I'd love to go out with you, Madison, but you don't need to treat."

"I don't *need* to, I *want* to. How about this Saturday night? I'll ask Cyndra if she can come over to sit with Mo."

"Saturday night sounds lovely. Six okay?"

"Perfect. I'll swing by to pick you up. There's a great ocean-side seafood restaurant across the highway."

They'd walked as far as Madison's house.

"Well, I should get back to tell Eva goodbye. Thank you for the walk and for coming over. I'm glad we talked."

"Me, too." Still worried about Gabrielle's stamina, Madison motioned with her chin toward Gabrielle's house. "Would you like me to walk you back?" She glanced at her watch. "I have enough time before I pick up Mo."

"I'm fine, but thanks for the offer." She leaned in and placed a soft kiss on Madison's cheek. "See you soon."

Gabrielle headed in the other direction. She turned once to give Madison a little wave and continued on her way. As Madison started for the steps leading up to her deck, she couldn't keep the grin off her face.

Eva was standing at the door, her bag at her feet, when Gabrielle entered the house. "Everything okay?" She looked up from her cell phone. "I'd say by your smile, it is."

"We had a good talk." Gabrielle didn't realize she was beaming until Eva pointed it out.

Eva held up her phone. "Checking on the flight. It's on time, so I better get a move on." She opened her arms. Gabrielle didn't hesitate in welcoming her embrace. "I'll always remember our time together. Always."

Gabrielle had wondered if she'd feel a little pang of longing when Eva's arms went around her. Instead, she felt a slight loss of what could've been but was never meant to be.

Eva slipped from the embrace and picked up her bag. "I'll call you when I land in New York." She opened the front door and took a couple of steps. "I wish you the best with everything, Gabrielle. But especially with Madison."

"I don't know what's there between us."

"Oh, I think I do, and I think it'll be all you hope for. Stay well." With that, Eva put her bag in the car, climbed in, and backed out of the drive. When she'd pulled completely out onto the road, she tooted her horn.

Gabrielle shut the door and walked to the kitchen. She grabbed a bottle of juice and carried it out to her chair on the deck. As she took a sip, she thought about her life, all of the twists and turns it had taken. She thought about her mother. About her dad. And she thought about a dolphin and the magic he was weaving into her heart, as surely as a master weaver creates a tapestry.

Chapter 16

"Where are you taking her again?" Cyndra asked as she ladled out another helping of fresh green beans onto her plate. She'd invited Madison and Mo over for dinner Friday night. Mo was of course in the den slaying dragons with Cyndra's Xbox. Cyndra hadn't even attempted to hide why she'd scheduled a dinner the night before Gabrielle and Madison were going out. She wanted details.

When Cyndra took a bite of green beans, Madison had a flashback to when she and Cyndra would snap the beans for their mom. It was one of the bonding "moments" of their childhood. "Hey, where'd you go?" Cyndra said.

"Oh, thinking back to when we used to clean and snap beans for mom."

"Those were the days." Cyndra snorted.

Madison quickly got back to Cyndra's question before she started on a rant about their mother. "You asked me where I was taking Gabrielle for dinner."

"Please don't disappoint me with your answer."

"You think I don't know how to pick a nice place?"

"Well…"

"It's the new seafood restaurant across the highway. Sherry's Shrimp Shack. We went there once, remember? You loved their crab legs."

"I do remember. You'd never think a place with a name like that would be good, but it is. You have my stamp of approval." Her lips twitched in amusement. "So, how do you feel about your first date with her?"

Madison's stomach flip-flopped at the word "date." "It's not a date. It's a dinner to celebrate that she's cancer-free."

"Oh, really? It's not a date?" Cyndra ticked off the points on her fingers. "You've gotten to know her in the time since she moved in next door. You invited her to your home for a cookout, although you managed to screw that one up later."

Madison glared at her smug sister.

Cyndra leaned her elbow on the table and rested her chin on her fist. "So, what would you call tomorrow night's outing then, oh sister dear, if it's not a date?"

Madison sighed. "Oh, all right. It's a date. Happy now?"

"Only if you are." Cyndra turned serious. "Are you?"

Madison pushed her food around on her plate with her fork as she thought about Gabrielle's shining face when she'd told Madison her scan came back clean... and how pleased she was when Madison asked her out for dinner. "Yeah, I am."

"Good."

Madison was about to respond when Mo trounced into the dining room. She leaned over the table and snatched a dinner roll.

"How many does that make?" Madison asked, raising one eyebrow.

"Two," Mo answered as she took a big bite.

"Montanna..."

Mo's shoulders slumped. "Three."

"No more."

Cyndra put her arm around Mo's waist. "I baked an awesome angel food cake, munchkin, so listen to your mom."

"Okay, Aunt Cyn," Mo mumbled as crumbs dribbled down her chin.

"What do you want to do tomorrow night? See a movie? Rent one on Netflix? It's up to you."

Mo plopped down in the chair next to Cyndra. "I still don't know why I can't go to dinner with Mom and Gabrielle. Mom, you said it was to celebrate her not having cancer anymore. Can't I be there, too?"

Madison shot Cyndra a pleading look across the table.

"Now, Mo. This will be a special night for your mom. I think she'd probably like some alone time with Gabrielle."

Mo's eyes widened. "You mean it's a *date*?"

"Thanks, Cyn," Madison said, her voice dripping in sarcasm.

"Eh, what are little sisters for except to annoy their big sister?"

"I thought you outgrew that."

"Oh puh-leze. It never gets old. It's one of my greatest achievements in life, and I plan to carry on the tradition for several more years, if not into our ripe old age. Well, *your* ripe old age since you'll get to old-agedom much, much sooner than I."

"Seriously, Mom. It's cool you're going out with her."

"That's what I told her, too, Mo."

"I'm sitting right here, you know," Madison said, trying to remain serious but failing to keep the smile off her face.

"Where?" Cyndra made a show of looking around Madison's chair and then under the table. "I don't see you."

Mo giggled.

Madison balled up her napkin and tossed it at Cyndra, scoring a perfect "ten" by hitting her square on the nose. Cyndra promptly tossed it back at her. Mo grabbed a napkin from the napkin holder, wadded it up, and hit Madison on the forehead.

"Oh, that's how it's going to be, huh?" Madison snatched more napkins and a napkin war ensued for several seconds.

"Enough, enough!" Cyndra said. "I don't have that many napkins left in the pantry. I don't need you both wasting them."

"She started it." Madison pointed at Mo.

"Really, Madison? You're resorting to, 'she started it'?"

"Hey, it worked when we were kids."

* * *

Madison smoothed down the collar of the light-blue, silk shirt over the lapels of her navy-blue suit jacket. She straightened the seams of her khakis and checked her hair in the mirror. Mo was watching her from Madison's bed.

"You look nice, Mom."

"Thanks, baby. I thought I'd dress up some for Gabrielle since she's only seen me in jeans and shorts."

"Mom?"

"Yeah?"

"Do you think Gabrielle will come live with us?"

Madison lifted her head, and the lighthearted quip died on her lips when she saw how serious Mo was. She sat down next to her on the bed.

"Hey, what's this about?"

Mo leaned her head against Madison's shoulder. "She'd like it here, and I think Free wants her to be with us."

"He does? How do you know?"

"He told me in a dream."

Again, Madison stopped before teasing Mo. "Honey, I'm not saying I don't believe you, but Free is a dolphin. Even though he seems like he's talking to us, he really isn't. And besides, it was only a dream."

"But, Mom, in my dream, I *saw* Gabrielle living with us. He showed me."

"Sweetheart, I think you're hoping for this, and it came out in your dream."

"Nuh-uh. He wouldn't lie to me. Free's not mean."

Mo had such a fierce expression on her face, Madison decided not to push it. She encircled Mo's waist with her arm. "Even though you dreamed about her living here, remember we're getting to know each other, and it's not something you rush. I already feel like we're friends. I like her."

"Me, too, and Free likes her." Mo waited a beat. "I think Mama would like Gabrielle, don't you?"

Madison pictured Callie meeting Gabrielle. "I could see the two of them being good friends."

"You know how you always say Mama's an angel, and she's watching over us?"

Madison nodded.

"I think she sent Gabrielle."

"You do?"

"Uh-huh. Mama knows you've been lonely and sad. She wants you to be happy again."

Sometimes the wisdom of her nine-year-old daughter humbled her. "You know how much I love Mama, though, right?"

Mo bobbed her head in agreement. "We'll always love her."

Madison brushed her suit jacket with her fingertips. "You don't think this is too dressy? Or not dressy enough?"

Mo jumped to her feet, thrust her fists to her hips, and with a furrowed brow studied Madison's appearance. "I think it's fine for a date."

Madison almost burst out laughing at Mo's serious expression. "Thank you, Montanna."

The doorbell rang. "I'll go get it. I bet it's Aunt Cyndra." Mo sprinted out of the room.

Madison stood, checked herself one last time in the mirror, and headed down the long hall leading into the living room. Cyndra waited in the foyer, sporting a smug grin when she saw Madison's attire.

"I'm glad this isn't a date."

"Oh shut the f—" Madison clamped her mouth shut

before the word slipped out.

"Yes?"

"Never mind." Madison glanced up at the clock over the couch. "Gotta go. She's expecting me at six." She grabbed her billfold off the table and slid it into the inside breast pocket of her jacket.

"I told Mom she looked very nice," Mo said as Madison walked to the front door.

"She most certainly does. I like teasing her and have that right as her sister. It's under the Sister Rules, Rule Number 28."

Mo stared up at Madison with a look of wonder. "Wow, there are Sister Rules, Mom?"

"No, sweetheart, there aren't. Your aunt is being facetious."

"Fa... fa... what-ish?"

"She's being a smart aleck." Madison gave Mo a quick peck on her cheek. "Have fun with your aunt. Be sure and mind."

"She always does." Cyndra tapped the side of her face for Madison to place a light kiss on her check as well. "Seriously, have a wonderful time tonight. Don't worry about staying out too late. We always find something to do, don't we, kiddo?"

"Yup."

"I'll see you later, although you might be in bed," she told Mo.

"Aw, Mom."

"Remember, I know what a bear you are the next morning if you stay up too late. Aunt Cyndra gets to go home and misses out on all the fun."

Cyndra pushed her toward the door. "Go. Tell Gabrielle we said hi."

* * *

Madison inhaled deeply to steady her nerves before she pressed Gabrielle's doorbell. The door swung open. Gabrielle's gaze swept over Madison from head to toe and back up again. Madison couldn't help but do the same.

"You look wonderful, Madison."

"Th-thanks." Madison had to catch her breath after seeing what Gabrielle was wearing—black slacks and a long-sleeved, turquoise sweater cut low enough to show the briefest hint of cleavage. She didn't realize she'd allowed her gaze to linger too long on Gabrielle's chest until she caught her knowing smile. Without thinking, Madison let the words tumble out of her mouth, "You're absolutely stunning."

A faint blush rose from Gabrielle's neck to her cheeks. "Thank you." She turned to shut and lock the door, and when she faced Madison again, she seemed a little more composed.

Madison walked Gabrielle to her SUV and held the passenger door open before coming around to the driver's side and sliding in behind the steering wheel. "I think you'll love the food," she said as she keyed the ignition.

"I trust your judgment, and I already know what I want to order."

"I love a woman who... I mean I love that you know what you want." The collar of Madison's shirt suddenly seemed too tight. She unbuttoned the top button which didn't allow for that much more of her skin to show, but when she glanced over at Gabrielle, she caught her staring at the newly exposed skin. Gabrielle met her gaze and quickly found the passing scenery more interesting.

* * *

The hostess seated them at a small table in front of the expansive windows overlooking the ocean. She set their menus on the table and told them their server would be by soon. The words had barely left her lips when he arrived.

"Hello. My name is Henri. I'll be your server tonight." He zipped through the specials for the evening and left after taking their drink orders.

Gabrielle took in their view. "There's something about the ocean that always brings me such peace," she said wistfully. "I don't know why I didn't come down to Islamorada before now."

Henri returned with their iced teas. "Need a little time before you order?"

"I know what I want, and I believe you do, too, right, Gabrielle?"

"I do. I'll have Sherry's Seafood Platter with a baked potato, butter on the side, and balsamic vinaigrette for my salad, if you have that."

"We do. And for you, ma'am?"

"Eight-ounce sirloin, medium, with lobster tail. I'll also have a baked potato, sour cream and butter, and honey mustard for my salad."

"Thank you. Salads should be out shortly," Henri said as he took their menus.

As he walked away, the lighting dimmed in the restaurant and made it much more intimate. Servers went table-to-table lighting the small candles. Madison handed theirs to a young male server and set the glass-encased candle back at the end of the table to Gabrielle's right.

Gabrielle gazed out on the water. Fishing boats and sailboats bobbed on the horizon. Although the sun had set to the west, it still made its last presence known across the expanse of the Atlantic, visible as far as Gabrielle could see. The dying rays bathed the small whitecaps in a golden hue as if someone had painted them there. Madison's paintings came to mind—how she conveyed emotion through light. She wondered if Madison would be any more receptive to discussing her work.

She tore her attention away from the view and found Madison looking at her. The candlelight captured the deep planes of Madison's face—her high cheekbones and sensual lips.

"You seemed somewhere else there for a moment," Madison said.

Gabrielle motioned to the window. "This makes me think of your painting. The light on the water, the tranquil beauty, all of it brings to mind your work. I'd love to talk about your painting. You seemed reluctant before." At first, she was afraid she'd said something wrong, and Madison wasn't going to respond. Gabrielle could almost see the debate going on inside her head.

"I started painting when I was a kid." Madison's voice was distant, as if she were there in the past. "Even though we lived in Kansas City, I dreamed of the ocean and light. Always light on the water, in the sky, somewhere in each painting. I'm not sure where that came from, but it's something that's stayed with me."

"So different from your mother's style."

Madison chuckled. "Definitely. My mom always strived to be 'with it.'" She curled her fingers in the air as she said the words. "Mom's pretty calculated in how she paints. Just as she is in how she sees me, both in my personal life and in my painting. I told you before how she's not happy with my lifestyle, as she puts it."

Gabrielle caught the bitterness in her voice but waited for her to say more.

"Mom was in Europe for Callie's funeral. Work came first. Since she never recognized our relationship, I'm sure she didn't think there was a point in her being present at my wife's funeral."

Henri returned with their salads and a basket of bread with butter. Madison poured the dressing over her salad before continuing. "Cyndra still has contact with her. Barely. But she does manage to have a civil relationship with her. Definitely not warm and fuzzy, though. Our mother doesn't do warm and fuzzy."

"How was your relationship with your father?"

Madison smiled sadly. "He passed a year before Callie. Cancer. But we were very close. He'd take me to see the Royals play. He had season tickets with three of his buddies, but he made sure I got to go at least twice a month. He taught me a lot about the game. It wasn't just about baseball, though. While we sat there in the sun, we'd talk about everything. How school was going. How proud he was of my art. He was a great guy."

Gabrielle reached across the table and touched Madison's hand that fiddled with her silverware. "I'm sorry for your loss. I know how you feel. I told you about my mom passing away from breast cancer when I was fifteen. And losing my dad three years ago… well, I know I've not gotten over it and doubt I ever will."

"Were you close to your mom, too?"

"I was at that age when we were developing a friendship. A camaraderie. My dad and I had always been close but grew even closer when my mother passed." Gabrielle's voice caught.

It was Madison's turn to reach for Gabrielle's hand. "I can see how much you miss him."

"Every day. Although coming down here has eased some of the pain of his absence. It's almost as though he's still with me."

For the next several minutes, they concentrated on eating their salads. They'd just finished when Henri brought over their entrees. They took some time away from conversation to sample their dinners.

Gabrielle slipped a piece of crab meat into her mouth and groaned. "Oh my God. This is divine." She looked across the table. Madison was staring at her, her fork paused in front of her mouth. Her hand shook slightly as she swallowed her bite of steak.

"I think Mo might have asked you this, but how long do you plan to stay in Islamorada?" Madison kept her head lowered while she ate, as if she were afraid of Gabrielle's answer.

"At least through the winter. I plan to continue seeing Dr. Corrigan for the next few follow-ups. After that, I don't have plans."

"What about your modeling?"

Gabrielle had tried to push that from her mind. With her appearance, it was the least of her concerns. She wouldn't feel comfortable until her hair grew out. From a conversation she'd had with one cancer patient, Gabrielle learned her hair wouldn't fill in until spring at the earliest. She focused on the piece of flounder on her fork.

"I'll return to it at some point. It's what I do, after all."

"Will you go back to New York?" This time Madison raised her head and met her gaze.

"Yes."

Disappointment showed in Madison's expressive brown eyes.

"But it doesn't mean I'd live there permanently," Gabrielle hastily added. "Only for the photo shoots, which I can schedule for the summer months. Who knows? Maybe I can manage to work here on one of the beaches."

Gabrielle felt something growing between them, something she wanted to explore. She got the distinct impression Madison felt the same. She shifted the conversation back to Madison.

"Tell me about your teaching. I showed up after one of your classes, but I don't know anything about what you do."

"I teach two nights a week. They're mostly older students. Right now, I have a class of five women and one man, all in their forties or fifties. Even though their skills may have been rudimentary at the outset, they're at least learning to find their own style. It's fun to be a part of their progress."

"We've already discussed this, but have you given any further thought to returning to your own painting?"

Madison poked at a piece of steak on her plate. "My answer's still the same. I can honestly say I don't know. I have no problem demonstrating technique to my students, but that's different. It's not personal."

"Like I told you before, you'll return to it at some point. But it'll be when you're ready and will take you completely unawares. I can see the creativity flowing from your brush. It may even be different from anything you've painted before. But it *will* happen."

They were quiet as they finished their meals. Henri appeared at their table just as they set their forks down for the last time.

"Would either of you like desserts?"

"Not me. How about you?" Madison asked Gabrielle.

"No. I'm completely full. This was wonderful."

"I'll take the check," Madison said before he walked away.

"You really don't have to treat me."

"Remember, Gabrielle, I *want* to treat you."

Exhaustion washed over Gabrielle like a wave crashing into the shore, only she was but a grain of sand. *Damn. It always seems to come out of nowhere.*

"Why don't we get you home after I pay the check?"

Gabrielle shouldn't have been surprised that Madison recognized her fatigue, but she was surprised at how in tune Madison seemed to be. "You could tell, huh?"

"I've seen it before, remember?" Madison said in a gentle voice.

After Madison took care of the bill, they rose from their chairs and made their way out of the restaurant and to Madison's SUV. Madison walked Gabrielle to the passenger side, opened her door, and made sure she was seated comfortably before shutting the door and getting into the driver's side.

Gabrielle rested her head back on the leather seat as they drove the short distance home. When they pulled into Gabrielle's drive, Madison shifted into park and again got out to open Gabrielle's door. Before, Gabrielle thought it was gallant. Now, she was grateful because she wasn't sure she could've opened the door on her own.

Madison walked her to the front door where they stood under the soft glow of the porch light.

"I had a lovely evening, Madison. Thank you."

Madison stared at Gabrielle's lips. Gabrielle's breath hitched at the intensity she saw there. They leaned toward each other at the same moment. Her lips brushed Gabrielle's in a soft, sweet kiss. When they pulled out of the kiss, Madison's expression grew serious. "Please get some rest and call me if you need anything—anything at all."

"I will," Gabrielle said quietly. "Give my best to Mo and Cyndra."

Madison backed up toward the SUV. "I will." With a little wave, she pulled out of the drive.

Gabrielle entered her house. She shut the door and leaned her back against it—not for support because of her exhaustion, but for an entirely different reason. She touched her fingers lightly to her mouth, and her lips curved slowly into a smile.

Life was good again.

Madison still felt the tingling aftereffects of the kiss. She parked the SUV as she reminisced about the passing years. She was thirty-four. She'd expected to share her golden years with a woman who lit up her life in so many ways. As if it were onl y yesterday, she recalled being in the delivery room when Callie held Montanna in her arms for the first time. Madison almost couldn't fathom the beauty of the moment. Callie, her hair drenched in sweat, her face awash with tears, had whispered, "I love you." Madison had lost her heart just like the first day they met.

Now, she'd met someone who opened her heart up to the possibility of love again. But was she ready?

A sliver of light made its way into the darkness of the SUV. She raised her head. Cyndra was standing in the doorway. Madison got out of the car and walked up the path.

"Are you all right?" Cyndra asked when she moved aside for Madison to enter.

Madison didn't know what else to say other than, "I'm really not sure."

Chapter 17

Gabrielle woke up feeling refreshed and humming with excitement for what the day would bring. She stretched and lay there enjoying the quiet, interrupted only by the call of a bird and the faint sound of splashing water. Splashing water? She threw the covers aside and grabbed her robe from the chair next to the bed. Her heart pounded in her chest as she tied the sash and stepped out onto her back deck. Sure enough, Free had returned and was performing a show.

Ignoring the fact she was barefoot and only dressed in a thin robe, Gabrielle quickly stepped down the stairs to the sand and hurried along the shore to her dock. She stood on the end as Free progressed through a series of flips, spins, and swimming backwards on his tail. He dove down and reappeared directly in front of her, once again jabbering and bobbing his nose. Then he stopped and stared. The image of her swimming with him in the cove planted itself in her mind as if it had already happened and she was simply recalling the memory.

She shook free from the vision. "You still want me in there with you, huh?"

He again bobbed his nose.

Gabrielle debated the pros and cons. Despite insisting to Madison that she was an adult and she could do as she pleased, a small inkling of doubt crept in. What if she were to get an infection? Would her compromised immune system fight it off? Granted, it had been over a month since her last chemo treatment, but her body hadn't fully recovered and might not for quite some time. Her fatigue of last night was testament to this.

Water splashed the front of her robe.

"Hey, Free! Cut it out. This is thin enough as it is." She was glad, though, that the water he'd splattered on her stomach was at least warm.

He seemed to be admonishing her as he began his nonstop

chatter once again.

"Okay, okay. I'll do it."

She laughed as he launched into his acrobatics. He flew so high that she felt compelled to applaud him.

"I'll be right back." As she left for the house, she shook her head. "I still can't believe I'm talking to a dolphin."

She opened the back door and strode to one of the guest rooms where she'd stored a lot of her old clothes. In the walk-in closet, she searched through several boxes on the top shelf until she found what she was seeking. She opened the box and lifted out the wetsuit. Still not certain she even needed to wear it, she decided to play it safe and not take chances. This particular suit extended to the hands and feet. The only parts of her body that would be showing would be her hands, her face, and a little bit of her ankles.

Quickly discarding the robe, she grabbed her one-piece swimsuit and slipped it on. Then she stepped into the wetsuit and zipped it up. She dug around in the back of the closet for her flippers and goggles and headed outside to the small storage shed on the other side of the house. Although it'd been several years since she'd opened the shed, she was reminded how neat she was when she immediately spotted the small life vest resting on one of the pegs. After buckling the lightweight vest into place, she started back downstairs.

Gabrielle's stomach fluttered with an excitement similar to that which assaulted her when shooting a swimsuit issue for *Sports Illustrated*. Only this felt different... something life-altering. She sat down at the end of the dock to slip on her flippers and her goggles. Free circled the cove, waiting patiently for her to join him.

Staring down at the water, she smiled at the look of wonder and excitement reflected back at her. Without another thought, she dropped into the water. She only sank a few feet before the ballast from the life vest pushed her to the surface. She glanced around for any sign of Free and yelped when he surfaced in front of her. He tilted his head, and she marveled again at the blue of his eyes. One night she'd searched the Internet to find out if the color was an anomaly. Apparently it was because she found no evidence of blue-eyed dolphins. It made Free that much more intriguing.

He turned away from her and floated on his belly, his blowhole intermittently emitting little puffs of air. The invitation was there for her to grab hold of his dorsal fin.

"I hope you know what you're doing, Gabrielle," she said under her breath before gripping his fin. The feel of his rubbery skin wasn't a shock since she'd touched his nose during their initial meeting.

Free didn't jerk away, which was what she was afraid of—a wild, uncontrolled ride. Instead, he eased forward, barely making ripples with his body. He dipped below every few feet but never enough to submerge Gabrielle. His speed increased as he swam toward Madison's house at the other end of the cove.

As they neared Madison's side of the cove, a vision of Madison standing next to Gabrielle at an easel played in her mind. Madison held a paintbrush and was demonstrating to Gabrielle a technique to add light to her painting. Like the vision of joining Free in the water, this felt like she was simply reliving the moment. She stared down in wonder at Free's slick skin as he effortlessly carried them forward. She'd thought he was special, but this was so remarkable she could only describe it as spiritual, just like the first time she'd touched him.

Pure, unadulterated exhilaration about this moment, about her life, about the promise of her life to come, flowed through her veins. Laughter bubbled up inside of her until it burst forth like a geyser from her lips.

* * *

Madison stepped out of the SUV and shut the door. She'd dropped Mo off at school and was still a little irritated. Despite her best intentions, Mo had dragged her feet this morning and made them five minutes late. Mrs. Breckinridge stared Madison down once again. Madison barely refrained from flipping the old woman the bird, which wouldn't set much of an example for Mo.

Loud laughter rang up from the cove. It was the kind of laughter that made you want to join in without knowing why other than it felt freeing. She walked around the path to the back of the house where a small set of stairs led up to the deck. Rather than go that way, she continued until she stopped on the incline that sloped down to the cove.

She stared at the sight below. Gabrielle had latched onto Free's dorsal fin and was clearly enjoying the ride as Free swam around the cove. Her laughter made something in Madison's heart click over—as if someone had inserted a key into a keyhole and jiggled it until the lock tumbled open.

Gabrielle let go of Free in the middle of the cove, making Madison's heart skitter with apprehension. But then she spotted the bright-blue life vest keeping Gabrielle afloat.

Madison descended the slope and waded through the sand until she reached her dock. Gabrielle hadn't noticed her yet. She pushed her goggles up on her forehead and wiped her hand over her face. Free swam up beside her and allowed Gabrielle to stroke him. He dipped his nose and flung the water at Gabrielle.

"You're so playful." Free tossed his head a few more times and swam toward Madison's dock. Gabrielle looked over her shoulder. "Oh, hello there!" She waved.

Madison waved back. "Having fun?"

"Can you tell?"

"Maybe a little."

Free disappeared into the water and didn't resurface until he leapt over Gabrielle's head.

Again, Gabrielle's gentle laughter filled the cove.

"You're such a ham!" Gabrielle shouted.

Free swam up beside her and nudged her hand with his nose.

"I think he's ready for another trip around the cove. You should change and join us, Madison."

Madison shook her head. "No. This is your time with him. I'll join you another day. Maybe with Mo. He seems tame enough."

"You don't know what you're missing!" Gabrielle grabbed hold of his dorsal fin. Madison noticed how Free didn't break into a fast speed but built up to it. He seemed very aware of Gabrielle's frailty. Gabrielle allowed him to pull her along for a few passes in front of Madison. She eventually released his fin and swam over to the dock. Free continued to swim and jump before coming over to where Gabrielle was about to climb up the ladder to the dock. She took off her fins and goggles and tossed them up to Madison. As she lifted her foot onto the first rung, Free poked his head out of the water and nuzzled Gabrielle's neck with his nose.

"Now that's pretty precious," Madison said.

Gabrielle wrapped her arms around Free's body, although they didn't come close to encircling him completely. "I love you, too, big guy," she murmured. He pressed his nose against her cheek.

"Should I be jealous?"

Gabrielle laughed as she stroked him for a few minutes. Then she kissed his nose. Free fell sideways as if swooning from the smooch. He launched into a series of jumps and followed up by dancing on his tail.

Gabrielle started clambering up the ladder. She'd almost stepped up to the top rung when Madison reached for her. "Here. Give me your hand."

As Madison helped her onto the dock, Gabrielle stumbled. Madison gently gripped her waist to keep her from falling.

"Sorry," Gabrielle said. "I always forget how rubbery my legs feel after swimming. Especially with those fins on."

Madison's breath caught. The joy radiating from Gabrielle's face swirled around Madison's heart, holding it captive. Except now, Madison didn't want to be set free. For the first time since Callie died, she allowed herself the freedom to simply be in the moment. And this moment called for Madison to pull Gabrielle closer, tip her chin up with a slight touch of her fingers, and to kiss her... softly at first until Gabrielle responded.

Gabrielle lifted both hands to the back of Madison's neck and slid her fingers into her hair. She touched her tongue to Madison's lips until Madison parted them and allowed her inside. Madison thought her knees would buckle from the desire shooting through her body. She gripped Gabrielle's hips tighter and got lost in sweet surrender. Although she'd initiated the kiss, she allowed Gabrielle to set the pace. When Gabrielle drew away, they were both breathless.

"God, Madison," Gabrielle said, her voice rough.

"I know." Madison was about to say more, but they were suddenly drenched. Another sneak attack by Free. His mouth was open, showing his teeth in what appeared to be a smile. At least he seemed delighted with the show of affection. "I think our friend approves."

"I think our friend is much smarter than we give him credit for." Free jumped in front of them a few times before swimming toward the Gulf. Gabrielle opened her mouth but seemed to change her mind about speaking.

Madison grasped her hand. "What were you going to say?"

"Do you have an opening in your class for one more student?"

The request took Madison by surprise. "I'm flattered, Gabrielle, but if I may ask, why the sudden interest in painting?"

"I've dabbled in art. Nothing major, mind you. When we traveled for our photo shoots, I'd get bored sometimes waiting for my turn in front of the camera. I'd grab my sketch pad and sketch the other models, the locale for the shoot—anything that inspired me to draw."

Madison was still at a loss at what to say.

"If it would be inappropriate—"

"No, no. It's not that at all. You amaze me. Not only are you beautiful and incredibly brave in fighting your cancer, you have other talents I didn't even know you possessed."

Gabrielle rested her palm on Madison's chest and rubbed it lightly. "You'd be surprised at my other hidden talents."

Madison felt the heat of her touch as though Gabrielle were caressing her skin. She placed her hand on top of Gabrielle's. "Maybe I'll discover them one day," Madison whispered.

Gabrielle's eyes darkened even further with unspoken desire. "So... about the class?"

"I'll double-check with the head of the arts department, but considering I volunteer as an instructor, I can't see where it would be a problem at all."

Something passed across Gabrielle's face. What was it? Relief?

"Good, good." Gabrielle rubbed her fingers across her head, still wet from her dip in the cove. "I was so afraid I'd miss Free, I forgot to bring a towel."

Madison stilled Gabrielle's movement with a touch to her wrist. Gabrielle's hand dropped to her side as Madison brushed her fingertips over the hair that was beginning to grow back.

"It's coming in nicely," Madison told her.

"I don't know. Seems like it's taking forever."

"By March, you'll be sporting a very short cut."

"It's a little frustrating."

"Your hair doesn't define who you are."

Gabrielle leaned forward and brushed her lips against Madison's, causing Madison's heart to flutter. "I'd better get upstairs and out of this suit."

"Of course. My next class is tomorrow night. We could drive together."

"I'd like that very much. Thanks again for agreeing to teach me." She picked up her flippers and goggles and started down the dock.

"Have a good day," Madison called after her.

Gabrielle glanced over her shoulder. "You, too."

Joy again filled Madison's heart. She turned back to the cove to gaze out at the cut in the land that led to the open water of the Gulf.

"Thank you, Free," she whispered.

Chapter 18

Madison raised her head from her task to see Beverly walk into the kitchen. "Morning, Bev." She slapped a slice of ham on bread, grabbed the mayonnaise jar, and spread a thick dollop over the bread.

"Mo's lunch?"

"She surprised me and asked for a break from peanut butter and jelly."

Beverly chuckled. "I remember how Callie would get so frustrated with her insistence on eating PB&J sandwiches."

Madison bent down to get an apple from the bin in the refrigerator. She shoved it into Mo's lunch "pail"—an insulated container with Iron Man drawn boldly on the front.

Beverly lifted a couple mugs from the cabinet and poured coffee into one. "Want some, or have you met your quota this morning?"

"You know better. I consider coffee one of the major food groups."

Beverly poured Madison's coffee and carried the mugs to the island.

"Mo! Get a move on. You know how Mrs. Breckinridge is."

"Be there in a sec. I gotta find my English book."

"Check on the other side of your nightstand."

A shout of surprise rang out from Mo's room. Two minutes later, she was walking into the kitchen. "How'd you do that?"

"Moms know all things." Madison took a sip of her coffee. When she saw Mo's incredulous expression, she cut her some slack. "I saw it there when I was kissing you good night."

"Oh." Mo fidgeted in place as she watched Madison sip her coffee. "You said we needed to get a move on because of Mrs. Breckinridge."

"Right." Madison finished her coffee and pushed off the stool. She grabbed the car keys. "Bev, why don't you stay? I'll be back in about twenty minutes."

Bev lifted up her mug in a toast. "You got it." She tapped her cheek. "Mo? You forgetting something?"

"Sorry, Grandma." Mo bussed Bev's cheek. "Love you."

"Love you, too, sweetie."

"Be back in a few," Madison said as they walked out the front door.

Madison rapped the steering wheel with her thumbs while they headed down the road toward school. She had debated telling Mo about Gabrielle's swim with Free, knowing what it would start. But since she'd already made the decision it'd be safe for the two of them to go in the water with him, she decided to break the news.

"I know that this isn't a good time to spring it since you won't be able to concentrate in school, but how would you feel about swimming with Free?" Madison had anticipated excitement, but she didn't expect Mo to jump up so high in her seat that her head almost hit the roof of the car. So much for seatbelts.

"Really? We can? When? The next time he comes? How will we know when he'll be back? What made you change your mind? Wait, it really doesn't matter. But—"

"Whoa, whoa, Montanna. One question at a time. Yes, we can swim with him but only with our life vests. Yes, the next time he visits. I don't know... Free seems to have his own schedule. I changed my mind after watching Gabrielle swim with him yesterday morning."

"She did? And you're just now telling me? *Mom!*"

Thankfully, the discussion came to an end when they arrived at school. She shifted into park. "I probably should've waited, but I thought you'd like to know."

"Thank you, thank you, thank you!" Mo kissed her repeatedly on the check.

"I see Mrs. Breckinridge looking this way, so you better go." Madison reached across the console to give Mo a hug. Before Mo stepped out of the SUV, Madison said, "You have to promise to keep this to yourself, Mo. We don't want anyone else showing up and chasing Free off." *Or alerting "the authorities" to capture him and haul him off to a dolphin show.*

Mo made a motion of locking her lips and throwing away the key.

"Good. Have a fun day. I'll pick you up this afternoon."

"Love you, Mom." Mo bounded away and caught up with two of her friends who were waiting for her.

Madison waited until they disappeared into the building. "I think

I've created a monster," she muttered as she headed back home.

* * *

Madison dropped her car keys on the table in the foyer and glanced through the sliding glass doors. Bev stood by the railing, sipping her coffee. Madison went to the kitchen, poured another mug of coffee, and walked out on the deck to join her.

Beverly turned at the sound of Madison sliding open the doors. "I couldn't miss coming out here to enjoy the view."

Madison joined her at the railing. She cupped the mug in her hands and leaned her elbows on the worn wood. "It is a sight, isn't it?"

"I was hoping to catch a glimpse of the elusive dolphin." Beverly motioned at the water. "And the elusive next door neighbor," she added with a smile.

Madison studied Beverly's face to see if there was any censure there for her interest in Gabrielle, but there was none. It didn't surprise her since Beverly had encouraged Madison early on to pursue the friendship.

"Free was here yesterday morning, as a matter of fact. As for my neighbor, Gabrielle joined him in the water."

Beverly seemed startled at the revelation. "He's tame enough for that?"

"I wasn't so sure until I watched the two of them. You would've thought he really was an escapee from a theme park. You should've seen them. He was so gentle with her."

Beverly studied her a long moment. "She makes you happy, doesn't she?"

Madison was about to fire off a quick retort about how she was getting to know Gabrielle, that they'd only been on one date, but there was only one answer to Beverly's question.

"Very much."

Beverly gently clasped Madison's forearm. "It warms my heart to see you smile again."

"Haven't I been smiling before now?"

"Not like this. You have a sparkle to your eyes that's been missing. I look forward to meeting the woman who's put it there." Something over Madison's shoulder caught Beverly's attention. "I think I see her now."

Madison turned. Gabrielle was walking barefoot along the shore, her sandals dangling from her fingers. Madison hadn't noticed until now how much color Gabrielle had gotten in the Florida sun. Her tan contrasted with her white capris and the light-peach T-shirt she wore. She was about to call out to her, but Gabrielle lifted her head as if she were aware of the scrutiny. She waved.

"Stay there! We'll come down," Madison shouted.

"No, I'll come up to you!"

At first, Madison was a little worried about Gabrielle overtaxing herself, but there was a bounce to her step now. She appeared almost rejuvenated. It didn't take her long to reach the bottom of Madison's stairs. She slipped on her sandals before ascending the steps. When she stood in front of Beverly and Madison, she was barely winded, unlike other times when Madison thought physical activity had sapped Gabrielle's energy.

"Hello," Gabrielle said with a smile.

"Gabrielle, this is my mother-in-law, Beverly Carlson. Bev, Gabrielle Valenci."

Beverly held out her hand. "Pleased to meet you, Ms. Valenci. I have to admit you're even more beautiful in person than you are from the magazines."

"You're too kind, and it's Gabrielle, Ms. Carlson."

"It's Bev, please. How are you feeling? You look marvelous. I hope you don't mind, but Madison told me about your cancer and treatment."

"I don't mind at all. I had been feeling a little run-down, but I have to admit that since my swim with Free, I feel energized."

"From what Madison has told me of the dolphin, nothing surprises me. I'm glad to hear you're recovering, though. Callie had a rough go of it with the treatment."

Gabrielle's expression softened with understanding. "It's not an easy road to walk. Madison told me about Callie. I'm sorry for your loss."

"I miss her every day, but I'm so glad to have the love of this one here." Bev put her arm around Madison and pulled her close. "I'm also blessed to see my daughter live on through Montanna."

"You should be very proud of Mo. I can see the resemblance." Gabrielle gestured to her eyes. "Same blue."

The sun peeked in and out of the fast-moving clouds. Madison enjoyed watching the light play across Gabrielle's face. She didn't know she'd been staring until there was a lull in the conversation. Beverly was watching her with a bemused expression on her face.

"How about I pick you up around six tonight?" Madison asked Gabrielle. "You still want to come, don't you?" She hoped she didn't sound too desperate for Gabrielle's company.

"I'll be ready. Bev, it was nice meeting you. I hope we can all get together soon."

"I would like that very much."

"See you at six, Madison." Gabrielle went back down the stairs. She again slipped off her sandals and waded through the sand on her walk home.

Madison kept Gabrielle in sight until she reached her deck. She waved, and Gabrielle returned the gesture. Distracted, she looked at Beverly. "Did you say something?"

Beverly chuckled. "I said 'what a lovely young woman.'" She patted Madison's stomach. "But I really didn't need to repeat myself because I can see you already are quite enamored."

Madison's face warmed, and it wasn't from the sun. "I don't know…"

"Oh, but I do." Beverly picked up her mug. "I need to go grocery shopping. I have absolutely nothing to cook tonight for when I come over to watch Mo."

"Bev, if you have to go grocery shopping for your own needs, that's fine. But I have plenty of leftovers in the freezer. Plus, you can always order Mo's favorite."

"Pizza," they said at the same time and laughed.

* * *

Gabrielle tried to calm her nerves as she waited for Madison to show up. No, this wasn't a date, but she felt it was something even more important. Painting was such a part of Madison's life. If the only way Gabrielle could see Madison in her element was by watching her as she taught her class, it's what Gabrielle would do while hopefully learning some things herself—especially since it was Free's idea. Who was she to argue with the dolphin? She held back a snort. She'd better be careful with whom she shared that information. Others might think she had "chemo brain."

Madison's navy-blue Mazda SUV swung into her circular drive and stopped at the path that led to Gabrielle's front door.

Gabrielle stood up from where she'd been sitting on her porch swing and grabbed her purse. "Hi," she said as she settled into the passenger seat.

"Ready for the drive to Tavernier?"

"Yes, I am, and I'm especially ready to watch you at work, and to learn, of course."

"I'm not sure how exciting this will be for you."

Gabrielle touched Madison's hand that sat between them on the console. "Your art excites me. *You* excite me—your love of Mo, of Callie. I want to learn so much about you. It's important to me."

Madison slipped her hand more securely under Gabrielle's and entwined their fingers. "It doesn't bother you that I still love Callie?" She kept her eyes on the road as they pulled onto the Overseas Highway.

Gabrielle squeezed Madison's hand until she met Gabrielle's gaze. "On the contrary, it only endears you to me more."

Madison turned back to the road and blew out a breath. "You keep saying things like that, and I'm going to have a hard time concentrating tonight."

Gabrielle was happy when Madison didn't let go of her hand. "Don't worry. I'll sit quietly in the back and watch you weave your magic."

The drive from Islamorada to Tavernier was ten miles but only took a little over fifteen minutes since it was all a straight shot. Just after six-thirty, they pulled into the high school parking lot. Madison walked around the SUV to the trunk and opened it.

"Need some help?" Gabrielle asked as Madison began lifting out her easel.

"If you don't mind, could you grab that case there? It has my supplies in it."

Gabrielle grunted as she hauled it out of the back. "Lord, Madison, are *all* of your supplies in here?"

Madison looked mortified. "Damn. I didn't think about the weight. Let me—"

"I was *joking*." Gabrielle winked at her.

If Gabrielle didn't know any better, she'd say Madison was nervous the way she fumbled with the easel.

"Want me to grab that for you, too?" Gabrielle teased.

Madison jerked her head around and must have caught on. "Sorry. I don't know why I'm so flustered."

"Hey," Gabrielle said softly. "Put that down for a minute."

Madison leaned the easel against the bumper, and Gabrielle set the case, which to her resembled more of a tackle box, onto the pavement. She loosely gripped Madison's hips. "I think it may be because this is such a part of you and now you're about to open that up to me. It's a bit daunting, I'd imagine." Madison didn't dispute what she was saying, so Gabrielle went on. "Remember it's me. I'm attracted to you for so many reasons. What you're allowing me to be a part of tonight is only a small fraction of who you are to me. It doesn't define you, but for me, it completes you." Madison didn't say anything, and at first, Gabrielle thought she'd offended her. "I'm sorry."

"Please don't apologize. It's just that some of the things you tell me… you take my breath away and I'm at a loss. Thank you, Gabrielle. Thank you for bringing hope back into my life."

It was Gabrielle's turn to gasp. "No, Madison. You've brought hope into mine when I never thought it would be possible again." She leaned forward and brushed her lips against Madison's. Madison's eyes were hazy as Gabrielle drew back from the kiss. "Now how about we go in there, and you blow me away."

"Gee, no pressure there."

Gabrielle smiled and bent over to pick up the case of supplies. "None at all."

Gabrielle watched Madison lean over the shoulder of one of the younger women. "Nice, Alicia, nice. I like the color blend of the water. This looks like Key West. Am I right?"

"Yeah, I'm painting from memory, but I still don't think I did it justice."

"You did just fine. I have a place down there, and the view from the house looks like your painting."

Alicia ducked her head and murmured something Gabrielle couldn't hear.

"Keep up the good work. Don't hesitate to ask if you need help blending the colors of the sky." Madison approached her next student and offered some suggestions.

She talked to the older woman, who listened with quiet intensity to every word Madison said. Gabrielle watched Madison's fingers when she swept them above the painting. She had artist hands. Her long, slender fingers were almost a work of art on their own. Gabrielle was mesmerized, thinking about those fingers painting her body with soft, gentle strokes—like the fine caresses of a sable brush. She shivered and tried to focus on what Madison was saying. Madison had stopped speaking, though, and was staring at her, as if she knew exactly what Gabrielle was thinking.

The remaining thirty minutes of the class passed quickly. Gabrielle contented herself with being a quiet observer.

"All right, everyone, great job tonight. Keep up on what I've instructed each of you to do for your particular painting, and I'll see you here Thursday night."

Gabrielle waited until one of the students, another middle-aged woman, had finished talking with Madison before Gabrielle approached her.

"What'd you think?" Madison said.

"That it's fascinating to watch you teach." She wanted to add that it'd be even more fascinating to watch Madison paint, but she refrained.

Madison finished packing up her supplies. Gabrielle automatically reached down to pick up the paint-supply case.

"You weren't bored?" Madison asked as they headed out the door and into the parking lot.

"Not at all." Gabrielle laid the case next to the easel in the back of the SUV and walked around to the passenger side to get in.

Madison started the SUV and eventually merged onto the interstate. "I wasn't sure how much you'd enjoy it. Well, I was actually a little worried you'd hate it."

"I could never hate something that means so much to you."

Madison glanced over at her and smiled. On the way back to Islamorada, Gabrielle peppered her with questions about technique, choices of color, and the length of time it took her to finish a piece. As Madison spoke, she kept one hand on the steering wheel and used the other one to gesture as if she were holding a brush. Again, Gabrielle grew mesmerized with the simple, graceful movements of her hand.

About twenty minutes later, Madison pulled into Gabrielle's driveway. She shifted into park and turned off the ignition.

"I'm glad you came, Gabrielle. From what you've told me, it sounds like you might want to give it a try."

"I would like to, yes. I was wondering, though, if you'd maybe teach me at your house."

Madison seemed surprised at the request.

"I understand if you don't feel comfortable doing that."

"No. It's just I never thought of teaching you there." She stared out of the windshield and nodded. "I think it would work. We'll drive into town to Hobby World, and I'll get you set up with supplies. I have plenty of paint I'm not using, so there's no problem there."

The longer Madison talked about it, the more animated she became. Gabrielle couldn't help thinking that a certain dolphin would be proud of her right now. She realized Madison had stopped speaking and hurried to fill the silence. "Do you think we could go into town to the hobby store tomorrow?"

"Sure. I can swing by and pick you up in the morning after I take Mo to school."

"Sounds perfect." Gabrielle decided to be the one to initiate the kiss this time. She leaned across the console until she met Madison's lips. "I'll see you tomorrow." She reached for the door handle.

"I'll call you before I come over."

Madison waited until Gabrielle made it to her front door. Gabrielle waved as Madison backed out of the driveway. She already looked forward to tomorrow.

Chapter 19

The next day, Madison swung by Gabrielle's and picked her up as promised. On the way to Hobby World, they talked about what medium Gabrielle wanted to try. She'd only dabbled with sketching, but Madison thought she'd enjoy working with acrylics.

When they entered the store, they were bombarded by Christmas decorations and Christmas Muzak blaring. Normally, Madison would be feeling down this time of year, even though she tried to be upbeat for Mo's sake. This year felt different, and the reason was walking right beside her. As she thought of Christmas, Madison wondered if Gabrielle would like to spend Christmas Eve and Christmas with her, Mo, Cyndra, and Beverly. The gathering had become a tradition in the years that Callie was alive, and Madison had continued it after her death.

She glanced over at Gabrielle who looked festive with her long-sleeved, hunter green Henley and small, ruby stud earrings. Even without her long hair, she had the ability to turn the heads of the few men they came across in the store and even some of the women. Madison caught herself admiring the fit of Gabrielle's shirt and the snugness of her straight-legged jeans.

"Art supplies are in the back right corner of the store," Madison said. As they picked out some brushes, Madison hoped she wouldn't be subjected to another sneak attack by Rachelle. "Let's get a couple more tubes of white."

"Is that how you achieve the lightness in your paintings?"

"There are a couple of different ways to do it, but yeah, I mix in white—especially when I want to emphasize a particular section of the painting. Would you like to learn?"

"Well, I'm sure I won't be as accomplished as you are at it, but I'd like to at least try the technique."

As they were heading to the checkout, Gabrielle stopped at a rack of books about painting and ones that focused on various artists.

She picked up one entitled, *Madison Lorraine's Seascapes*. Madison watched while she flipped bright-colored pages full of her work. She shifted uneasily as Gabrielle paused on one page, afraid Gabrielle would ask her questions she wasn't prepared to address.

Gabrielle glanced up at her. "If I haven't told you lately, I love what you do." She shut the book and placed it back on the shelf. "Ready?"

"Ye-yeah." Madison, who'd been ready to defend her decision not to paint, didn't know what else to do but follow Gabrielle as she headed to the checkout. She tried to pay for the supplies, but Gabrielle insisted on purchasing the items.

Once they reached the cove, they carried everything into Madison's studio. She moved her desk over to make room for the easel. "It's been a long time since I had this in here." She'd set it up a few months after Callie died. But the easel, with its blank canvas, stood unused in the middle of her studio. Spotlighted by the sun, it became a silent witness to her despair. Madison had stared at it and then at her hands as she willed them to create something—anything—to assuage her grief. But nothing would come.

Madison didn't realize she'd stopped talking until she felt Gabrielle watching her. She broke away from her memories.

"Let's get your canvas set up. You can do this a couple of different ways—by buying the linen and making your own frame and canvas, or by buying the premade version, which is what we went with to save a little time." Madison propped the canvas on the easel. "First, I'll demonstrate how you coat the canvas in gesso to prepare it for painting. This will help familiarize you with the initial stage before you experiment with your background." She glanced over at Gabrielle. Her brow was deeply furrowed. Madison tried not to laugh at the serious expression. "Any idea what you want to paint?"

Gabrielle answered quickly. "I want to paint Free."

"All right, let's get down to business." Madison opened up the container of gesso and showed Gabrielle how to apply it to the canvas. She handed Gabrielle the brush to give her a feel of the process. Madison stood behind her and clenched her fists to resist the urge to take the brush from Gabrielle when it looked like she was spreading it too thickly.

"You want to thin it out some," Madison said. "That's it. Nice and even."

Gabrielle finished with one coat and stepped back to observe the canvas as if she'd created a masterpiece. "Is this okay?"

"Perfect. We need to let it dry. It should take an hour or two but usually closer to an hour. Would you like some coffee?"

Gabrielle followed her to the island in the kitchen. Madison poured two mugs of coffee. They settled over their mugs as they asked each other more "getting to know you" questions.

"Your favorite movie?" Madison asked.

"Drama or comedy?"

"Both."

"For drama, *The Godfather*, but *not* because I'm Italian."

Madison laughed.

"It's a cinematic masterpiece. It's about family—the relationships between the brothers, their love of their father." Gabrielle smiled. "And yes, it's about the family business. Favorite comedy would be *Tootsie*."

"Oh my God! That's my favorite one, too! 'Michael, I *begged* you to get therapy.'"

Gabrielle giggled. "What about Dustin Hoffman asking the soap actor if he was famous when the guy called himself a 'has-been'? 'Well, how can you be a has-been if you were never famous?'"

"Classic, classic comedy. Hoffman should've won the Oscar for that."

They chatted for another hour before they returned to the studio. By then the gesso had dried.

"This is one of the most important aspects of painting," Madison said. "What would you like your background color to be? What kind of mood do you want to create? If you want to create shadow, you'll use darker colors, like gray or blue. To create a lighter mood, you'd use yellows, oranges, or similar colors."

"I want it to be a light mood because that's how I see Free."

Madison reached for the tube of lighter yellow acrylic. "Let's try this." She again demonstrated how to brush a thin layer and handed the brush off to Gabrielle. This time, Madison was a little more patient in watching when she noticed Gabrielle's confidence growing as she became comfortable with the medium.

"This won't take as long to dry," Madison said, "but let's have a little more coffee." They returned to the kitchen and chatted some more until forty-five minutes had passed. Madison glanced at her watch. "Should be done."

She approached the canvas and touched it. "Give it a touch," she told Gabrielle. "You'll feel that it's not tacky, and we're ready to go."

Gabrielle pressed her finger onto the canvas. "Seems dry to me, too."

"What would you like Free to be doing?"

"Jumping, of course."

"It does seem to be his modus operandi." Madison dug around in her own supplies until she found her number two leaded pencil. She held it up. "I could do this, but I think it'd mean more if you were to outline the image you want to paint."

Gabrielle took the pencil from Madison and, without any hesitation, lightly sketched a very nice rendition of Free in action. She stopped with her pencil above the canvas and cocked her head. "What do you think?"

Madison tried to hide her surprise at just how well Gabrielle had drawn.

"You don't have to look so shocked, Madison," Gabrielle teased.

"You've done a wonderful job." To cover her embarrassment, Madison got Gabrielle started on adding contrast, showing her how to mix certain colors.

They stopped briefly for a lunch of half sandwiches and a salad that Madison whipped up. Then they went back at it. Madison finally had to stop Gabrielle.

"I need to pick up Mo."

Gabrielle rolled her neck and shoulders in a circular motion. "I can't do any more on this today anyway. How long could you work without stopping?"

Madison thought back to her halcyon days. "I'd get caught up so much that I painted until the early morning hours. Callie would have to come get me to drag me off to bed." She reached out and wiped a spot of paint off Gabrielle's cheek, and because she couldn't resist, she leaned in and kissed her, softly at first, but then with a little more passion. She eased away. "Let me drop you off at home on my way to the school."

After Madison picked up Mo, the day played out in Madison's mind. She felt something stirring deep inside that had been missing for the past three years. She was falling for Gabrielle. Of that fact, she was sure. Where they would go with the relationship was still as unforeseen and unpredictable as the currents swirling beneath the surface of the ocean.

Maybe that wasn't such a bad thing.

* * *

Gabrielle took a shower to scrub off the paint she hadn't noticed when she was working on the canvas. After she finished showering, she nuked some leftovers. While she waited for the timer to ding, she heard splashing from the cove. She hurried to her back deck and once again felt the thrill go up her spine at seeing Free frolicking in the water below. Her cell phone rang inside. She hustled to the dining room table where she'd laid it.

"Hey, Madison."

"Did you see he's back?"

"Yes, I did." She heard Mo shouting in the background. "I take it Mo knows, too?"

"What do you think?"

"Are you going to let her get in the water?"

"I promised her I would. We have some old wetsuits we've not worn since... well, in quite a while. Would you like to join us?"

She was about to answer "yes," but then thought better of it. "I think it's a nice time for you and Mo to bond with Free, but I'd be happy to watch from your dock. I need to grab a bite to eat, and I'll be right down."

"By the time you're here, we should just be getting into the water."

"See you there."

Gabrielle sat down and hurriedly ate so she could join Madison and Mo. As she was about to step outside, she thought of something and went into the spare bedroom to grab her old digital camera. When she made it down to Madison's dock, Madison and Mo had already donned their life vests and were slipping on their flippers. Like Gabrielle, they also had goggles. Free circled in front of them. He'd stop occasionally and poke his head out of the water. His focus was entirely on Mo and Madison.

Gabrielle held up her camera. "Thought I'd snap some shots if you don't mind."

"Not at all." Madison glanced out at the water. "Hope I'm not making a mistake," she muttered under her breath, so only Gabrielle could hear her.

"You'll be fine. He won't hurt either of you. Trust him."

Mo edged up to the end of the dock.

"Hold on. I'll jump in first, Mo." Madison slid on her goggles, took a deep breath, and jumped into the water. Free had swum away, as if knowing she needed room to get comfortable. Eventually, he approached her, nudging her with his nose. She reached out to pet him. He nodded his head and playfully splashed Madison. Gabrielle captured the shot as Madison laughed. Free moved toward the dock and shook his head at Mo. Madison swam over to her. "Jump in. I'll be right here."

Mo inhaled and pinched her nose before jumping into Madison's outstretched arms. Free edged closer and rolled on his side, allowing Mo to stroke his belly. "He feels like rubber." She giggled. "Mom, he's so gentle."

"He is, isn't he?"

They rubbed his belly until he rolled back over, slid under the surface, and burst out of the water in front of them.

"Can I ride him?" Mo asked.

As soon as the words left Mo's lips, Free swam back over to them and presented his back, as if welcoming one of them to grab hold of his dorsal fin.

"That's how he let me grab hold," Gabrielle said as she lowered herself to the dock and hung her legs out over the water.

"I'm still not sure about Mo doing this." Madison rubbed Free's back a few times and seemed to come to a decision. "Let's give it a try, but if he goes too fast, let go, okay, Mo?"

"Sure, Mom." Mo grabbed hold of his dorsal fin.

Free started out smoothly without jerking Mo. He began a slow circle of the cove. He never increased his speed, as if knowing how careful to be with Mo's smaller body. Mo's laughter was infectious, and soon Gabrielle and Madison joined in. Gabrielle clicked away on her camera, capturing Mo's joy. After three circles of the cove, Free slowed to a stop in front of Madison, and Mo let go. She raised her goggles.

"That was sooo cool! Oh my God! I wish he would've gone a little faster."

"He went fast enough, Mo."

Madison debated about giving it a try.

"You'll have fun, Madison. Trust us."

"Mom, you *have* to ride him."

Free took that moment to start his jabbering. He directed his nonstop "dialogue" at Madison.

"Okay, okay," Madison said with a laugh. "You convinced me."

As if Free understood her words, he slid next to her and offered his back. She gripped his dorsal fin and off they went. Gabrielle noticed that with each pass, he picked up speed. She clicked away on her camera. Soon, he was moving as fast as he had when Gabrielle swam with him. After five trips around the cove, Madison let go in front of the dock.

Free circled a few more times, leaping and flipping in the air, before making his way toward open waters.

"Aw, he's leaving," Mo whined.

"Come on. Let's get out." Madison gestured for Mo to swim to the ladder. She followed close behind. She pulled off Mo's flippers and tossed them on the dock, then pulled hers off. Madison held her hand to Mo's lower back until Gabrielle helped Mo up onto the dock. Madison stepped up after her.

"So?" Gabrielle asked as Madison slid off her goggles.

"That was fun."

Gabrielle believed her, but there was something else in Madison's expression she couldn't read. "Are you okay?"

"Hmm? Oh yeah, fine." Madison ruffled Mo's wet, blonde hair. "What did you think, kiddo?"

"I wish he'd stayed longer."

Gabrielle glanced at her watch. "You both were out there about an hour. Wasn't that long enough?"

Mo gave Gabrielle an incredulous look. "No!"

"Free must know tomorrow is a school day for you," Madison said. "Time to go take a shower and wind down before bed."

Mo grumbled a little more before starting for the house.

Madison hung back. "I enjoyed our time earlier today. I wanted to thank you."

"For what?" Gabrielle asked.

"For reminding me how much fun art can be. I think I let it slip away from me." Madison stared out at the water and then met Gabrielle's gaze.

Gabrielle's breath caught. "You felt something with Free, didn't you?" She waited for Madison to offer up what had happened, but after a long moment, she accepted it was something private between Madison and the dolphin, just as her own vision would remain private.

Madison motioned with her goggles toward the house where Mo had almost reached the top of the stairs that led to the back deck. "I'd better get up there." She started to walk away but stopped. "Hey, would you like to join us in celebrating Christmas. Like Thanksgiving, it'd be Cyndra, Beverly, and of course Mo and me. We have a dinner Christmas Eve and stay up late to open one gift apiece at midnight. Cyndra and Beverly usually stay over. The next day, we wake up bright and early to finish opening presents. I didn't know if you'd be here for the holiday or if you were heading to New York."

"No, I planned to stay here and spend a quiet day at home."

"Oh. If you change your mind—"

Gabrielle touched her arm before she finished. "But with your kind invitation, I'd love to spend Christmas with you and your family."

"Good. We missed you for Thanksgiving. That's my fault. I'm still kicking myself about it, too."

"I would say it's water under the bridge." Gabrielle grinned. "How about we say it's water under the dock."

Madison laughed. "Let's call it exactly that."

"You coming, Mom?" Mo shouted from the deck.

"Be right there!" Madison turned back to Gabrielle. "Thanks for sharing this with us."

"It was fun watching you let go and laugh, but before you go..." She cupped Madison's cheek and gently pressed her lips to Madison's.

"Have a good night," Madison said, her voice raspy.

Pleased with the desire she saw swirling in Madison's eyes, Gabrielle started for home.

As Madison got to the bottom of the stairs, the images that had flashed through her mind while she swam with Free appeared again as a movie reel. With each step she took, she saw herself standing in front of an easel, painting and lost in her art, just as she used to be. While she painted, Gabrielle and Mo's laughter drifted in from the living room as they watched something on TV.

She smiled. Because in her vision, it wasn't simply that she'd returned to her work. It was the comfortable feeling of family.

Chapter 20

The weeks before Christmas passed quickly for Madison. She enjoyed time with Gabrielle, especially the hours Madison taught her about painting. One evening when Beverly came over and shared dinner with the three of them, Madison asked Beverly to stay a little longer while she walked Gabrielle home.

"Go ahead. I'll clean up and get this one ready for bed," Beverly said as she put her arm around Mo.

"Bev, the one stipulation I have is that you do *not* clean up. You fixed dinner."

"I believe I'm an adult and have my own mind as to what I can and can't do."

"Uh-oh, Mom. Grandma sounds like you when I'm in trouble."

They all shared in the laugh. "All right. I give up. I won't be long, though."

"You take all the time you need." Beverly had picked up her dish and was standing behind Mo. She winked.

Madison felt her face flush and hurried to get out of the house before Mo caught on. On their way down the street to Gabrielle's place, Madison took hold of her hand. She savored the silence between them, something that had become natural in the days since Madison had started teaching Gabrielle. They reached Gabrielle's front door.

Gabrielle pulled her key from her pocket. "Would you like to come inside for a glass of wine?"

Madison tilted her wrist toward the porch light and glanced at her watch. "Let me give Bev a quick call. I know she said to take our time, but I should let her know."

"Oh, sure." Gabrielle unlocked the door and they stepped inside.

Madison dialed home. "Mo, let me talk to Grandma."

Madison held the phone away from her ear when Mo screamed for Beverly.

"Hi, Bev. Listen, would you mind staying there a little longer? Gabrielle has asked me in for a drink."

"You enjoy your time with her," Bev said.

"Okay. Thanks. I should be over in about an hour." She ended the call. "Guess we're all set."

"Make yourself comfortable." Gabrielle motioned to the couch. "I'll be just a minute with the wine."

Madison sat down at the end and sank into the soft cushion. She crossed her legs, then uncrossed them as she tried to get comfortable. *God, you're only having a drink with her.*

"Here you go." Gabrielle came back from the kitchen and held out a glass of wine. "Hope white is okay."

"It's fine." Madison took a sip of the chilled wine. "Excellent." She should've known Gabrielle would have only the best.

"My father's family has a small vineyard in Italy. I was glad to see we still had some bottles on the wine rack, because I haven't gone shopping for any wine since I've been here." Gabrielle settled back into the cushion at the opposite end of the couch, pulled her legs up under her, and faced Madison. The light from the lamp sparkled off the glass of wine as she lifted it to her lips again. She stretched out her arm on the back of the couch and rubbed Madison's shoulder. "If I haven't told you before, I want you to know how much I enjoyed the time I went to school with you."

Madison was having a hard time concentrating on Gabrielle's words as the touch from her fingertips warmed her skin through her long-sleeved T-shirt.

"I don't know how good I am at teaching."

"Oh, Madison. Maybe you didn't see the expressions on your students' faces. They hang on your every word. And with me? You are so patient with my questions and never make me feel I'm making a mess of things."

Madison took another sip of wine, a little embarrassed by Gabrielle's compliment.

"You're cute, you know that? You're such an accomplished artist, and yet you're so modest. I can see you don't know what to do with compliments. How were you at your shows?"

Madison thought back to her last show, which was more than four years ago, a year before Callie died. "At the shows, I have to put myself out there. Callie used to coach me on how to interact with the public, but it was still hard. It's funny how artists and writers are probably some of the most introverted people you can meet. Yet, part of our jobs is to either show our work or read from our books. I would joke with Callie that maybe it'd be better if I smoked a joint before a show."

Gabrielle had just taken a drink and held her hand over her mouth as she started laughing. "Don't say things like that without warning me."

"Sorry."

Gabrielle slapped her lightly on her shoulder. "No, you're not."

They stared at each other until Gabrielle leaned forward and took Madison's glass and set it on the table. She set her own beside it and scooted closer. Cupping Madison's jaw, she rubbed her thumb softly against her cheek. "I'm not sure where we're going with this, but I need to know if you're feeling the same thing I'm feeling."

Madison's gaze dropped to Gabrielle's full lips which glistened with the remnants of wine, as if begging to be kissed. In answer to Gabrielle's question, she brushed her lips against Gabrielle's, then licked the sweet taste of wine from them before gently entering Gabrielle's mouth with her tongue.

Gabrielle whimpered. Her hand that had been cupping Madison's jaw moved to the back of Madison's neck. She ran her fingers through her hair and pressed into Madison's body.

It was Madison's turn to whimper. As she deepened the kiss, she pushed Gabrielle onto her back and draped her body over her, amazed at how well they fit. She rocked into Gabrielle's body, her thigh in between Gabrielle's legs. Trailing kisses down Gabrielle's throat, she felt her pulse throbbing against Madison's lips. She cupped Gabrielle's breast and rubbed her nipple until it hardened in her palm. "Oh, God, Gabi," she choked out.

"Madison, Madison, Madison..." Gabrielle wrapped her leg around Madison's calf and yanked her flush to her body. She gripped Madison's hair and pulled their mouths together again.

Madison was losing control. But the buzz of desire quickly turned into the clanging of an alarm inside her head. *Not like this. I want to make love to her, but not like this.* She slowed the kiss down until she gently pulled away.

Gabrielle's eyes were almost black now as they questioned Madison. "Wh-why are you stopping?"

Madison slowly pushed up to a seated position. Gabrielle did the same, her expression now troubled.

"Hey," Madison said in a soft voice. She brushed the back of her fingers against Gabrielle's cheek. "I want this so much. You have no idea what you're doing to me."

Gabrielle gave a shaky laugh. "No, I think I do." Her hand trembled as she pushed her fingers through her short hair.

Madison grasped both of Gabrielle's hands and ducked her head to meet Gabrielle's eyes. "I want to make love to you, but I want to do it properly." She grimaced at her choice of words. "I don't mean properly, I mean I want to do it right. Ah hell…"

Gabrielle's lips slid into a slow and sexy smile. "You're incredible. Thank you for having the will power to wait until we can at least make love in bed. Am I right? That's what you want?"

"First of all, I wouldn't call it will power. It's pretty stupid on my part because you've made me so wet, I'm a little out of it here."

Gabrielle drew in a quick breath. "God, don't say things like that."

"I want nothing more than to lead you to your bedroom. But Bev is watching Mo, and I don't want to keep Bev out too late." She leaned forward to kiss Gabrielle and waited for Gabrielle's eyes to flutter open before speaking again. "Once we start making love, I have no intention of leaving your bed or you leaving mine. I want to share the night with you, to wake up in the morning with you in my arms." She touched Gabrielle's cheek with the back of her fingers. "To watch the morning light as it plays across your face while you sleep."

Gabrielle took Madison's hand and pressed her lips to her palm. "You've just described the perfect night."

"Thank you for understanding."

"Please don't thank me, Madison. I think we have something special going, and like you, I don't want to ruin it."

"Oh, believe me. You could never do that." Madison slowly rose to her feet. "I should be getting home."

Gabrielle walked her to the door. Madison stepped out onto the porch, and Gabrielle gave her one last kiss. "Tonight was wonderful."

"It was."

"Same time tomorrow afternoon for my lesson?"

"As long as it works for you." Madison had only walked a few feet away when Gabrielle's voice stopped her.

"Madison?"

She turned, her breath catching in her throat as she took in Gabrielle's sensuous body outlined by the porch light.

"Sweet dreams," Gabrielle said.

"I couldn't have anything but sweet dreams."

* * *

Gabrielle knocked on the door. She heard Madison yell, "Come on in! I'm back here." She walked toward the sound of Madison's voice, which she recognized was coming from the studio. Normally, Madison greeted her at the door, and they shared a cup of coffee before they started. When she got to the doorway of the studio, Gabrielle stuttered to a standstill.

Madison was painting. She wasn't preparing the supplies for Gabrielle or readying her canvas on the easel. No... she was painting.

Madison looked over her shoulder. "Oh, hi. Sorry I didn't greet you, but I got a little caught up in this." She was about to set her brush down.

"No, no. Keep doing what you're doing."

That was all the encouragement Madison needed. She turned back to the canvas. Gabrielle stepped closer, trying to be as quiet and inconspicuous as possible to not break the fragile mood. But when she saw what Madison had painted, she gasped.

It was again a seascape, but the blues and greens Madison had used leapt from the canvas and right into Gabrielle's heart. Because in the midst of the bold color was the outline of a pod of dolphins. She saw one that looked very familiar.

Madison made one more broad sweep of her brush and stopped. She pushed a lock of hair off her forehead and in the process, added a touch of paint to the other paint specks on her face. She looked adorable, and even better, she looked happy.

"Did you stay up all night painting?" Gabrielle asked as she continued staring at the canvas.

"Almost. I got a couple of hours of sleep before I took a shower and drove Mo to school. Then, I hurried home to get back to this." Madison grabbed a small towel and wiped at her hands. "So, what do you think?" she asked, her voice small and tentative.

"It's beautiful, Madison. Looks like Free with some of his friends." This was better than the vision Free had shown her. Much better. She reached out her hand until her fingers hovered inches from the canvas. She traced the swirl of colors in the air. She almost felt the energy Madison had put into her work leap from the canvas to her fingertips.

"It's how I picture him when he leaves us because I can't see him as a loner. Not only would that be highly unlikely for a dolphin, he seems too outgoing to strike out on his own." Madison was about to set the canvas aside and lift Gabrielle's canvas onto the easel. Gabrielle gently grasped her arm.

"Please keep painting. That is, if you don't mind," Gabrielle added quickly. She didn't want to spook Madison and cause her to be self-conscious.

"Are you sure? I mean, I can always come back to this later."

Gabrielle wanted to say it'd be almost sacrilege to halt Madison's burst of inspiration, but she kept her thoughts to herself. Instead, she said, "We can always come back to mine later. Would it bother you if I sat over there in the recliner and watched? If it would, I'll leave you to it."

"You know, before it might have bothered me. Callie would join me at times, though. But since I've been teaching, I don't think I'll be as aware if someone is watching. If my students can do it, then I should be able to."

"Can I get you anything? Coffee? A soda? Water?"

"Water's good," Madison answered distractedly as she returned to painting.

Gabrielle brushed her fingertips lightly through Madison's hair as she passed by on her way to the kitchen. When she brought a cold bottled water back to Madison, Madison didn't take her focus away from her painting.

Gabrielle curled up in the recliner and let herself soak in the beauty of an artist at work... an artist she was falling for. Last night, yes, she was overwhelmed by desire. But something else was stirring deep inside. As she watched Madison's delicate hand sweep over the canvas, she thought back to how those fingers had touched her the night before.

Time slowly ticked by as the shifting sun filtered through the skylight with each passing hour. Still, Gabrielle didn't move for fear she'd break the spell woven by an encounter with a dolphin. She wasn't presumptuous enough to think that she alone had this effect on Madison. She would like to think she'd brought some joy back into Madison's life, but there was more at work here.

Madison set her brush down and rubbed her hands with the towel. She took a drink of water and stared at the painting at length before facing Gabrielle. She blinked a few times, as if she'd completely forgotten Gabrielle was in the same room.

Gabrielle got to her feet and walked to her. She loosely draped her arms around Madison's neck.

Madison gripped her hips to hold her back. "I'm pretty messy."

Gabrielle tugged Madison to her body. "I don't care. I dressed to paint, remember?"

"About last night…"

Gabrielle tensed as she waited for her to finish, a little afraid Madison would say it was a mistake.

"I'm not rushing you, am I?"

"Believe me, that's impossible." Gabrielle kissed her, pleased with the desire that washed over Madison's face. "If I didn't make that plain enough last night, then I wasn't doing a very good job."

Madison chuckled. "I think you did just fine."

Gabrielle glanced at the clock on the wall behind Madison. "I should go. It's almost three."

Madison spun around to check the time. "Oh, my God. It is? What happened to the day? I didn't even ask if you wanted something to eat."

Gabrielle placed her hand on Madison's chest. "I'm fine."

"But still, you shouldn't be skipping meals."

"To be honest with you, I've been feeling much better. Today, it was a pleasure to watch you at work. I completely forgot about lunch, too."

"You really do look refreshed. There's a glow to your cheeks that wasn't there before."

"I'd like to think you had something to do with that," Gabrielle said, kissing her again before pulling away. "Now, I need to let you go so you can pick up Montanna."

"Can I drop you off at home?"

"No, I think I'll walk back." Madison left for the front door, while Gabrielle moved to the sliding glass doors that led to the deck. "Do you mind if I go out this way? A walk along the water sounds nice."

"Not at all." Madison accompanied her to the back. "I'm not sure how much we'll see of each other the rest of the week. A lot of my students are finishing up on their paintings because they're giving them as Christmas gifts. I've offered to stay late to help some of them."

Gabrielle stepped out onto the deck. "I understand. But please tell me you'll keep up on *your* painting."

"You know, I never thought I'd hear myself say this again, but you couldn't keep me away from painting now if you tried." Madison caressed Gabrielle's check. "I have you to thank for that. You've

brought something back into my life I thought was lost to me."
Gabrielle started to duck her head, but Madison tilted her chin up. "I
thank you… my heart thanks you." She leaned in and pressed her lips
to Gabrielle's in a soft kiss.

"Sounds like I may not see you until Christmas Eve?"

"Probably not. Can you come over around six? We usually eat
dinner about that time and then hunker down to watch Christmas
movies until midnight."

"As long as one of those movies is *It's a Wonderful Life*, I'll be
here."

Madison grinned. "It's my favorite. 'Merry Christmas'…"

"'Bedford Falls!'" Gabrielle finished for her.

They both laughed. "I'm such a sucker for that movie."

"So am I." Gabrielle knew Madison needed to get going, but she
hated to end their day.

"I'll miss you, too."

"Am I that obvious?"

"It's not like I don't feel the same way," Madison said. "Have a
good week, though, and call if you need anything."

"That goes both ways."

Gabrielle started down the stairs. As she liked to do, she slipped
out of her sandals and waded in the water lapping onto shore. She
stopped when she got to her house and stood facing the cove. Her life
had changed in so many ways. Cancer had changed her, yes. But it
didn't define who she was as a woman.

She'd thought she'd eventually return to her career, but now she
wasn't so certain. Was that life so important now? Did she want to
return to the glitz and glamour, to the pressure of being "on" all the
time? Or did she want to remain in Islamorada where she she'd found
what had been missing for so many years. Love. Here in this cove
with Madison and Mo.

Chapter 21

"Are you sure Gabrielle will like her gift?"

"For the twentieth time, yes, Madison. She'll not only like it, she'll love it," Cyndra said in an exasperated tone. "Chill, okay? It's Christmas. It's supposed to be fun and lighthearted."

Madison had debated about how personal the gift should be. Jewelry didn't seem right. So, she'd buckled down and finished the painting of Free with his pod.

"It's the first thing I've painted since Callie died." She watched out the back window as the setting sun's dying rays played across the Gulf of Mexico in the distance. She heard Cyndra move away from where she'd been preparing a plate of chips and dip for movie snacks.

Cyndra stepped behind Madison and touched her shoulder. "Honey, I know it's your first painting. It's gorgeous. I'm a little jealous you're giving it to Gabrielle and not to me, but it tells me just how much she means to you. And *that* is very comforting."

Madison turned to meet her gaze. "She's special, Cyn."

Cyndra brushed a lock of hair off of Madison's forehead. "I gather. Especially since you asked me to watch Montanna on New Year's Eve."

"Is it too much for you?"

"Again, chill. I'm more than happy to have Mo stay with me. I don't have a date for the night. It'll be fun to visit with my niece."

"I haven't asked Gabrielle yet if she'd like to share the evening with me, so it all depends on her answer. I wanted to ask you first."

Cyndra playfully slapped the shoulder she'd been rubbing. "Of course she'd like to share the evening with you."

"I'm glad you're so confident."

"Trust me on this one."

The front door opened. "Hello and Merry Christmas!" Beverly called out.

"We're back here!" Madison yelled.

There was a rustling sound of paper as Beverly rounded the corner and reached them in the back. She was hauling two bags full of presents.

"Beverly, you always do too much." Cyndra went to help her with the bags. "Do you want these under the tree?"

"If you don't mind."

"Not at all." Cyndra left for the living room, toting bags overflowing with brightly wrapped gifts.

"Don't you look festive," Madison said as she took in her mother-in-law's appearance. "I see you have on your favorite sweater." Beverly was wearing a red knit sweater with stitched-on ornaments and a Christmas tree.

"Yeah, I drag it out each Christmas. Callie gave it to me years ago, but I can't seem to let it go." Beverly blinked several times.

Madison reached for her and enveloped her in a hug. "I still miss her, too."

Beverly squeezed her tight. "But it sounds like you're moving on with your life." She held Madison at arm's length. "As you should. Your happiness is what matters, Madison. From what I hear from Mo, she absolutely adores Gabrielle."

"She does."

"That's enough for me." As she patted Madison's cheek, the doorbell rang. "I believe she's here."

The three of them went to the door. Madison opened it and tried not to stare. Gabrielle was beautiful, as always, but tonight in her black slacks and red silk blouse, she looked stunning. The top button was undone, and a small diamond pendant nested delicately above her cleavage. The diamond stud earrings she wore shimmered in the glow of the porch light.

"Aren't you going to ask her in?" Cyndra elbowed Madison's side.

Madison shot Cyndra a look as she let Gabrielle enter. Like Beverly, Gabrielle was also bearing a bag of gifts.

"Merry Christmas, everyone."

Beverly and Cyndra hugged her and wished her Merry Christmas. Madison hesitated for just a moment before leaning in and giving her a quick kiss. "Merry Christmas," she murmured.

"Merry Christmas, Madison."

Nobody moved while Madison shared a long look with Gabrielle until Cyndra gripped each of them by an elbow and urged them toward the dining room. "Enough goo-goo eyes. Time to get this show on the road. Let's eat."

Mo slid around the corner and skidded to a halt on the tiled floor in the foyer. Madison glanced down at her feet.

"Where are your shoes?"

"I wanted to show Gabrielle my Christmas socks. Aren't these cool?" Mo pointed to her green socks with individual red toes.

"Those are ultra cool."

"Mom got them last year for me. I only wear them at Christmas time. That's just a little out of each year, but I still think they're fun. The toes feel kind of weird, but—"

"Mo, how much candy have you had?" Madison asked.

Mo ducked her head and scuffed her foot against the tile. "I dunno. Four or five chocolates maybe?"

Gabrielle covered her mouth with her hand, and her nose crinkled with humor.

"We're having dinner in about thirty minutes. Do you think it was smart to eat candy right before dinner?"

"No, ma'am."

"Come on, Madison. Give my niece a break." Cyndra draped her arm around Mo's shoulder. "Christmas only comes around once a year."

"But no more candy."

"Yes, ma'am."

"Would you like me to take your bag?" Madison motioned at Gabrielle's gifts. "I can put them under the tree."

Gabrielle handed over the bag.

"You didn't have to bring anything," Madison said as she pulled the packages out and set them next to the other gifts.

"I know I didn't have to bring anything, but I wanted to participate in the opening of one gift at midnight tradition. There's a present for each of you."

Madison rose up from her kneeling position and stood in front of her. Cyndra and Beverly, with Cyndra tugging Mo with them, had moved on into the kitchen. Madison didn't think her mother-in-law and sister were subtle in allowing them a quiet moment alone.

"We seem to be by ourselves," Gabrielle said in a soft voice.

Madison's heart rate increased—like it always did when she anticipated a kiss from her. She wasn't disappointed. She closed her eyes as Gabrielle's lips descended on hers in a sweet, soft caress.

"It's good to see you again. I missed you this week," Madison whispered into Gabrielle's ear. She breathed in Gabrielle's scent—a perfume as light and as promising as the woman she was holding.

"Missed you, too."

They gently rocked together until a voice interrupted their private moment.

"Ahem."

Madison released Gabrielle. Cyndra was standing at the entrance to the living room.

"I think I've allowed you enough time to get reacquainted. And good Lord, it's only been a week." Cyndra looked like she was trying to maintain a stern face, but her lips tugged into a smile.

Madison linked hands with Gabrielle and followed Cyndra into the dining room where already a large plate of turkey sat in a place of prominence in the middle of the table. Mo, with her tongue sticking out of her mouth, was carrying in a bowl of dressing.

"Here. Let me help." Gabrielle took the bowl from her and placed it next to the turkey.

Beverly brought out a bowl of green beans and the cranberry sauce. Madison grabbed them from her and added them to the feast.

"You two go ahead and sit down. We've got this," Cyndra said when she carried in the bowls of mashed potatoes and gravy.

Madison pulled out a chair for Gabrielle and took the seat next to her. Before long, they were all seated and eating.

As Madison listened to the free-flowing conversation, she marveled at where she was now in comparison to the other Christmases since Callie's death. Yes, she, Beverly, Cyndra, and Mo had wonderful holidays together. But this was different, and Madison felt it deep inside. Her thoughts returned to Callie, and as they did, a warm, tingling sensation struck her right hand that lay on the table next to Gabrielle. As if someone had touched her. But Gabrielle was using both hands to describe how Free had taken each of them around the cove.

Peace settled over her soul, an understanding that this woman sitting beside her had received the blessing of the one who'd once been Madison's world. She felt Callie's presence and could almost see her nod and smile.

Gabrielle had finished her story and was listening to Cyndra talk about the trouble Madison used to get into growing up. As she laughed at Cyndra's exaggerations, Madison reached for Gabrielle's hand. Gabrielle turned to Madison. With a smile, she intertwined their fingers before returning to the conversation.

Madison's heart swelled with gratitude and hope—thankful for the time she'd shared with Callie and hopeful for a future with Gabrielle.

After dinner, they settled in front of the sixty-one-inch TV and watched *Rudolph the Red-Nosed Reindeer*, followed by *A Charlie Brown Christmas*. Then it was time for the "adult" movie, *It's a Wonderful Life*. Gabrielle had more fun watching Madison watch the movie. The enraptured expression on her face was worth sitting through the well-loved movie for at least the twentieth time in her life. When Clarence the angel earned his wings, it was only minutes before midnight.

As Madison passed the gifts around, Bev hurried to grab her camera. Gabrielle quickly discovered that the "opening of one gift at midnight" policy was going to be seriously skewed in her favor. She had gifts from Cyndra, Beverly, and Mo to open.

"You'll get mine when you're done with those," Madison said.

Cyndra had finished ripping the paper away from her gift. "It's beautiful, Gabrielle." Her voice was touched with wonder as she turned the crystal Christmas ornament in her hand. The multicolored lights from the Christmas tree sparkled in the glass.

"It's from Milan. I found it in a boutique in Miami."

"I love it and thank you. I would say you shouldn't have, but since I have no intention of giving this back to you, I won't."

Gabrielle laughed.

Beverly opened her gift and lifted out a similar ornament from the small box. "This is remarkable craftsmanship. Thank you."

"You're very welcome."

Mo ripped open her gift with all the fervor a child could muster. "Oh, thank you, Gabrielle. How'd you know I like Selena Gomez?" She flipped over the CD and read the song list. "It's her newest one, too."

"A lucky guess." Gabrielle winked at Cyndra.

Gabrielle had already opened her gifts from Mo, Beverly, and Cyndra. There seemed to be a theme. Beverly and Cyndra had gotten her glass dolphin statues. Mo had given her a carved wooden dolphin riding a wave's crest. The only gift left for her to open was from Madison.

"Let me go get your gift." Madison jumped to her feet. She returned carrying a large square package wrapped with shiny green paper and topped with a big red bow.

Gabrielle's heart skipped a beat when she thought about what it might contain. Madison turned her gift over and over in her hands and shook it. She was grinning like a kid. "Open yours first," Gabrielle said.

That was all the encouragement Madison needed. Beverly took her picture as she tore open the package. Madison sat back in her chair. Gabrielle had captured a moment with her camera when Madison and Mo were laughing as Free flipped them with water. Madison touched the glass of the picture frame reverently, as if it were a treasure from an ancient time.

"I don't know what to say, Gabrielle." She raised her head. "Except, thank you." She pointed at the large package sitting at Gabrielle's feet. "Now yours."

Beverly readied her camera again. Unlike Madison and Mo, Gabrielle carefully opened her gift, running her thumbnail along the seams of the tape until she had the paper pulled aside. She stared at the finished painting of Free with the pod of dolphins. Then, the significance of the gift hit home.

"Madison, it's remarkable, but are you sure you want to give it to me? It's your first painting in years. Shouldn't it be in one of your shows?"

Madison stood up to sit beside Gabrielle on the couch. She took her hand. "No. I can think of no other place I'd rather this be except with you. That is, if you want it."

"Want it? I'll treasure it with my heart." She placed a chaste kiss on Madison's lips. "It's the best Christmas gift I've ever received."

Madison's cheeks flushed.

"Aw, Madison's blushing," Cyndra teased, which made Madison's cheeks turn even redder.

Madison glared at her sister. "You know, if it weren't Christmas, I'd tell you to shut up."

Cyndra stuck her tongue out.

"Really mature, Cyn."

"Enough, you two," Beverly cut in. "Gabrielle, sometimes I have to act as their mother. This would be one of them."

"I think it's adorable."

"I don't mean to change the subject," Cyndra said as she gathered the wrapping paper from the floor, "but what time do you want me here next Saturday to pick up Mo?" She kept her head down as she stuffed the paper into a large trash bag and didn't catch the expression on Madison's face.

"I still don't know why I can't stay home with Gabrielle and

Mom," Mo grumbled.

Cyndra raised her head. Her face was bright red. "Oh, God. I forgot that you hadn't asked her, Madison."

Madison looked anywhere but at Gabrielle.

"Asked me what?" Gabrielle said.

Finally, Madison met her eyes. "New Year's Eve. Would you like to come over to spend it with me?"

It was Gabrielle's time to blush. "Yes," she said in a soft voice. "I'd love to."

"Munchkin," Cyndra said, "you're going to have a blast with Aunt Cyn. You'll hurt my feelings if you keep complaining. We'll make a homemade pizza, pop popcorn, and eat junk food. Since Mom won't be there, she can't scold us."

"Yes!" Mo pumped her fist.

"I'll be spending a nice, quiet evening with some friends, so don't worry about Grandma."

"We would've loved for you to come over, huh, Aunt Cyndra?"

"Absolutely."

While Mo and Cyndra discussed their New Year's Eve plans, Gabrielle couldn't look away from Madison who was staring at her.

"Is it okay?" Madison asked quietly.

"I can't think of anywhere else I'd rather be."

Chapter 22

Christmas day, Madison insisted that Gabrielle join them again. She agreed, but only if she came over at noon, well after they'd opened the rest of the Christmas gifts. They had a light lunch of leftover turkey sandwiches. She and Madison spent some time alone on the deck.

"I'm sure you've had shows in New York," Gabrielle said.

"I have. Quite a few, actually."

"What do you think of the city?"

"Every time I've been there, it amazes me how people are out and about at one in the morning." Madison shook her head. "I'm dead tired from being 'on' for three hours at a show. I look out my taxi window and see couples sitting at tables in front of restaurants, laughing and drinking."

Gabrielle reached over and tickled her side. "Not the party girl, huh?"

"What do you think?"

Gabrielle squinted. "Uh… no. Can't say I see you as that type."

"Don't get me wrong, though. I love New York. Loved the theater when I had time to go to a few musicals. Callie and I…" She stopped. "Sorry."

"Don't do that, Madison. You had a life with Callie. It's okay to talk about what you did together as a couple."

They grew quiet for several minutes.

"Think you'd ever like to visit?" Gabrielle finally asked.

"I'd love to. Especially with you. I mean, to visit you if you're there. Or—"

Gabrielle took hold of her hand. "We have a lot to talk about, but for now, let's enjoy this time."

* * *

During the week, Madison taught her classes but also allotted time to Gabrielle and her painting of Free. Madison's encouragement spurred Gabrielle's confidence, and by the end of the week, she'd finished the painting. Despite her protests, Madison insisted on hanging it in Gabrielle's living room. After Madison had told her she'd surpassed all of her students in just that one painting, Gabrielle had finally acquiesced.

With Gabrielle focused on finishing the painting, New Year's Eve had snuck up on her. As she pulled on her jeans and long-sleeved T-shirt, she couldn't stop the butterflies in her stomach from flapping their wings. Or her heart from pounding out of her chest. Or any other cliché for nervousness that she couldn't think of because she was... well... nervous.

She stood at Madison's door and lifted her hand to knock, but the door flew open before she had a chance to follow through.

Madison held onto the door with one hand and reached for her with the other. "Hi," she said and placed a soft kiss on her lips.

Gabrielle let the kiss linger before pulling away.

"Cyn has already picked up Mo. Do you want anything to drink?"

"Diet Coke if you have it."

"No alcohol?"

They walked back to the kitchen. Gabrielle leaned on the counter as Madison lifted a Diet Coke from the bottom of the refrigerator. Handing it to Gabrielle, she grabbed a bottle of water.

Gabrielle motioned at the water with her can of Diet Coke. "I could ask you the same thing."

Madison wet her lips.

Ah. She's nervous, too.

"I think I'll wait until we share a glass of champagne later. That is, if it's okay with you that we have a drink at midnight."

Gabrielle took a sip of her soda. "Drinking champagne at midnight is only appropriate."

Madison walked over to her and mimicked Gabrielle's stance in leaning against the counter with one hip. "I want this evening to be something special, Gabrielle. But it doesn't mean we have to make love. It's special simply sharing this holiday with you, creating memories together."

"Don't you want to make love to me?"

Madison blew out a breath. "God, yes."

Gabrielle set her soda can on the counter and did the same with Madison's bottle. She gripped Madison's hips and yanked her forward.

"Good. Because I want you to make love to me." She slowly trailed her finger down the middle of Madison's chest to her abdomen, pleased when the muscles there rippled and tensed. "I want to make love to you, and I don't want to wait any longer."

Madison swallowed hard. "Same here."

Gabrielle suppressed a smile and held out her hand. "Come on. Let's get comfortable and start watching the music shows. Someone always makes a fool of themselves before the ball drops on Times Square. We can make fun of the performers we don't like."

Madison grabbed her hand. Gabrielle tugged them toward the living room and the big-screen TV.

Melissa Etheridge finished singing her newest release as Madison watched the light from the television play off the delicate planes of Gabrielle's face. Her hair had begun to fill in even more. Her lips curled up at something one of the announcers said. Madison had a vision of what she wanted to do to that mouth.

Gabrielle met her gaze. Electricity surged between them. Madison had felt it before, but this time, it was different. This time it held a promise of the tempest to come.

She cleared her throat and stood up. "Can I get you anything? More chips? Another Diet Coke?"

Gabrielle glanced at the digital clock on the cable box. "How about that bottle of champagne since it's going on midnight."

"Right. Makes sense." Madison left for the kitchen, hoping with every step she took that she didn't sound as nervous as she felt. She retrieved the bottle from the refrigerator. No, it wasn't Dom Perignon, but it was pretty damn close: a 2003 Ca' del Bosco's Cuvee Annamaria Clementi. Not only was it a mouthful to say, it had cost her almost a hundred dollars. She wanted something Italian, and she called Angie Cantinnini, her friend in Key West, for advice. Madison and Callie had become friends with Angie and her partner, Meryl, through Madison's art and Callie's love of Angie's writing. Madison had to drive to Miami to find the wine, but it was worth it. At least she hoped it was. She tore away the foil and carefully worked the cork until it popped free.

As she set the bottle and glasses on the table in front of the couch, Gabrielle's small gasp was all she needed to confirm she'd chosen well. She made a mental note to call Angie to thank her.

"Madison, this is too much."

"Tonight's a special night. Not only are we celebrating a new year, we're celebrating you being cancer-free." She poured the bubbling wine into the flutes, handed one to Gabrielle, and lifted hers up in a toast. "To a New Year, to your health..." She paused as tears threatened to make an appearance. "And to us."

"To us." They clinked glasses.

Madison closed her eyes as the exquisite liquid slid down her throat. It might be the only bottle she ever bought, but damn, it was worth every penny.

Gabrielle moaned. "Oh my God. I forgot how wonderful this tasted."

They finished one flute, so Madison poured them another. They turned to the TV when Ryan Seacrest announced the countdown to midnight. They took one more sip of champagne before Madison stood and pulled Gabrielle to her feet. Seacrest began chanting, "Ten... nine... eight..."

He reached "one" and exclaimed "Happy New Year!" Madison brushed her fingertips against Gabrielle's cheek, cupped the back of her neck, and pulled her close.

The kiss started slowly, their tongues moving together in a gentle dance until Gabrielle's deep moan nearly brought Madison to her knees. She increased the pressure of her tongue against Gabrielle's while her hands drifted down to press against the sides of Gabrielle's breasts.

Gabrielle broke away with a gasp. "Remember what you said about wanting to make love in the bed?"

Madison grasped Gabrielle's hand and led her to the bedroom.

Gabrielle took even breaths to try to calm her racing heart. Madison squeezed her hand, as if knowing Gabrielle's nervousness. Or was it anticipation? Or a little of both? They entered Madison's bedroom. Madison reached for the light switch on the nightstand lamp, but Gabrielle stopped her progress by grabbing her arm.

At Madison's questioning gaze, Gabrielle dug down deep to find her courage. "Can we leave the light off? This scar..." She motioned at her stomach.

Madison drew nearer and caressed her cheek. "That means nothing to me, Gabrielle. You know that, don't you?"

Gabrielle bit her lip to try to quell her anxiety.

"All right," Madison said in a gentle voice. "We'll leave the lights off." She leaned in for a kiss which quickly became heated. She curled her fingers under the hem of Gabrielle's shirt. "May I lift this?"

Gabrielle stepped back and without another thought, pulled the shirt over her head. Madison held her gaze before staring at Gabrielle's lace-covered bra. Gabrielle reached behind her back and unclasped it, letting the straps fall down her shoulders. Madison tugged the bra the rest of the way and let it drop to the floor.

For a long moment, Madison simply stared. She licked her lips and rasped out, "You're breathtaking." She cupped both breasts in her hands and rubbed her thumbs against her nipples until they hardened. Gabrielle couldn't stifle the groan as the move shot all the way to her groin.

In a matter of seconds, they'd shed their clothes. Thankfully, the moon cast enough light in the room for Gabrielle to admire Madison's muscled form from her shoulders and arms to her tight abdomen and her strong thighs. Her breasts were small but perfect for her lean body. Gabrielle moved forward and brushed the back of her hand against Madison's nipples. She smiled when Madison shivered at the touch.

Gabrielle grasped Madison's shoulders and backed toward the bed until she felt the mattress behind her knees. She pulled Madison down with her, not wanting to lose the connection. When their bodies pressed together, Gabrielle became even wetter.

Madison leaned on her hands and rose above her. The expression on her face was one of desire, but Gabrielle saw something else there… something Gabrielle was afraid to name for fear what she was seeing was her own wishful thinking.

Madison brushed her lips against Gabrielle's before trailing her kisses down Gabrielle's neck and to her chest. She encircled one nipple with her tongue and sucked it into her mouth. Gabrielle's hips rose off the bed, but Madison's body kept her firmly in place. Madison lavished her other nipple with the same attention. Then she touched her mouth to Gabrielle's scar. Gabrielle immediately tensed.

Madison shifted to her side. "What is it, sweetheart?"

"It's the scar. I…" Mortified, Gabrielle tried to hold back her tears.

"Hey."

The one word, spoken so softly and with so much feeling, threatened to shatter what was left of Gabrielle's composure.

Madison pulled Gabrielle into her arms. "Do you know what your scar signifies to me?"

Gabrielle shook her head into Madison's shoulder.

"Life. It represents life. The surgeon removed the cancer, and your scar is a badge of honor you should wear proudly." Madison gently pushed Gabrielle onto her back. Her hand drifted lower, brushing lightly against the scar. "You're a survivor, Gabrielle, and you're beautiful." She lowered her hand even farther until she rested it between Gabrielle's legs. With a trust she didn't question, Gabrielle opened herself to Madison.

She sighed when Madison slipped into her folds and dipped her fingers through her wetness.

Madison moaned. "Oh, God. Is this for me?"

"Ye-yes."

"What do you need? Tell me."

"Inside. Go in—" Madison pushed one finger deep inside. Gabrielle lifted her hips to meet her with each stroke. "More." Madison added another finger to the steady thrusts. Gabrielle felt the fluttering of the beginnings of her orgasm. As if knowing exactly what she needed to send her over the edge, Madison pressed her thumb against Gabrielle's clit. Just as she climaxed, Madison covered her mouth with her lips and plunged her tongue inside, synchronizing the movement of her tongue to the thrusting of her fingers.

As the throbbing lessened inside, Madison slowed and brushed her thumb against Gabrielle's clit one last time before withdrawing her fingers. Gabrielle tried to slow down her breathing and the fierce pounding of her heart. Madison placed a soft kiss on Gabrielle's lips and pulled her once again into her arms.

With her ear against Madison's chest, Gabrielle heard the rapid beating of her heart. She threw her leg over Madison's and pressed her knee into the wetness below. Madison drew in a breath.

"Do you need something, baby?" Gabrielle asked as she leaned on her elbow and tweaked Madison's nipple. Madison opened her legs wider. Gabrielle settled over her with her hands on either side of Madison's body.

"Move higher."

Gabrielle shifted up in the bed. Madison cupped her breasts and lifted one to her mouth. Gabrielle bit her lip as the pleasure began building again. With great effort, she pulled away from Madison's lips.

"Oh, no you don't. This is about pleasing you." Gabrielle brushed her lips against Madison's temple, her cheek, her mouth. But she didn't linger. She continued exploring Madison's body. She sucked one nipple into her mouth and rubbed the other between her thumb and finger. Madison squirmed and moaned. Gabrielle trailed her kisses lower until she reached the soft, downy hair below. She inhaled Madison's scent before she parted her lips and slid her tongue through her wet folds. Madison gripped Gabrielle's head and pulled her closer. Knowing how much Madison needed release, Gabrielle didn't let her wait. She sucked her clit into her mouth and plunged two fingers inside her. Madison's grip became even tighter. Gabrielle pulled every ounce of passion from Madison's body until she tensed and cried out.

"Oh, Gabi! God!"

Feeling the throbbing of Madison's inner walls against her fingertips was enough to make Gabrielle climax again with her. She kept up the movement of her lips and fingers until Madison loosened her hold on Gabrielle's head and weakly tried to pull her away.

Gabrielle eased out of her, slid her tongue once more through her wetness, and placed a gentle kiss on her mound. She moved up in the bed to lie beside Madison and hold her in her arms. She sifted her fingers through Madison's thick, soft hair as Madison's breathing gradually evened out.

Madison's breath warmed Gabrielle's chest as she spoke. "I haven't felt like this in such a long time."

Gabrielle tensed. Was Madison remembering Callie? If Madison sensed her tension, she didn't let on. Instead, she said, "I feel safe with you. Safe and loved."

Afraid to speak the three words that would set her free, Gabrielle pressed her lips to Madison's forehead. "I know. I feel the same way." She kept petting Madison's hair until her body grew heavier and she drifted off to sleep. Gabrielle lay awake a little while longer, watching moonbeams shifting on the ceiling until she could no longer keep her tired eyes open.

Madison stirred awake as the sun's rays streamed through the large bedroom windows that faced the cove and the Gulf beyond. The light yellow paint she and Callie had chosen for the bedroom was burnished gold in the soft light of a new day.

Callie. She hadn't thought of her last night as she celebrated New Year's Eve with Gabrielle, nor had she thought of Callie as she made love to Gabrielle. Which surprised Madison. With Rachelle, the only woman she'd been with since Callie, the memory of Callie would appear unbidden at some point as if she were a sentry standing watch while they made love. Madison thought back to Christmas dinner and how she'd sensed Callie next to her as she gave her blessing of Gabrielle's place in Madison's life.

Madison touched her lips. Gabrielle's taste lingered. She still felt Gabrielle's soft skin under her fingertips, still felt the skipping of her own heartbeat with each of Gabrielle's climaxes. And now, with Gabrielle asleep in her arms, her heart swelled with love. With the passion Gabrielle had shown last night and in the early morning hours, Madison was certain Gabrielle felt the same way. Perhaps they were a little afraid to actually speak the words out loud. Madison wondered whether other women had told Gabrielle they loved her and whether Gabrielle had believed them.

A light touch on her arm shook her from her musings. She turned to find Gabrielle studying her.

"You seem far away," Gabrielle said.

Madison heard the worry beneath Gabrielle's quiet observation. She moved to face Gabrielle completely. She raised her hand and traced the soft contours of her cheeks, her lips, letting her index finger slide down her neck and between her breasts. She saw no need to hide from the truth or to keep it from Gabrielle.

"I was thinking about Callie." She felt Gabrielle tense beneath her fingertips. "No, it's okay. I didn't think about her at all last night while we were making love. That's never happened to me."

Gabrielle raised one eyebrow. "Never?"

"No. I haven't told you this, but at Christmas dinner, I swear I felt Callie beside me and her touch on my hand. It was like she was giving us her blessing." She shook her head slightly. "Maybe that sounds unbelievable…"

Gabrielle lifted Madison's hand to her mouth and pressed her lips to each knuckle. "I don't think so. If you truly felt she was with you, I'm more than honored she's happy for you."

In answer, Madison slipped her hand out of Gabrielle's grasp and cupped her breast. She watched in fascination as Gabrielle's eyes darkened with desire. She didn't speak as she caressed her nipple and brushed her fingertips farther down her body. Gabrielle drew in a shuddering breath when Madison stroked her hip and slid her hand between her legs.

"Do you need me, Gabi?"

"Yes," Gabrielle whispered and opened her legs.

"Here?" Madison asked as she parted Gabrielle's folds. She smiled when she felt the wetness already pooled there. "Oh, yes. Most definitely here." She savored each twitch of Gabrielle's lips, each flutter of her eyelids as she sank her fingers inside.

"God," Gabrielle gasped.

Madison kept up a steady rhythm with Gabrielle's thrusting hips. When Gabrielle tensed, Madison lowered her head and took Gabrielle's nipple into her mouth, sucking until Gabrielle screamed her name. Madison stilled her fingers and relished the pulses throbbing against them. It was as if she were feeling the very beating of Gabrielle's heart.

She released Gabrielle's nipple and slowly slipped her fingers out. Gabrielle's eyes flickered open. She held Madison's gaze before pulling her forward for a sweet, lingering kiss. Pressing her forehead against Madison's, she whispered, "Wow." They shared another long look until Gabrielle glanced at the clock over Madison's shoulder. "I hate to do this, but I should probably go before Montanna gets home."

Madison checked the time which was now nine. "She won't be back until around noon. How about I make us some breakfast? We can take it out on the deck to enjoy the weather."

"Do you mind if I shower?"

"Not if you let me join you."

Gabrielle rose from the bed and stood in front of Madison in all her naked glory. Madison's mouth went dry. With her crooked grin, Gabrielle seemed to be very aware of the effect she was having on Madison. "I think that can be arranged."

Gabrielle set her fork down after swallowing the last of her omelet. "Oh my God. No more. This was wonderful, but I'm full."

"You don't want another?"

"Are you serious? That's the biggest omelet I've ever seen. It covered my entire plate."

Madison shrugged. "Have to make sure you keep up your strength."

"Well, you've done an admirable job, and you should be commended."

"There are other ways you can reward me."

"I'm sure there are, but I need to get home." As the words left her mouth, a splash sounded from the cove. They jumped to their feet and peered over the railing. A large ripple circled out from the middle of the cove. Suddenly, Free shot through the water and performed a series of pirouettes before lunging nose first into a graceful dive below the surface.

By unspoken agreement, they headed down the stairs and to the end of Madison's dock. Free seemed content to not approach them but continued his acrobatics, much to their delight.

"He's pretty happy today, huh?" Madison said as he rode his tail across the water then dove out of sight.

"Mmm." Gabrielle gazed at him in amusement while he continued his antics.

Madison glanced over at her. "What's that 'mmm' about?"

She motioned at Free. "Doesn't it seem to you that he's performing more today than he has before?"

Madison looked back to the water. "I guess. Wait. You don't think…"

Gabrielle's lips slipped into a smile. "I think our friend's happy for us."

Free leapt from the water and flipped twice in one large arc as if to say, "Duh."

Madison shook her head. "You know, I'm not even going to argue the point."

He eventually tired of his fun—or of emphasizing his stamp of approval—and swam back to the opening that led to the Gulf.

Madison slipped her arm around Gabrielle's waist. Gabrielle leaned into her solid strength, content as they shared a quiet moment. She sighed as she felt peace settle over her, not unlike the same peace she felt while swimming with Free.

Chapter 23

The weeks rolled by quickly, and before Gabrielle knew it, early March had arrived. The days were full of love and laughter and with the joy of watching Madison brandish her brush with abandon. Of seeing her face light up as she talked about another idea for a painting.

And there was Free. Some weeks, he'd show up daily. Other weeks passed without a sighting. During the absences, Mo would fret that he'd never return. Gabrielle and Madison would try to reassure her, although Gabrielle shared the same concern. The days that he did appear, they'd don their wetsuits and join him in the water. When he'd swim toward open water, Gabrielle would wonder about his life away from the cove. She knew enough about dolphins that they swam in pods. Madison's artistic rendition of Free's "family" was exactly what Gabrielle envisioned.

Gabrielle had been a little worried at Mo's reaction to Madison having a new woman in her life. Despite Madison's assurances that Mo had wanted to see them together, Gabrielle was still reticent. She never wanted to be Callie's replacement to either of them.

But there was no need to worry. When Madison had told Montanna that she and Gabrielle were seriously dating, Mo jumped up from her seat on the living room chair and flung herself into Gabrielle's arms. "I'm so happy," Mo had said and then whispered in Gabrielle's ear, "and I know Mama would be, too."

Cyndra and Beverly had also been supportive. In a quiet moment between them, Cyndra had told her she was glad Madison had finally found someone worthy of her love. Gabrielle hadn't responded. Even though she felt in her heart what she and Madison shared was love, they still hadn't spoken the words. She'd come close, only to shy away and resort to saying how deeply she "cared for" Madison. Why was it so hard to acknowledge what was plainly true? Was she afraid that Madison wouldn't reciprocate?

One evening, Madison suggested a short trip to Library Beach.

She said the beach was secluded and thought Gabrielle would appreciate the privacy. As they walked hand in hand along the sandy shore, Madison suddenly turned to face Gabrielle. She reached for Gabrielle's other hand.

"I want to ask you something, but I wasn't sure how you'd feel about it, so I've been a little reluctant in bringing it up."

"You can ask me anything."

"Would you like to drive down to Key West and stay at the beachside cabin I own?" The words came out in a rush, as if Madison was afraid Gabrielle would interrupt her.

"It sounds wonderful. When and for how long?"

"We could leave Friday and maybe stay until Wednesday. Beverly's already said she'll watch Mo."

"Kind of sure of yourself, aren't you, Ms. Lorraine?" Madison's face fell. Gabrielle quickly changed her tone. "I was joking, honey. I'd love to go with you. But don't you think Mo would want to join us?"

"I'm sure she would, but I wanted it to be only the two of us for your first trip to the cabin. We can always go down again with Mo."

Gabrielle pulled Madison into her arms and kissed her, first gently, then with a growing urgency as she slid her tongue inside.

"Guess that's a definite yes," Madison murmured.

"If you still doubt it, then obviously I'm doing something wrong."

"Oh, no. You've made yourself perfectly clear."

* * *

"Tell me again how you know Angie Cantinnini?"

Madison had asked if Gabrielle would like to meet Angie and Meryl. Although she had originally thought it would just be the two of them, the more she thought about it, the more she wanted Gabrielle to meet her friends. They'd been so good to her when she was at her lowest. She wanted to show them she'd moved on and found happiness again with such a wonderful woman.

"Angie came to one of my shows in Miami and introduced herself. Callie was blown away at meeting her favorite author. She went off in a corner with Angie and talked with her for over an hour about her writing." Madison smiled as the memory played in her mind. "Later, when Meryl reappeared in Angie's life, we of course became friends with her and shared a lot of laughs in Key West."

Madison briefly looked away from her driving and met Gabrielle's gaze. "You sure you don't mind spending time with them? Because I'd love for Angie and Meryl to meet you."

"It's important to you, Madison, so that makes it important to me. I'm honored you'd want to introduce me. Besides, Angie's my favorite author, too. So smack my arm or something if I start acting like a star-struck teenager, will you?"

"She's Italian, you know."

"Really? Never could've guessed with the last name of Cantinnini," Gabrielle teased.

"I thought you might catch on."

They reached Key West in just under two hours. Madison hadn't made many trips down since Callie's death. There'd been too many reminders of their time spent there, either with Mo or on their visits alone when they'd wanted to share a romantic getaway. Traffic was heavier—a sure sign that college students were making their spring-break trek to the resort.

She turned off the main highway and made a series of other turns until they drove up to a gated entrance on the Gulf side. She slowed to a stop and punched in the code. They passed several stately houses and made another turn down a secluded road leading to a beachside home. Madison pulled the SUV to a stop in the drive.

"This is a cabin?" Gabrielle asked as she got out and stared at the house.

"That's what we've always called it since it's smaller." Madison tried to see the home from Gabrielle's point of view. Other homes in the gated community were more expansive, but she and Callie had never thought of getting anything bigger. The peach-colored stucco exterior was attractive with its wrap-around porch, and the three-bedroom residence suited their needs.

"It's beautiful." Gabrielle walked until she faced where a parting of the palm trees allowed a clear view to the Caribbean blue waters of the Gulf.

Madison popped the trunk and lifted out their bags. She carried them over to stand next to Gabrielle. "This view sold us on it. It wasn't cheap."

"I don't imagine so. I know how much property is down here. My father owned a home for a few years until he realized he rarely spent time in the place. But I'm sure it was worth the peace of mind that you, Callie, and Mo enjoyed while you stayed here."

Something passed over Gabrielle's face but was quickly gone.

Madison had a feeling she knew what it was. She decided to wait until they were inside and settled before they talked.

She dug her keys out of her pocket and unlocked the front door, moving aside so Gabrielle could enter first. Madison followed and left Gabrielle to explore on her own while Madison took the bags to the master bedroom. When she returned to the living room, Gabrielle was running her fingers along the cover cloaking the couch. It'd been since late last spring that she and Mo had taken the trip down. This time it felt different and again, it surprised Madison how smoothly she'd eased into this relationship. She accepted that was what this had blossomed into—a relationship. She never thought she'd feel this way again. Truly happy to love free and easy, without worries about any consequences of sharing her heart. She simply hadn't spoken the words aloud, but first she needed to address something she thought was troubling Gabrielle.

"Hey." Madison approached her. "Are you all right?"

"Hmm? Oh yeah. I'm fine."

"Gabrielle," Madison said and brushed her cheek with her fingertips, "you can tell me anything."

"I don't know. I guess I was worried that this might be too much for you. I mean, this is where you spent intimate moments with Callie. I know you did at the house, too. But this feels different. Maybe it's because it's such a romantic setting. Maybe it's because you've painted the same exact scene out there." She waved toward the window that faced the beach. "It somehow feels... sacred."

"You're right. It is sacred." Madison cradled her face with both her hands. "It's a sacred place where I shared my love with my wife. Where we brought our daughter. Now, I want to share it with you." Madison took a deep breath before speaking again. "I love you, Gabrielle." Gabrielle's lips parted in obvious surprise. "I don't know what's taken me so long to tell you. Maybe I was afraid it was too good to be true that I could find someone to love again and to share my heart. But God has blessed me with you." She leaned in to softly brush her lips against Gabrielle's.

She waited for Gabrielle's response and grew concerned when Gabrielle didn't speak right away. Without warning, Gabrielle crushed her mouth against Madison's in a bruising kiss. After several seconds, she slowly eased away. Her eyes filled with tears. "I love you, too, Madison. You have no idea how long I've wanted to tell you, but I was afraid."

Madison's mouth curled into a slow smile. "We're quite the pair, aren't we?"

Gabrielle laughed. "We are."

Madison glanced around the room. "How about we take the covers off the furniture, open the windows to air out this place, and then head to the beach?"

In answer, Gabrielle went to one side of the couch while Madison took the other. Together, they began the task of reclaiming the house.

* * *

Gabrielle was nervous about dinner. Not only would she be meeting her favorite author, she also would be meeting close friends, ones whose opinions mattered to Madison. She smoothed out the nonexistent wrinkles in her white linen pants as they stood on the stoop of Angie and Meryl's house.

Madison glanced back at Gabrielle. "Don't worry. They're going to love you. Trust me." Gabrielle gave her a timid smile as Madison knocked twice on the door. It swung open, and Gabrielle tried not to gape at the beautiful woman standing before them.

Meryl's blonde hair brushed her shoulders. Her hypnotic blue eyes drew Gabrielle in. The color matched the blue of the water surrounding the island. Like Gabrielle, she wore a sleeveless cotton blouse—hers a light blue in contrast to Gabrielle's forest green. Gabrielle tried to keep her gaze from drifting down from Meryl's khaki shorts to her tan and well-toned legs below—but it was difficult.

"Madison!" Meryl opened her arms and embraced her. "And you're Gabrielle." Without missing a beat, Meryl enveloped her in her long arms. "Angie has been so excited about your visit. In fact, I've had to scold her because she's slacked off on her writing since you called to tell us you were coming. She's out back firing up the grill. Follow me."

They reached the French doors that led out to a patio. Angie stood at the grill with her back to them.

"Look who I found, Ange," Meryl said.

Angie whipped her head around. She grinned as she spotted Madison. "Hey, dudette!" She gave Madison what looked like a bone-crushing hug.

Madison held out her hand for Gabrielle. "This is Gabrielle."

"Of course she is," Angie said as she gave Gabrielle a hug. "I would've recognized her anywhere."

Gabrielle was suddenly tongue-tied, embarrassed at her inability to form a response. Madison came to her rescue.

"Gabrielle's one of your biggest fans, Angie, but not in a *Misery*-Kathy Bates's creepy kind of way."

Angie burst out laughing, instantly relieving Gabrielle's pent-up anxiety.

"I've read all your Derek Barker books, including the last three you wrote under your own name." Angie had used the pen name "Zach England" before she revealed herself as the author of the detective series. Gabrielle knew she was babbling like a star-struck groupie but couldn't help it. "I also love your lesbian romances. Especially the first one, *Together Once More*." She sensed it was autobiographical but didn't want to broach the subject. No need. Angie addressed it for her.

Angie put her arm around Meryl's waist. "It always makes me feel good when someone says they love that book since it's about us getting back together. Right, honey?"

Meryl gave Angie a peck on the cheek. "Right."

Angie gave Meryl such a look of adoration, Gabrielle felt as though they weren't even aware of Madison's and her presence. Gabrielle's breath caught in her throat when she noticed Madison directing that same heated look at her.

Angie broke the spell. "I'd say we're all mad and crazy in love with our significant others, and it looks especially good on you, Madison."

They'd finished their steaks and were seated around the dining room table sharing a bottle of wine.

"Gabrielle, how have you been feeling since your treatment ended?" Meryl asked. "I hope you don't mind me asking, but Madison shared your story with us. You look fantastic. Although, I'm sure our friend here has something to do with that." She winked at Madison.

Madison felt herself blush. Callie had always accused her of having a mild crush on Meryl, but hell, it wasn't hard at all to develop one. The woman was drop-dead gorgeous. Then she caught Gabrielle's smirk as if she knew exactly what Madison was thinking.

Gabrielle answered Meryl's question. "I'm doing very well, thank you. My three-month follow-up appointment is next week. So far, so good on the reports I've gotten from the oncologist."

A pang of anxiety gripped Madison's stomach. She'd been so wrapped up in their romance, she'd forgotten about the appointment, even though Gabrielle had reminded her two weeks ago that the date was fast approaching.

Meryl held up her wineglass. "Here's to further good news."

Everyone joined her in the toast.

"I caught your latest book review for the *New York Banner*, Meryl," Madison said. "I have to say I agree with you on the biography of Lincoln. I've always felt the man is fascinating, but the author seemed to delve deeper than any other biography I've read on him and the Civil War era."

"You're right. The biographer definitely had a refreshing take not only on Lincoln but also on that period in our nation's history. I'm just grateful the paper allows me to work here virtually. I can't fathom working in New York after living here with Angie." She turned to Gabrielle. "Although I'm not knocking the city. I know you're usually there when you're working. Do you plan to return to modeling?" She must have noticed Madison's expression. "I'm sorry. Maybe this is something you haven't discussed."

"You're fine," Gabrielle said. She reached for Madison's hand. "I plan to work out something with the agency when I'm able to return. It won't be an issue."

Madison's heartbeat returned to its normal rate with Gabrielle's soft assurance. She decided to shift the conversation back to her friend. "How's your writing coming along, Angie? Meryl was saying earlier you hadn't been able to concentrate this week because of our visit."

"Oh, she did, did she?" Angie gave Meryl a mock glare.

"Face it, sweetie. When I'm right, I'm right."

"I concede the point. However," she said and emphasized the word, "I've already written three chapters of the next Barker book and have some ideas for another romance."

"Care to give us a hint about the romance?" Madison asked.

"Let's just say a story is formulating in my mind about an accomplished artist who finds love again when she thought it an unattainable dream." Angie took a sip of wine and stared at Madison over the lip of her glass.

Madison suddenly choked up. Gabrielle patted her thigh under the table, giving her the strength to find the words. "That sounds like a great storyline."

"How about your painting, Madison?" Meryl said.

Gabrielle cut in before Madison had a chance to answer. "You should see the work she's been doing these past few months."

In a sudden move, Angie jumped up from her chair and threw her arms around Madison. "God, buddy, you can't believe how glad I am to hear that."

Madison gave in to the tears.

They shared the rest of the bottle of wine and many more laughs before Gabrielle and Madison decided to call it a night. Meryl and Angie walked them to the door.

Angie clapped Madison on the shoulder. "How about you two joining us at the Cozy Conch sometime?" Angie's bar was the second love of her life. She'd often said those exact words to Madison.

"You feel up to it, Gabrielle?"

"Sure."

"Call us when you think you'd want to go. Tuesday night is a lot of fun with Sage's drag show."

Gabrielle's eyes widened. "Sage? As in Sage Starr from the TV show?"

"The very same." Angie stood a little straighter, obviously proud of her friend. "He shoots that show in LA for six weeks in the summer. He said he always has a blast. Even though he comes across as a bitch on the show, he's really not." Angie paused. "Most of the time."

They laughed.

After sharing embraces, Madison and Gabrielle began the walk back to their house, arm in arm. The air was still warm and surrounded them like an old friend. As they left the main drag and the brighter-lit streets, the stars became more visible. Madison gazed up at them and sighed with contentment.

Gabrielle leaned into Madison. "I like them."

"They're special friends. They were there for me when Callie died and have kept in touch since her death. They made sure I didn't hole myself away. Angie even drove up to Islamorada a few weekends to stay with me and Mo. Mo adores her and calls her Aunt Angie. Meryl's especially good with Mo. I asked her once if she and Angie had ever thought about having kids. She told me they were content watching Mo blossom with each passing year. God, do they spoil Mo, though." Madison shook her head as she recalled how long it took Mo to decompress after a stay with her "aunts."

Gabrielle broke into her thoughts. "You know, talking about your painting made me think of something. I love the painting you did for me of Free, but wouldn't Mo like one, too?"

Madison stopped walking and slammed her eyes shut. "Damn. Why didn't I think of that?"

"Have you ever painted anything for her before?"

"No, it's always been about my work. Or, if I've painted personal pieces, Mo was a part of the painting. *A Good Day* is the most intimate painting I've done, and I sold it because I couldn't bear to look at it."

Gabrielle gripped her arm. "I'm sorry, Madison. I didn't mean to bring up those painful memories."

"It's okay. You haven't. You've just reminded me that Mo would appreciate a painting of Free, too." They began walking again in silence as Madison started imagining what she'd paint for Mo.

After a long moment, Gabrielle asked, "Tired?"

"Not really. I'd like nothing more than to show you again tonight how much I love you."

Gabrielle smiled. "I'd like that, too… a lot."

They didn't speak when they arrived at the house and walked back to the bedroom. Gabrielle tried to control her breathing but wasn't successful. Not when Madison, standing across the bed from her, was slowly removing her clothing, piece-by-piece. Her own fingers trembled as she fumbled with the buttons of her blouse. Gone was any thought of being smooth and in control.

Madison came around the bed. She stilled Gabrielle's hands. She creased her brow in concentration as she undid each button. She reached the last one and slid the blouse off Gabrielle's shoulders. Gabrielle's heart rate felt like it had doubled as her gaze lowered to Madison's dark nipples. She was so lost in admiring Madison's body, she didn't notice Madison had removed her bra until she felt it fall at her feet. Madison knelt in front of her. Gabrielle didn't miss the shaking of Madison's hands as she gently tugged down the zipper of Gabrielle's slacks. The idea that Madison was just as caught up in desire as Gabrielle caused moisture to pool between her legs.

Madison hooked her thumbs in the waistband and pulled the slacks down to join the pile of clothes on the floor. She placed a gentle kiss on Gabrielle's stomach. When she pressed her mouth against Gabrielle's mound, Gabrielle had to grip Madison's shoulders to keep from crumbling to her knees. Another gush of wetness soaked her panties, and she tried not to squirm as Madison slipped them off.

Madison rose to her feet. She ran her thumb across Gabrielle's lower lip. Emotion swirled in the golden hue of Madison's eyes. She slid her fingers behind Gabrielle's neck and pulled her down so their mouths were but a breath apart. Gabrielle waited in anticipation for the kiss and moaned when Madison skimmed her tongue along her lips until she delved inside. She sought out Gabrielle's tongue, and they began a slow dance that built in intensity. Gabrielle gripped the hairs at the nape of Madison's neck with both hands, shivering when Madison gasped. They stumbled toward the bed and struggled at first for dominance.

Gabrielle won the battle and grinned in triumph as she straddled Madison's hips. She lowered her body, sucking in a breath as their nipples met.

"I can feel how wet you are," Madison said in a ragged voice. "Let me—"

"No." Gabrielle surprised herself at the forcefulness of her response and was pleased to see Madison's pupils darken even further in desire at her utterance of that one word. She grabbed Madison's wrists and pinned them above Madison's head. Then she pressed the length of her body against Madison's and began a slow grind. She felt the evidence of Madison's desire as their hips thrust together. They quickly picked up a mutual rhythm, building toward something glorious. Madison's body tightened. Gabrielle stopped her movement, and Madison groaned in obvious frustration. "Not without me, baby." Madison only gave her a slight nod. Gabrielle started her thrusting again and felt the stirrings of her orgasm. "Now. Come with me now." It wasn't a request.

Gabrielle drove her body against Madison one last time and cried out as her climax erupted from deep inside some primal place. A place she'd never reached before. Madison screamed Gabrielle's name as she joined Gabrielle in her release. In contrast to the intensity of their orgasms, Gabrielle lowered her head, placed the gentlest of kisses on Madison's lips, and slipped her tongue inside briefly. She kissed Madison's forehead before rolling off her body and slumping beside her. They lay like that for a long time, both breathing hard as they stared up at the ceiling.

"I love you, Gabi," Madison whispered.

Gabrielle thought she heard tears behind Madison's words. She touched Madison's cheek with her knuckles and felt moisture.

"Oh, sweetheart." Gabrielle pulled Madison into her arms. She didn't tell Madison not to cry because tears were trickling down her own cheeks. If ever there was a perfect moment in Gabrielle's life, it was this moment she was sharing with the woman she knew, without a doubt, was her destiny. She ran her fingers through Madison's soft hair. "I love you, too."

Madison emerged from her deep slumber like a bud emerges for its first breath of spring. She blinked in the pale light of dawn that blanketed the room. Sensing she was alone, she felt the empty space beside her. She inhaled the tangy scent of sex, and images of last night's lovemaking rushed through her like a torrent of floodwater. Rising, she walked to the window that overlooked the Gulf and saw a figure of someone standing at the shore. She went to her dresser and pulled out a pair of boxer shorts and a T-shirt. At the back door, she slid on her sandals before stepping outside.

As Madison approached Gabrielle, she noticed Gabrielle had dressed in a baggy sleep shirt which dropped down to her thighs. It was a tantalizing sight—enough to make Madison wonder if Gabrielle wore nothing underneath.

Madison finally reached her. "Everything okay?"

Gabrielle remained facing the water, as if searching for answers from the waves pushing against the shore.

"It's perfect. So perfect, it's a little scary."

Madison slipped her arms around Gabrielle's waist so that she faced Madison. She tried to gauge Gabrielle's expression in the early morning light. She waited for Gabrielle to say more, sensing she needed a little time to gather her thoughts.

"My life changed almost a year ago when I was diagnosed with cancer. I felt so alone as I struggled through the treatment. I never missed my dad as much as I missed him in those months of fatigue and side effects that go along with treatment." She ducked her head and swiped at the dampness on her cheeks. "I'm not telling you anything you don't already know. You've gone through this with Callie. But I'm almost afraid to dream. That if I allow myself to hope for a life with you and Montanna, it will all come crashing down on me. Last night was…" Gabrielle's voice trailed away.

"Yeah, it was." Madison rubbed her fingers up and down Gabrielle's back, offering gentle encouragement with her touch to say the rest of what was on her mind.

"There was a moment when I knew without a doubt that my being here, meeting you, and falling in love… all of it was meant to be." Gabrielle shook her head slightly. "Then this morning when I watched you sleeping, I thought, can this really be happening? Is God or the universe offering me this chance at happiness? Or will something snatch it all away? Will I be knocked down again right when I thought my life had truly begun?"

There was such anguish in Gabrielle's voice that Madison pulled her close and hugged her. "Baby, I understand how you feel. I've wondered how I could be so lucky to find love again. I thought Callie would always be the only one for me. Yet, here you are."

Gabrielle eased out of the embrace and touched Madison's face. "You're real, aren't you?"

Madison stared at Gabrielle's lips before kissing her softly. "Yes," she whispered. "And so is our love."

What Madison didn't express was her own deep, underlying fear about Gabrielle's cancer possibly returning. What then? Could she again survive the agony and helplessness of watching her partner suffer? As she looked into Gabrielle's eyes, so full of emotion that Madison felt as though she were seeing into the very depths of her soul, she accepted that she had no control over the future. Like Gabrielle, she only prayed that fate wouldn't be so cruel.

Chapter 24

"I'll greet you with my standard question—"

Before Sage Starr uttered another word, the crowd at the Cozy Conch shouted, "How're all you bitches doing tonight?"

He shook his finger at them. "That's my line, bitches!"

Gabrielle and Madison sat at a table in the back of the bar with Meryl and Angie. They'd enjoyed the opening number with Sage leading his "girls" on the stage in a rousing rendition of Madonna's "Holiday." Earlier, they shared some laughs with Sage over drinks before he had to transform into his drag persona.

He introduced the first queen who strutted downstage to Aretha Franklin's "Respect." Three other performers followed. Then the lights dimmed, and the place grew hushed. The spotlight blinked on and focused on Sage, now in a blonde wig and a red, sequined gown. The opening notes of Barbra Streisand's "People" drifted down from the speakers. Although he was lip synching, he poured so much emotion into the performance, it was as if he'd channeled Streisand herself. He ended the song to thundering applause and whistles. He raked in the dollars, tens, and twenties, then blew kisses to the crowd before calling out the rest of the queens for one last number. After they walked off the stage, the lights came up and the DJ started playing a dance mix.

Gabrielle glanced over at the small dance area and marveled at the energy of the twenty-somethings who showed no sign of letting up—even at midnight.

"I think we'll head home," Madison said over the music.

"I don't think we'll stay, either." Angie stood and held out her hand to Meryl.

Duvall Street was still bustling but wasn't nearly as loud and boisterous as the Cozy Conch. Gabrielle's ears adjusted to the relatively quieter nightlife outside the bar. By unspoken agreement, they started walking toward Angie and Meryl's house.

"What'd you think of the show?" Angie asked.

Gabrielle slipped her hand into Madison's. "It was every bit as good as I thought it would be."

"Glad you enjoyed it. I didn't want you going back home without seeing Sage perform."

As they walked, they discussed when Angie and Meryl might make a trip to Islamorada to visit Madison and Gabrielle. When they arrived at Angie and Meryl's gate, they shared embraces.

"Take care of our friend," Meryl whispered into Gabrielle's ear as they hugged.

Gabrielle nodded.

She and Madison gave them a little wave before heading on to their house. When they entered the bedroom, they didn't speak as they undressed. They made love unhurriedly, as if memorizing each soft curve of skin. Gabrielle felt Madison hold back a little in her passion. When they cuddled afterward, she looked up at Madison. She was studying the ceiling as she caressed Gabrielle's shoulder. Gabrielle almost questioned her about her quiet contemplation but decided against it. Madison would let her know if anything was bothering her... at least Gabrielle hoped she'd earned that trust.

Chapter 25

When they arrived home from Key West, Montanna threw herself into Madison's arms as soon as she entered the house. Gabrielle felt a slight pang of guilt for keeping Mo's mom away, but then Mo ran up to her and hugged her.

"I'm glad you and Mom are home. Did you have fun?"

"We did. We missed you, though."

They made it a point that week to spend quality time with Mo. Madison helped Gabrielle start on another painting, this time of her memory of the sun dancing off the water in Key West. Gabrielle was glad when Madison jumped right back into her own painting. She'd immediately started the one of Free for Mo. Only it wasn't just of Free. Madison included Mo in the painting. She'd captured the moment Mo had rubbed Free's belly the first time they swam with him. The painting was meant to be a surprise, but the ever-curious Mo had spotted it when she came home from school one day. Her squeal of delight reached Madison and Gabrielle in the living room. "I think she found her surprise," Madison said with a shake of her head.

Mo sprinted into the living room and stood in front of Madison. Her body vibrated with excitement. "Oh, please, please, pleeeeease can I have that painting for my own?"

Madison glanced over at Gabrielle. "Should I make her wait a little longer?"

Gabrielle slapped her lightly on the shoulder. "Quit teasing her, Madison."

"Yes, I'm painting it for you."

Mo hugged Madison. "Thank you, thank you, thank you, Mom!"

"Mo, you're strangling me."

Mo pulled back. "Oh, sorry. Where can we hang it? Can we hang it in my room? Because I think it'd look great over my bed, and I'd see Free every day. Don't you think that'd be a good place for it, Gabrielle?"

"If that's where you want it to go and as long as your mom

agrees."

Mo turned to Madison. "Mom?"

Madison made a serious face like she was really thinking hard about it. Then she grinned. "As soon as it's done, we'll hang it there."

Madison grew quieter as Gabrielle's follow-up appointment approached. She'd asked if she could drive Gabrielle to get her blood drawn for the CA-125, but Gabrielle didn't want to take Madison away from her work. Soon, Madison would have enough for a show—one long-anticipated because of her over four-year hiatus.

* * *

The day after her short trip to the lab, Gabrielle was home and was about to grab a juice to take out on the deck and enjoy the warm temperatures. Her cell phone rang and vibrated on the kitchen counter. She checked caller ID. Her heart did a little flip when she saw it was her oncologist's office.

"Hello."

"Gabrielle?"

"Yes."

"This is Allison Bennett, Dr. Corrigan's nurse. Your lab work came in this morning, and I wanted to call you right away."

Gabrielle reached behind her for the stool and sank into the cushion.

"Are you still there?"

Gabrielle realized she hadn't responded. "Is there a problem?" She already knew the answer but held her breath anyway as she awaited Allison's response.

"Your CA-125 came back elevated."

"How elevated?"

"It's jumped from four on your last visit to fifteen."

Gabrielle gripped the counter in front of her as she tried to calm her racing heart.

"These things happen sometimes, so please don't be too alarmed. But Dr. Corrigan wants you to come into the hospital for a CT scan. He'd like to get that scheduled before your appointment."

"I see him Tuesday. It's Friday, so that only leaves—"

Allison cut her off. "Let's get you scheduled for first thing Monday morning. He'll still be able to have the results read before your appointment Tuesday afternoon. Here's radiology's number."

Gabrielle grabbed a pad of paper and scribbled down the number.

"Even though they may be full, they're aware that appointments like these come up. Let them know Dr. Corrigan's office has requested the scan and to call us if there are any questions."

"Okay." Gabrielle hated that her voice trembled.

"Gabrielle, I know this is easy to say and hard to do, but please try not to worry. As I said, this does happen occasionally, and it usually turns out to be nothing but a glitch in the lab work."

Gabrielle disconnected from the call and stared mindlessly out the window, feeling nothing but numbness. She was about to dial Madison's number but hung up before the call went through. The conversation they'd shared in Key West earlier in the week ran through her mind. She'd tell Madison once she processed the information, if there was any right way to process these things.

She made the call to radiology and was given an appointment for eight Monday morning. Picking up her juice, she stood out on her deck and stared out at the water. How long, she had no idea. It took a while for her to register the splashing in the cove below. Free had made an appearance, which was a relief. Not only because she was scared and needed his comfort, but it had been a couple of weeks since they'd last seen him. She finished her juice and headed down the deck stairs. She walked to the end of her dock and sat down with her feet dangling over the water. Free performed a few more jumps and flips before swimming toward the dock.

"Hey, big guy," Gabrielle said in a soft voice.

He bobbed his nose a few times and flipped his head back as if to motion her into the water.

"Not today. Sorry. But it's good to see you. We wondered if you were coming back."

Free chattered at her as if to question the audacity of the statement.

Gabrielle held up her hands. "I know, I know. But you have to admit, you've been gone longer than before."

He stared at her and became very still. Gabrielle almost felt like he was probing her mind. She still wondered about her sanity, or at least common sense, when it came to Free. She couldn't explain the things he did or the visions he planted in her mind any more than she could explain the intricacies of the stock market. But she felt a quiet assurance from her aquatic friend that everything would be okay.

"You think so?"

He nodded, flipping water on her legs in the process.

"Should I tell Madison?" Gabrielle motioned toward Madison's house.

Again, he nodded. This time, he backed it up with some more chatter, which very well may have been, "Why wouldn't you tell her?" Then he swam away and performed two perfect flips in the middle of the cove. With one last nod of his head, he swam toward open waters and disappeared from view.

Gabrielle pushed off the wooden dock and rose to her feet. Slowly and with a quiet dread, she started for Madison's house.

Madison thought she heard tapping on the glass of the sliding back doors, but she was too caught up in her painting to answer. Soon, Gabrielle's voice drifted into her studio.

"Madison?"

"In here!" She set her brush down and wiped her hands off with a paint-stained towel. Her breath caught as it always did when Gabrielle entered the room. She was dressed simply in white shorts and a Key West T-shirt she'd bought on their trip. It didn't matter. Gabrielle made any outfit shine with her beauty.

Gabrielle approached the painting, her face becoming animated as she got closer. "Oh, Madison. It's gorgeous." She held her fingers over the painting but didn't touch the canvas. "It's Duvall Street, isn't it?"

"Yeah. It's been a while since I painted something that wasn't a seascape, but I did manage to paint some seagulls. That's as close as I got to anything related to water. At least they're always by the shore, right?"

Gabrielle didn't answer and seemed a little distracted.

"Gabrielle? Are you all right?" She watched as Gabrielle took in a deep breath before facing her again. Madison blanched at the tightness of Gabrielle's lips and her troubled expression. She swallowed down the sudden rise of bile in her throat. "What is it?"

"Let's sit down first."

Madison stayed rooted in place when Gabrielle tried to pull her toward the couch. "No. Whatever it is, I want to hear it standing up." Gabrielle didn't speak right away. "Tell me."

"My CA-125 is elevated."

Madison gripped the back of a nearby chair. "How... how much?"

"It's jumped from four to fifteen."

"Fuck." Madison's legs felt as though they were about to give out, so she quickly made her way to the front of the chair and slumped into the cushion. Gabrielle knelt in front of her and took her hands.

"It's going to be okay. Allison, the nurse, said sometimes when this happens, it's nothing more than a glitch in the lab work."

"You don't know that." The words came out harsh and raspy. She cleared her throat to try to sound stronger. "You can't know for sure."

"Which is why I'm having a CT scan done first thing Monday morning." Gabrielle's grip tightened on her hands. "Will you go with me?"

"Of course."

Gabrielle reached out a trembling hand and touched Madison's cheek. "Let's stay positive, honey. We have to. Because I can't bear to think of the alternative."

In answer, Madison took Gabrielle into her arms. Her throat burned with the effort to keep from sobbing. *This can't be happening. Not again.*

* * *

Madison had been mostly quiet on the drive to Miami Monday morning. She and Gabrielle had spent the weekend together. Although they were a couple, Gabrielle had cautioned about moving too fast for Mo. She would stay over a few nights and then stay at her own house. The weekend had been a quiet one, as well. Mo and Gabrielle played video games together. They attempted to get Madison involved, but she hadn't been in the mood. On occasion, Gabrielle would offer Madison what Madison had thought was an attempt at a reassuring smile. She tried to return the same smile but couldn't pull it off.

Now, they were seated in the waiting area of the cancer center's radiology department. Gabrielle had already downed three of the Styrofoam cups of prep and had almost finished with the fourth and last.

Madison observed the others in the waiting area. She saw the worried expressions that loved ones wore, almost like masks of despair. If she had to paint what despair and fear looked like, it would be these faces. Gabrielle slipped her hand over Madison's and gave it a little shake.

"You going to be okay?" Gabrielle asked.

Madison could only nod. Gabrielle was about to say more when the technician called her name. Not caring where they were, Madison pulled her forward to kiss her lightly on the lips. She watched as Gabrielle went behind the door with the technician to a place of mystery to Madison. A place that held all the answers to their future...

Madison hated it. She hated the total loss of control she had over the situation. There was nothing to do but wait. Wait and pray.

Monday night was one of the most agonizing nights of Gabrielle's life. The only thing comparable to it was awaiting the pathology results after her surgery, especially after the surgeon had described the lymph nodes as "gritty," a possible indicator of cancer outside the uterus. She spent Monday night with Madison and discovered again how withdrawn she could be. Gabrielle attempted to get her to talk about her fears but eventually grew as quiet as Madison. Mo, always the perceptive one, picked up on the tension in the house. She did her best to make Gabrielle laugh as she challenged her to a game of bowling on her Wii. Mo glanced over with a hopeful expression at Madison as they played the game. But Madison didn't acknowledge her.

Tuesday morning finally dawned. Struggling with her own fears, Gabrielle spent the day at home until Madison picked her up in the afternoon for her appointment. On the way to Miami, they barely spoke. Instead, Madison punched through the satellite radio stations before settling on one that played eighties music.

They'd just settled into their seats in the waiting area when the attendant called for Gabrielle. After she measured Gabrielle's weight and checked her blood pressure, she escorted them to an exam room. Madison tapped her sneaker in a staccato beat on the linoleum floor as the minutes slipped by. The door swung open. As soon as Gabrielle saw the expression on Allison's face, she knew it was okay. Madison, however, remained tense beside her.

Dr. Corrigan followed Allison into the exam room.

"Allison, Dr. Corrigan, this is my girlfriend Madison Lorraine."

They each shook her hand. Dr. Corrigan opened Gabrielle's chart and without preamble said, "Good news, Gabrielle. Your blood work came back this time at five for your CA-125. Better yet, your CT scan is completely clean. No sign of cancer."

"Oh, thank God." Madison slumped against her and started

crying.

Gabrielle put her arm around Madison's shoulders. "Don't cry, sweetheart. This is good news." She tried to sound lighthearted, but Madison's tears continued to flow. Gabrielle glanced at Dr. Corrigan and Allison who seemed unfazed with Madison's reaction. Gabrielle imagined they'd seen the complete gamut of emotions from their patients and their loved ones.

Eventually, Madison composed herself and straightened in her chair. Allison held a box of tissues in front of her. Madison took one and dabbed at her eyes and nose. "Sorry."

"Don't apologize," Dr. Corrigan said. "It's understandable, given the circumstances. I'm only sorry you had to worry until you received the results, Gabrielle. As Allison probably told you, sometimes the blood work can be off. This was one of those times. Since you didn't have any other symptoms—no fatigue or pain anywhere in your abdomen—I was optimistic this would be the result. We'll recheck your CA-125 next month. After that, you'll be fine until your next three-month follow-up."

Gabrielle barely absorbed what he was saying. She was more concerned with Madison who stared at the wall with a faraway expression.

Allison handed Gabrielle a script for the blood work. "Give me a call when you go in. I'll let you know the results the next day."

She took the script as she rose from her chair, but Madison didn't stand immediately. "Come on, honey."

Madison rose to her feet and followed Gabrielle out of the office. On the drive home, Madison again turned on the radio and only spoke when Gabrielle asked her how she was feeling.

Madison stayed focused on the road. "This has all brought back a lot of bad memories."

Gabrielle waited for her to elaborate, but that was extent of the conversation. As the wheels churned up the miles back to Islamorada, she sensed Madison building a brick wall around her emotions. Gabrielle sat there, feeling helpless to knock down the bricks before they became a fortress.

* * *

The cove was still tonight, the water a mirror reflecting the moon's glow. Free never visited them at night, but Madison longed for their friend to make an appearance to calm the storm raging inside of her.

Gabrielle had attempted further conversation when they got home. Madison feigned fatigue and dropped Gabrielle off at her place. Now, sitting in the dark after putting Mo to bed, guilt was eating at her. The confused and hurt look Gabrielle gave her as she got out of the SUV was almost enough to make Madison follow her into the house. But she remained glued to her seat.

So here she sat out on her deck. She'd asked Cyndra, who'd come over to watch Mo while they were in Miami, if she'd stay for dinner while Madison took some time to decompress—or at least attempt to. As she stared out at the water, she thought about the months she'd spent with Gabrielle. A woman she'd grown to love when she thought it impossible. She thought about Callie and the love they shared. But mainly, the painful memories of Callie's last months played over and over in her mind in one continuous loop of chemo treatment, of pain and fatigue, of Callie making the decision to live the remainder of her days the way she chose, treatment-free.

Madison felt the first tear hit her cheek. In the time that had passed since Gabrielle had told her she had to go in for a scan, every nightmare scenario had balled inside her stomach like a fist. She knew she was wrong to shut Gabrielle out, but she couldn't help it.

Because the one person she thought of even more than herself was her daughter. She remembered the nights of holding Mo while she cried for her mom. Mo had suffered through more heartache than any nine-year-old ever should. When Mo was six, her biggest worry should've been who to play with that day—not the impending death of one of her mothers.

Madison went inside and walked into the living room. Cyndra stirred on the couch and glanced up from the book she was reading.

"You doing okay?"

Madison had already shared with her Gabrielle's good news, but afterward, she'd shut down when Cyndra had asked what was bothering her.

"I'm fine." She headed down the long hallway to Mo's room. The door was cracked open, as always. She pushed it open farther and peered in at the sleeping form of her daughter, the nightlight casting a soft glow on Mo's face. Madison wanted to go to her and rock her in her arms. To tell her pain and death would never visit their lives again. That Madison would protect her from any future harm. She would stop it before the hurt even reached out its angry tendrils to entangle her daughter.

Madison approached the bed, brushed Mo's hair off her face, and planted a soft kiss on her forehead. Mo stirred in her deep slumber, murmured something unintelligible, and rolled to her side. The innocent movement, a reminder of Mo's vulnerability, cut into Madison's heart.

Madison walked to the doorway, turned back to look at Mo one last time, and left for the living room. "I know it's late, but can you give me just a few more minutes?" she asked Cyndra.

Cyndra's expression softened. "However much time you need."

Madison left through the sliding glass back door. She headed down to the cove and their dock and sat down on the end. It was almost ten. She didn't want to keep Cyndra up any later, but she needed a few minutes to be near the water, as if to draw strength from the still and peaceful inky blackness. Madison glanced up at the full moon and wondered what it would be like to be up there looking down. Maybe from that vantage point, their lives would be an insignificant afterthought in the universe. A blip in time. But from here, in the midst of day-to-day living, everything was magnified. Every emotion. Every worry. Every memory of the loss of someone she'd held so dear.

And Gabrielle... what if this were a mere indicator of what was to come? What if it was God in His infinite wisdom warning Madison to pull away now before it was too late? She closed her eyes and choked back a sob. *I'm so tired.* Attempting to compose herself before she returned inside, she took one last deep breath of the night air and started back.

Gabrielle sat in the shadows and watched Madison make her way up the stairs to her deck and into the house. Noticing the slumping of Madison's shoulders, Gabrielle struggled not to go to her. To sit beside Madison and hold her hand. Even if Madison wouldn't talk, simply touching her would've been a comfort to Gabrielle. Instead, she'd fisted her hands until her nails dug into her palms to keep from going down to the dock. Wherever Madison had gone in her solitude, she was the only one who could find her way back.

Gabrielle went into the house. She poured a glass of wine from the bottle on the dining room table she'd opened earlier. Carrying the glass into the living room, she sat down on the couch and tucked her legs under her. Before taking a drink, she rolled the glass between her fingers and stared at the liquid that captured the light from the table lamp. She couldn't help but think her emotions mirrored those of the swirling wine.

With every sip, memories of Madison flooded her mind. The way Madison touched her as they made love. The way she looked at her as if there was no one else in the world. How treasured and safe Gabrielle felt when being held by her.

Sighing, she set the empty glass on the table. Exhaustion poured off her shoulders in waves. The day had taken its toll. After checking to make sure the house was secure, she made her way to her bedroom and stripped down. Settling between the sheets, she tried to empty her mind of all thoughts of Madison. But as she closed her eyes, the image greeting her was Madison's golden brown gaze staring down at her as they made love.

Chapter 26

In the next two weeks, Gabrielle shared awkward dinners with Madison and Mo, but she and Madison were never alone. It was obvious Madison was using Mo as a buffer. Frustrated beyond measure, Gabrielle had no clue how to break through Madison's defenses. She'd thought about seeking out Cyndra for advice, but she decided it was inappropriate. Maybe she herself was just as stubborn with showing her feelings.

One morning, as she was fixing a light lunch in her kitchen, her cell phone rang. She picked up the phone from the counter. Although vaguely familiar, she didn't recognize the New York number. She only knew it wasn't Eva calling.

"Hello?"

"Hello, Gabrielle."

"Dirk?" She hadn't heard from her agent in months. He'd called to check on her after her surgery and on occasion afterward during her recovery. Eventually, those calls dwindled down to nothing.

"How are you?"

"I'm well." She thought about that simple statement and the power behind those words. She truly *was* well. If only Madison could see it, too...

"Listen, I know this might seem out of the blue." He cleared his throat. Gabrielle realized he was nervous, which was uncharacteristic for the demanding, sometimes overbearing, agent. "I've been contacted by *Glam & Fashion*. They're planning a spread on cancer survivors. They have a couple of actresses lined up, but they really want to focus on you. You were one of the most sought-after models and will be again," he hastily added. "They want to show how beauty also lies within and to detail your treatment and recovery, anything you'd be inclined to share. Not only do I think this is a great way to shine the light on cancer survivors, I also think it would jumpstart you back into work. That is, if you're ready to get back out there."

Gabrielle had to bite her tongue. Although Dirk Wesley was at times kind and caring, mostly his duty was to see her on as many magazine covers as possible. She walked over to the back window that looked out over the cove and watched the water gently lap against the shore. She scanned the area for any sight of their friend, but Free had been AWOL for the past three weeks. She didn't think it mere coincidence that his absence began with Madison's withdrawal.

Madison. To feel so strongly in love with someone, to speak the three simple words and have them returned to you, all of that paled in comparison to the emptiness she now felt. Suddenly, the mood to get away and flee the tension of her present situation coursed through her body like an electric current.

Dirk apparently took her silence as her reluctance to take the work. "Gabrielle, I really think—"

"Yes."

"Excuse me?"

"Yes, Dirk. I'll take the job. Where do I need to be and when?"

* * *

"So how are you and Gabrielle? You haven't talked about her much lately." Cyndra looked at Madison over her glass of iced tea. They were seated at one of their favorite restaurants. Cyndra had threatened to tie Madison up and toss her in her backseat if she didn't come out. Madison squirmed under her sister's penetrating stare. She had always been perceptive.

"We're okay." Madison had tried to put some enthusiasm behind her words, but from the look on Cyndra's face, she had failed miserably.

"Oh, no, Maddie, you're not pulling away again, are you?"

A flash of anger riled up inside Madison. She swallowed it down before replying. "I don't know what you're talking about."

Cyndra sat back in the booth across from her. She set her glass down and folded her arms across her chest.

Madison raised a hand. "Don't. Please don't lecture me about this."

Cyndra relaxed her posture and reached across the table to take Madison's hand. "What happened, sweetie?"

Madison fought back the sudden urge to burst into tears. "I got scared," she said in a choked voice. She grabbed her ice water and took a big drink.

"About the cancer? But you said she's okay and all the tests came back clear." Madison wiped the sweat from her glass. Cyndra stilled her hand. "Maddie?"

"Yes, the tests came back fine. But it brought back old stuff for me, and I haven't been able to get past it."

"Don't tell me you broke up with her."

"No, we didn't break up, although to her, I'm sure it feels like we have. I've been so distant these past few weeks. She's come over for dinner, but we've not been, well, you know…"

"I understand. I mean I understand you're struggling with your fears, but that's when you talk it out with the one you love." Cyndra held her gaze. "You *do* love her, right?"

"Very much." Cyndra was ready to say more, but Madison spoke before she had a chance to. "It's not so simple. I worry the cancer can come back. I worry about how much Mo has gotten attached to her. I worry about sitting on the side of Mo's bed and holding her as I explain to her that yet one more woman we've loved was taken from us too soon."

"That's a lot of worry and conjecture on your part. If you do love her as much as you say you do, you *have* to fight your way through to the other side." Cyndra dipped her head to get Madison to look at her. "Because there *is* the other side. You can't always be waiting for the worst, Madison. It could happen to any of us. It's called life."

Madison let Cyndra's words sink in. It wasn't like she didn't know the logic of what she was saying was true. The trick was getting her heart to believe it, too.

* * *

Mo fought her on going to bed. Occasionally, Mo was cranky about her eight o'clock bedtime, and this was one of those nights. Finally, she settled down.

Madison sat in her recliner and attempted to shut down her racing thoughts. Cyndra's advice from earlier was still rolling around in her brain. A soft knock on the door shook her from her reverie. She dropped down the leg rest, approached the door, and opened it. She almost stumbled backwards to have the object of her turmoil standing there.

Gabrielle, dressed in a pair of cut-off sweatpants and a baggy T-shirt, gave her a tentative smile. "Can I come in? I know it's late, but I noticed your lights were still on."

Madison hated that Gabrielle was hesitant to come over and that

Madison was the source of her hesitancy. In answer, she stepped aside for Gabrielle to enter. "Would you like something to drink?"

"No, thank you."

Madison sat down on the couch and motioned for Gabrielle to join her. Gabrielle fidgeted, and Madison immediately picked up on Gabrielle's nervousness. Suddenly feeling uneasy, she awaited the reason for Gabrielle's visit.

The speech Gabrielle had prepared died on her lips when she came face-to-face with Madison. She took a deep breath and plunged ahead.

"I have a modeling opportunity. *Glam & Fashion* contacted my agent about doing a spread on cancer survivors, but they want to feature me."

Madison sank back in the cushion. "When do you go?"

"I leave by the end of the week for New York."

Sadness shimmered in Madison's eyes. Then, just as quickly, she shut down her expression. "That's great, Gabrielle," she said quietly. "I'm happy for you."

Gabrielle hesitated before continuing. "I'll be there for a while. My agent has some other shoots set up for me. He'd been waiting until I completely healed. He hadn't been sure about my desire to come back to New York."

Gabrielle watched the emotions play across Madison's face. She was staring down at her hands in her lap, clasped so tightly that her knuckles had whitened. *Tell me not to go, baby. Tell me to stay. Or at least ask me how long. How long before we're together again.* She waited for Madison to say something—anything—but Madison wouldn't meet her gaze. Gabrielle finally spoke into the silence.

"I don't know yet how long I'll be there."

Madison raised her head. "You'll be back?"

Gabrielle took the plunge to be the braver of the two and address the tension between them. "I guess that depends." Her gaze never wavered.

"Depends…"

"Oh, Madison. You're making me work for this, and it shouldn't be this way. It shouldn't be me." She sighed. "It depends on *you*. You're the one who's withdrawn. Tell me I'm wrong."

"No." Madison's voice was hushed. "No, you're not wrong." She clenched her hands into fists. "I know it's me."

Gabrielle decided to wait her out this time.

"I know it's me," Madison repeated as she slumped her shoulders.

"Do you still love me?"

Madison's light brown eyes swirled with pain. "God, yes."

Gabrielle's heart had skipped a beat and settled back into rhythm with Madison's confirmation. She rose to her feet. Madison quickly stood to join her.

"Do you still love me?" Madison choked out.

The desperate sound of Madison's voice cut into Gabrielle's heart. She caressed Madison's cheek. "Yes, I love you, but you have to be the one to decide what you want." Brushing a stray lock of hair off Madison's forehead, she said, "Until you're ready to work through your fears, we can't be together. I won't have fear and doubt as our constant companions, especially in our bed. There has to be no questioning of our love or where we're going."

Madison was about to speak, but Gabrielle touched her fingertips to her mouth. "You know I'm right."

Gabrielle leaned forward and captured Madison's lips with a soft kiss that grew into something more. Before it became too passionate, she pulled away. She caressed Madison's cheek once more and turned to leave, fighting the strong urge to rush back into Madison's arms. She shut the front door behind her and stood there for a moment to steady her shaky legs until she could walk home without stumbling.

Madison stared at the door as if to will it to open and see Gabrielle rushing through. She sank to the couch and held her head in her hands. Everything Gabrielle had said was true. But that didn't mean it hadn't cut her to the core to see Gabrielle walk out the door. Despite her assurances that she still loved Madison, Madison couldn't help but think she was letting something precious slip through her fingers.

Chapter 27

"*What?*"

Madison braced herself against the counter with her back to Cyndra. She'd pulled two beers out of the refrigerator and probably should've waited until Cyndra had at least downed half a bottle before she broke the news.

"She left for New York Friday."

"Madison Kay Lorraine, bring those beers over here and sit down."

She carried the two Samuel Adamses to the island and pushed one bottle to Cyndra who sat on a stool across from her. She remained standing and raised the bottle to her lips. Maybe she should've had a couple of drinks before Cyndra came over.

"Go back and tell me what the hell happened," Cyndra said.

Madison gulped some more beer.

"And guzzling your beer isn't going to help."

Madison set the bottle down, none too gently, on the counter. "Gabrielle came over Tuesday night. She told me she had an offer for a photo shoot for *Glam & Fashion* magazine—a feature spread. She also has offers for more shoots."

"Did she say when she'd be back?"

"No."

"You didn't ask?" Cyndra's voice kept rising, and it was already at a pitch that dogs from three miles away would whine about. Madison was glad Mo wasn't home to hear this. Beverly had picked her up earlier for a "girl's night out." Beverly had questioned her with raised eyebrows, but Madison wasn't ready to get into it with her. Now, not surprisingly, she was hearing it from her sister.

"No, I didn't ask her."

"Jesus, Maddie. Why not?"

"Mainly because she told me it was up to me to work through this fear, and we wouldn't make it if I wasn't able to."

"Gee, that sounds familiar."

Madison squinted at Cyndra. "Sarcasm has never been one of your finer attributes."

"How's this for sarcasm. You know the saying, 'If you love something, let it go...'" She made a circular motion with her finger for Madison to finish.

"'If it comes back to you it's yours. If it doesn't, it was never meant to be.' That one?"

"Yeah, well, it's bullshit!"

Madison jerked back at the vehemence of Cyndra's words. "I'm thirty-four. I think I have it figured out by now, Cyn!" she shouted back. "I'm not completely clueless." She held up her hand before Cyndra disputed the statement. "It may appear that way, but I'm not." She finished off her beer, rinsed it out in the sink, and dropped it in the recycle bin. When she returned to the island, Cyndra had calmed down.

"All right. I'm sorry I'm jumping your case so much, but Gabrielle is so special. I can see it, Bev can see it, and Mo absolutely adores her. Hell, even the dolphin knows you two should be together."

"Funny you should mention Free. He's not been around since we returned from the oncologist appointment."

Cyndra furrowed her brow. "Don't you think that's odd? I mean I was sort of joking about him believing you should be together. But I honestly think he does. He shows up right before Gabrielle moves into the house next door. He practically pushes you two together, swims with you all. It's like it's his quest or something." She shook her head. "God. I'm losing it. I know dolphins are smart, but this one's like some sort of Dalai Lama of the Deep."

Madison laughed. "Dalai Lama of the Deep?"

"You know what I mean." Cyndra stared at Madison for a long time. "Sis, promise me you won't let Gabrielle slip away. You are so happy with her." She softened her tone even more. "You've not looked at another woman like that since Callie."

Madison tried to speak around the tightness in her throat. "I know." She rubbed her thumb back and forth on the granite counter and raised her head to meet Cyndra's gaze. "I need to get past this feeling of being scared shitless of losing her to cancer."

Cyndra reached over and gave her hand a gentle squeeze. "Just don't wait too long."

* * *

Gabrielle approached the baggage claim at LaGuardia. She craned her neck to search for her limo driver and spotted a tall, dark-haired man holding up a sign with her name on it. She smiled when she saw who was standing next to him. She'd called Eva and told her she was flying back to New York, but she hadn't expected her to show up at the airport. She waved and walked over to them.

"Hi," Gabrielle said as she leaned in to kiss Eva on the cheek. "I never thought you'd show up here. I would've called you after I got settled in the apartment." She caught the driver's attention. "I'm Gabrielle Valenci. I only have one bag."

As they approached the baggage claim, Eva put her arm around Gabrielle's waist. "I didn't want to wait until then. I called the service you always use and asked the driver to swing by my apartment to pick me up. I know there's more to this than you coming back to the city to work. You need to fill me in."

"I will," Gabrielle told her as she pointed out her bag to the driver. "Let's wait until we're in the car."

They followed the driver to a dark Lincoln sedan parked with the lineup of other limos and cabs. They settled into the backseat as he put the bag in the trunk. He slid into the driver's seat, tapped his electronic tablet, and glanced up at Gabrielle's reflection in the rearview mirror. "The Intrigue Lofts in Tribeca?" he asked her.

"Yes."

He checked his side mirror and pulled into the traffic leading out of the airport.

"So?" Eva entwined her fingers with Gabrielle's and lightly shook her hand.

"So... I came back for the work, but you're right. I'm taking some time away from Madison."

"Why? You seemed so happy with her."

Gabrielle laughed without humor. "Oh, I was. I am. But she had a meltdown when there was a chance my cancer had returned."

"Wait. What are you talking about?"

Gabrielle winced. She hadn't contacted Eva when she'd had the scare. "A few weeks ago, my CA-125 came back high. I had to go in for another CT scan."

Eva gripped her hand tighter. "Please tell me—"

"Everything's fine, Eva. I'm sorry I didn't call. I was so scared and so out of it, I didn't know if I was coming or going. But everything's fine." She patted Eva's arm with her other hand. "It was a false reading on the CA-125. It can happen, I guess. Unfortunately, it happened to me."

"And Madison freaked out?"

"You can say that. She completely shut down. It brought back so many bad memories of Callie, her late wife."

"She has to know this is different because you're okay."

Gabrielle stared out the window and watched the scenery fly by as they approached the bridge into Manhattan. "I think deep down she knows it's different. But she has to get past the fear before we can be together again." She turned to Eva. "I can't have her looking at me like she did, like I was going to leave her and die just like Callie. She has to accept there are no guarantees in life for any of us."

"But for her, the fact you both had the same cancer brings it all back."

"Right." Gabrielle heard the frustration in her voice. It was more than frustration, though. *Her* very real fear was Madison wouldn't be able to move past this.

"Hey," Eva said softly. "You're not giving up on her, are you?"

"No, I'm not."

They became quiet for a while until Eva spoke again.

"Tell me about this shoot you're doing…"

* * *

"Your chin a little to the left, Gabrielle," Raul said. She complied with the photographer's wishes.

"Now, a little up… a little more… there. Perfect!" The camera erupted with a series of shutter clicks. "Lilly, could you fix her hair on the right side." One of the assistants, a diminutive, whirling dervish, rushed over and brushed Gabrielle's hair back. It was such a simple gesture, but it was of immense importance to Gabrielle. Only a couple of months ago, there would be nothing to brush. Her hair, although still short, had reached the point where she could style it. Much to her delight, her dark, wavy tresses had grown back as thick curls.

Gabrielle at first had balked at wearing a bikini for the last segment of the shoot. They'd set up a faux beach background. Raul had positioned her so that she was leaning back on her hands, facing the camera, with one leg straightened in front of her, and the other drawn up to her chest. Of course, it wasn't the first time that she'd been photographed in a bikini, but it was her first time since her surgery. After listening to Mel Tripoli, the woman writing the piece for *Glam & Fashion*, she understood Mel's purpose for the bikini shot. Yes, Gabrielle had cancer, but her scar was a permanent reminder she was a survivor. As Mel had told her, there was nothing more beautiful than that.

After Gabrielle spent a few more minutes of lying in different positions for Raul, he said, "Okay. That'll do it."

She stood up and stretched to work out the kinks from remaining in various poses for lengthy periods. Lilly handed her a terry-cloth robe. Gabrielle was thankful. Although it was a "beach" theme for this particular segment of the shoot, there was a chill in the air-conditioned studio. Mel approached her.

"Fantastic," the tall, thin blonde said. "Exactly what I was hoping for. You have such a healthy glow about you. I don't know if you're aware of how it just radiates from your face."

She'd heard this from others, but it still pleased her. In her business, Gabrielle received many compliments, but this one pleased her more than if someone had told her she was one of the most beautiful women in the world—and she'd made the list more than once in her career. Mel's words resonated within her because it was an acknowledgement of how far she'd come since she'd first started the treatments.

Once they entered the dressing room, Mel sat down in one of the canvas folding chairs while Gabrielle stepped behind a screen to slip out of the bikini and pull on her jeans and loose-fitting, cotton shirt. As Gabrielle was finishing with buttoning her shirt, Mel said, "We should get the rest of the photos ready to go this week for the layout and in time to meet our deadline. *Good Morning America* has requested an interview the day the magazine hits the stands and online. I haven't called your agent yet. Would you mind doing the interview?"

Gabrielle came around the screen. "No, not at all."

"I'll call Dirk this afternoon." She pulled out her Blackberry, tapped on the keys, and kept pace with Gabrielle as they pushed through the door to the outside.

A limo was waiting curbside to take Gabrielle back to her apartment. The driver had stepped around the car to hold the door open for her. Mel stopped Gabrielle with a touch to her arm before she had a chance to slide into the backseat.

"Would you like to talk about the spread over lunch? Maybe go over what Tina Ramirez might ask in the interview on *Good Morning*

America?"

Gabrielle was about to answer that she and Dirk would discuss the interview when she noticed a spark of something else in Mel's expression—something more than a professional interest. She quickly squashed this before it had a chance to go any further. She flipped her wrist to glance at the time.

"Actually, I have a lunch date with a friend. From what you've shown me of the galley proofs, I'm quite happy with the photo spread. I think we've covered anything that might come up in the interview on the show, don't you? " She redirected the conversation to maintain a professional distance between them.

Disappointment flitted across Mel's face until her expression became blank. "Yes, you're absolutely right." She held out her hand to Gabrielle. "It was pleasure working with you. Thank you for your honesty about your cancer." When Gabrielle took Mel's hand, Mel held on a little longer than necessary. "Perhaps another time for lunch or dinner?"

Gabrielle gently tugged her hand out of Mel's grip. "It'll be hectic for me the next several weeks, but I appreciate the invitation. I've enjoyed working with you, too, Mel. Thank you for your kindness and sensitivity during the interview." She glanced at her watch again. "I better get going." She slid into the backseat. "Take care."

"You, too, Gabrielle."

Gabrielle breathed out a sigh of relief when the driver shut the door and they pulled into traffic. The conversation with Mel caused a stab of loneliness to hit her chest. Reaching into her purse, she lifted out her phone. She stared at it and thought about calling Madison. She jerked when it rang, her heart stuttering when she saw Madison's number on the display. She gathered herself before answering.

"Hello."

"Is this Gabrielle?"

"Montanna? How did you—"

"Please don't be mad at my mom. She doesn't know I'm calling. She's inside painting. I got her phone when she wasn't watching." Mo's words tumbled quickly out of her mouth. "I'm on the deck. I wanted to talk to you and found your number in her phone."

"Honey, you can call me anytime," Gabrielle said in an effort to ease Mo's anxiety.

"When are you coming home?"

Gabrielle drew in a breath. *Home.* Where was her home now?

"I'm working, Mo. I don't know when I'll be back to Islamorada."

"But you *are* coming back, aren't you? Because Mom has been so sad since you left."

"She has?"

"Uh-huh. And her paintings have gotten kind of weird."

"What do you mean?"

"They're dark with a lot of storms and rain. I asked her about the sunshine. She told me she was painting what she felt. She misses you. She didn't tell me that, but I know she does. I miss you."

"I miss you, too, sweetheart, but your mom and I, we... well, we..."

Mo sighed loudly into Gabrielle's ear. "I know, I know. I'm a kid, and it's adult stuff." Before Gabrielle could speak, Mo went on. "I can tell when mom's sad, though, and she is. She doesn't smile. She picks at her food like I do when we have broccoli. And you know the pictures Grandma took of us at Christmas?"

"Yes."

"Mom stares at the one of you opening your gift... a lot."

Despite Mo's obvious frustration, Gabrielle was hopeful for the first time since she'd arrived in New York. "Listen, Mo. Your mom and I love you very, very much."

"You still love my mom, too, don't you?" Mo sounded like she was about to cry.

"Yes," Gabrielle answered gently.

"She still loves you, so come home soon, okay?" This time, Mo's voice cracked.

Gabrielle answered the only way she knew how. "I'll be there when I can." Like Mo said, this was "adult stuff" that couldn't be explained to a kid despite how much Gabrielle loved Mo.

"Okay. Love you," Mo choked out and hung up before Gabrielle could respond.

Gabrielle gripped the phone so tightly she was surprised it didn't splinter into a hundred little plastic pieces. She leaned her head back on the leather seat and tried her best to clear her mind. Instead, a little blonde-haired girl danced across her vision like the whims of a dolphin.

Chapter 28

Madison stepped back, tilted her head, and stared at her latest painting. "God, I suck." She tossed her paintbrush down in disgust. She'd painted another scene of a boat—this one a yacht—in the throes of a raging storm. Even though she was very aware of why her painting had become dark, she couldn't stop it if she tried. She glanced over at the other paintings she'd completed when Gabrielle was still with them. It was some of her best work, and she wasn't one to compliment her painting. She left that to others. But she'd felt so good about the paintings she'd finished while Gabrielle had been in her daily life, she'd called her agent and told Noah she was ready for a show. She had to hold the phone away from her ear while he screeched in joy.

The phone rang. That might be him now, she thought, calling back with information on where and when the show would be. She never offered advice on such matters, always going along with Noah's wishes.

"How does New York sound two weeks from Saturday?"

Madison moved some paper aside on the couch and sat down. "New York, huh?"

"Where'd you think we'd hold your first show in years? Lubbock?"

"I don't know. I've heard Texas is nice this time of the year," Madison said as she ran her fingers through her hair.

"Honey, you've obviously never been to Texas in the summer. Now, be serious. What's wrong with New York?"

"Nothing, Noah. It's fine." But already, Madison's mind was racing with "what ifs" about seeing Gabrielle again. Even though they'd left it with Madison needing to be the one to make contact, there was a small part of her—well, more than a small part—who'd hoped Gabrielle would've phoned. She realized how ridiculous she was being. She'd missed what Noah was saying. "I'm sorry, what?"

"Chanelle is very excited to be the gallery that brings Madison

Lorraine out of retirement. I thought the poor woman was going to hyperventilate while she was talking to me on the phone. Please tell me you're not backing out of this."

"No, I'm not backing out of it. What time is the show?"

"Eight. How many new pieces did you say you had ready?"

Madison glanced over at the paintings stacked against the wall. She'd put them in two groups—good and what she considered crap, or her "I'm trying to paint away my sadness" work.

"Fifteen, I believe. Ten four by eights and five or six smaller pieces."

"Okay, good. That'll work for the gallery without overcrowding it."

Madison pictured the roomy gallery owned by Chanelle Burgundy, which surely to God couldn't be her real name. "I think you're right."

"Darling, you get some rest. You sound horrible."

"Gee, thanks." Madison clicked off the phone. She stood up and walked over to the still-wet canvas. "Maybe I can use these in class as an example of how *not* to paint," she muttered.

She left the studio and headed to the kitchen to grab a bottle of water. Twisting off the cap, she walked over to the island where she'd left the magazine. She stared down at the *Glam & Fashion* cover, not even trying to hold back her longing. Yes, Gabrielle was beautiful, but here she was breathtaking. She was wearing a gauzy, light-blue, long-sleeved blouse over a white chemise, along with a pair of white capris. The colors brought out her dark, Mediterranean skin tone, darkened even further from her months in Florida. Her left hand settled on her hip, her right held her curls off her face. Her hair had gotten so much fuller since Madison had seen her last. Madison's hand twitched as she thought how it'd feel to sink her fingers into Gabrielle's thick tresses.

But what Madison noticed more than anything was how clear Gabrielle's eyes were. They sparkled with joy, her lips drawn up in a half smile. She looked so happy… and healthy. When she spotted the magazine at the checkout stand in the grocery store, she gasped— loud enough for the woman behind her in line to ask if she was okay. Slightly embarrassed, Madison assured her she was. She picked up the magazine and placed it on top of her box of Wheaties.

That had been last week. She'd resisted the urge to open the copy of *Glam & Fashion*. It hadn't prevented Mo from opening it up, however, and exclaiming how pretty Gabrielle was, adding with more than a hint of annoyance, "Aren't you even going to look at it?" This was followed shortly by a phone call from Cyndra, uttering the same words when she'd found out Madison hadn't bothered to open the magazine.

She didn't know what she was afraid of. Perhaps it was finding out as happy as Gabrielle appeared on the cover, she was that much happier in her personal life. Maybe she'd even met someone, although Madison doubted the interview would've gotten that personal. Still, Madison wasn't thinking too rationally these days.

"Jesus, Madison, grow up." She snatched the magazine off the counter before she had a chance to talk herself out of it. She carried the copy, along with her bottle of water, to the deck outside and flopped down on the lounge chair. With one last brief moment of hesitation, she opened to the photo spread and interview. She flipped through the photos of other celebrity cancer survivors until she came to Gabrielle's photo spread and accompanying article. Before she read the article, she feasted on every single photo in the layout. Her favorite shot was of Gabrielle in swimwear and not because she was wearing a bikini. It was the expression painted on her face. One of a victorious survivor.

Madison began reading and quickly became engrossed in Gabrielle's frank answers about her cancer and treatment, including the dark hours of crippling fatigue from the chemotherapy and of total humility at losing control of her bowels when she was finishing up on radiation treatment. But above all, she talked about her quest to live life to its fullest, especially after the recent scare with the elevated CA-125.

"Obviously, I'm not alone as a survivor of this disease, and believe me, I know how blessed I am that they caught my cancer in the first stage. Like my sister and brother survivors, we're realistic and accept there are no guarantees in life. No promises that everything will be rosy. We can choose to be victims and prisoners to our fear that the cancer will return. Or we can embrace and be thankful for each day, each moment, and each breath we take. We choose life."

A drop of moisture hit the page. Madison glanced up, at first thinking one of Florida's unpredictable rainstorms had snuck up on her. The sky was clear. Another drop hit the page. It was then she realized she was crying. As she read the article, the chains of fear shackling her heart fell away. She read the paragraph again, caught up in the passion of Gabrielle's words.

A series of splashes in the cove drew her attention away from the print. She stood up, already anticipating the reappearance of their friend. She wasn't disappointed. He sped along in the middle of the cove, his dorsal fin almost a blur. She hurried down the deck stairs and rushed toward the dock, almost afraid Free was a mirage. But suddenly, he leapt high into the air, turned his body, and smacked hard against the surface.

Madison reached the end of the dock. She squinted against the glare on the water and cursed under her breath. She'd left her sunglasses on the dining room table. Feeling a little foolish, she cupped her mouth with her hands and shouted, "Free!" *Like he knows his name...*

Free popped his head out of the water right in front of her and startled Madison. She flailed her arms to regain her balance and prevent an unwanted bath.

"Hey, my friend. Where've you been these past few weeks?" Madison wouldn't have been shocked if the dolphin answered her back in English to explain his absence.

He bobbed his nose and chattered at her. It sounded very much like a drill sergeant dressing down a raw recruit.

"Yeah, sorry about that. I kind of screwed things up, didn't I?"

He nodded, dipped his nose in the water, and flipped it at Madison.

"You didn't have to splash me," Madison said as she wiped the water off her face. "I said I was sorry."

Free dove into the water and stayed submerged. She thought maybe he left her, but he surfaced in the middle of the cove in a perfect arc high above the water until he dove back in. He appeared in front of her. Instead of "talking" to her, he captured her with his intense gaze.

Unable to move, Madison stared into the swirling, hypnotic blue of the one eye turned toward her. She no longer saw Free. A video of Madison and Montanna's last Christmas with Callie played in her mind. She saw how drained Callie appeared, her head bald, her skin an unhealthy pallor. Madison hadn't watched the DVD since the first time she'd watched it with Mo. Mo had insisted on seeing it a few months after Callie died. Madison had balked at first, but Mo became almost hysterical in her insistence at seeing the video again. Madison gave in, slid the DVD into the player, and prepared for the onslaught of sadness at seeing her dead wife in her last days on earth.

Madison shook her head to clear it of the images. "You want me to watch that video?" Free didn't bob his head this time, but continued to stare at her. "I can't, Free. Please. I'm just now healing. I'm afraid if I—"

Free dove into the water and stayed submerged until he leapt at the opening to the Gulf.

"Wait!" she shouted. "Don't go!"

The cove was quiet, the water tranquil. The silence was almost deafening as it pressed down on her. Could she go through the pain of watching the DVD again? Would she be right back where she was before she read the magazine article? Somehow, she knew she didn't have a choice. She straightened her shoulders, and with a confidence she didn't quite feel, she made her way to the house.

Madison watched the DVD with detachment, as if she were watching a movie starring actors in the roles of her and her family. It was the only way she thought she could make it through to the end. As she'd feared, seeing Callie so broken by the sickness that had eaten away at her vitality and left her as fragile as a dandelion gone to seed had reminded Madison of Callie's death sentence. Why would Free ask her to watch this? Had she only imagined his insistence and instead set out to sabotage her chance at happiness?

The video reached the end. She'd never gotten this far with Mo because she'd shut it off when Mo had begun crying. Madison was so emotionally exhausted she couldn't bring herself to lift the remote and point it at the DVD player. Just as she gathered the energy to reach for the remote, the image on the screen wavered. Mo was no longer opening presents while Madison and Callie watched. That scene had been replaced by one of Callie propped up in her hospital bed. They'd gotten the bed when Callie had started hospice care. Madison had to tell herself to breathe, afraid if she did, Callie would disappear from the screen.

"Thank you, Renee. I'll call you when I'm through," Callie told the hospice nurse who was out of camera view.

Madison heard the bedroom door shut. Callie turned back to the camera. The same pain Madison felt when seeing Callie's health deteriorate day by day returned to Madison in an instant. So much so that she gripped her stomach as if someone had sucker punched her. Callie was bald. She'd never wanted to wear a wig or the colorful scarves so many cancer patients wore. With dark circles shadowing her eyes, her cheeks sunken, and her skin sallow, Callie was a woman literally on her deathbed.

Callie focused on the camera in front of the bed. "Hi, sweetheart. I was finally able to get you to take a break and go with Montanna to the beach. It gave me the time to tape this. I don't know when you'll watch it. It could be while I'm still here, but I believe I know you well enough that it will be too hard to watch what will surely be my last Christmas." Madison's lips trembled when she saw Callie's eyes well with tears. Callie's hand shook as she reached for a glass of water and took a sip. "Sorry. I guess I can't always be brave. I try for your sake and for Mo's, but it's so hard when I think about the two of you and the pain you'll face when I'm gone." She swiped at her cheeks.

"I still remember the phone call from the surgeon when I was first diagnosed. I remember where I was standing. We'd been waiting for the call all day. You'd stepped outside on the deck for just a moment when it came through. You rushed in, and your face fell when you heard me ask about scheduling the oncologist appointment. We both knew what it meant. I hung up, and you held me. From that day on, our world was no longer the same. Then when Dr. Gillespie gave us the results of the pathology report in the hospital..." Callie's voice faltered. "Well, we both know how that turned out. These two years have been so, so hard for you. Don't think I ever took for granted what all you did for me. How you cared for me. How you loved me each and every day we were together."

It didn't escape Madison that Callie was talking in the past tense.

"And now I'm leaving you and Mo much, much sooner than either of us had thought when we first met. We thought we'd have years together and joked about sitting in our rocking chairs in our eighties and sipping iced tea while watching our grandkids play. Because even then, we knew we wanted children." Callie offered a sad smile. "But it wasn't meant to be." She reached again for the water and took another drink before continuing. "This is where I want you to listen carefully to me, Madison. I've not been able to talk to you about this. You've stopped me each time I've tried. I understood your reasons, but it needs to be said." She laughed lightly. "You can't interrupt me now, so here I go...

"Sweetheart, when I'm gone, you need to open your heart up to love again. You're young. You deserve to be happy. Please don't close yourself off to the possibility of meeting someone, a woman who will love you as you should be loved. Who will love Mo as if she were her own daughter. She's out there, honey, this woman who will capture your heart. But only if you let go of your sadness and move on in your life." Callie's voice wavered again. "I think that's all I can manage to say. I feel this damn fatigue setting in."

Callie had always put on a brave face for everyone, so the undercurrent of anger in her voice was surprising. It reminded Madison that Callie was human.

"There you have it, honey. Live your life to the fullest. Embrace each day. Raise your face to the sun and, yes, remember me. Remember how much I loved you and Mo. But take all the love you've stored away in your heart and share it with that special woman. You deserve it." Callie winced and called for Renee. Madison heard the door open and the sound of Renee nearing the microphone. Then the camera shut off.

Madison stared at the screen through blurred vision, as if she could magically conjure up Callie to reappear. It wasn't what Callie had told her in the video. Cyndra, Bev, Angie, and Meryl had all tried to tell her the same thing. But this was Callie. *Her* Callie telling her what she'd tried to tell Madison while she was still alive. Madison smiled through her tears when she remembered Callie's gentle laugh because this time Madison couldn't stop her.

Free had given her a gift, one she never would've seen without his insistence. She no longer questioned why he appeared in the cove months ago. Cyndra was right. It was Free's quest that she and Gabrielle be together. Madison wouldn't let him down, but more importantly, she wouldn't let Callie down.

It was time to make that call.

She grabbed her phone off the coffee table and, without another thought, dialed Gabrielle's number. She waited anxiously for her to answer, but after five rings, it clicked over to voicemail.

"Gabrielle, hi. It's uh… me. Madison. I have a show in New York in two weeks." She relayed the details. "If you can make it, I'd love to see you. I want to talk to you, but I don't want to do it over the phone. Anyway… I hope to see you there."

Madison hung up and offered up a plea to Callie. "Make this happen, baby. Please."

Chapter 29

"Quit fidgeting."

"That's at least the tenth time you've said that," Madison told Cyndra. She'd insisted on accompanying Madison to New York. She said it was because she wanted to see Madison's return to the art world. But Madison had a strong suspicion it was to make sure she didn't back out on seeing Gabrielle.

"If you'd stop fidgeting, I wouldn't have to repeat myself, now would I? And quit messing with your collar. Here. Let me." Cyndra took over Madison's nervous fumbling and straightened out Madison's starched white shirt. She'd helped Madison choose the clothes she was wearing. Madison had to admit Cyndra had a knack for making her look nice. She was dressed in a midnight blue jacket, tuxedo pants, and the white shirt with French cuffs.

"At least I look good even if they think my paintings suck."

"Lower your voice," Cyndra hissed. She glanced around at the patrons with a fixed smile before grabbing Madison by the arm and yanking her into an alcove. "Would you at least *try* to relax? Your paintings do not suck, Madison. It's the best work you've ever done, and I'm damn proud of you." She cocked her head. "Why don't you be honest and tell me why you're really so bent out of shape?" Madison didn't miss Cyndra's smug expression.

"All right. Yes. I'm scared Gabrielle won't show."

"I have no doubt she'll be here. She told you she would, didn't she?"

Madison thought back to the short voicemail Gabrielle had left earlier in the previous week. She told Madison she'd make it to the gallery. She'd also said Madison didn't need to call back. Gabrielle was finishing up a photo shoot and wouldn't be available. Madison had replayed the message at least ten times, listening to the inflection in Gabrielle's voice and attempting to judge if Gabrielle was still open to renewing their relationship. She'd finally given up and chided herself for thinking a voicemail would answer all of her questions.

"Aha." Cyndra was looking over Madison's shoulder.

"Aha, what?" Madison turned to see what caught Cyndra's eye and sucked in a breath. Gabrielle was talking with Noah as she gestured at a painting. Madison's heart was pounding so hard, she thought it would leap out of her chest. Gabrielle was dazzling in a short, black, cocktail dress, cut low enough in the front to show much more than a hint of cleavage. Madison's gaze dropped down to her black stiletto heels and traveled back up her long, shapely legs. Her mouth went dry. She grabbed a flute of champagne from the tray of a passing waiter. She was about to walk over to Gabrielle when Noah moved and revealed who was standing on the other side of him. Eva. Madison stayed rooted in place.

"Stop," Cyndra said in a lowered voice.

"Stop what?"

"Stop thinking what you're thinking."

"What if she's with Eva now, Cyndra? Maybe that's the real reason she didn't want me to call her back. Maybe—"

Cyndra cut her off. "Hey, isn't that painting over there called *Conclusions*?" She pointed across the room.

"What are you talking about?"

"Your painting. That one. Didn't you entitle it *Conclusions*? Why don't you jump on over there?"

"What the fu... Oh, cute, Cyn. Real cute." Madison scowled at her.

"Because that's exactly what you're doing—jumping to conclusions. Good God, Madison. Get a grip, march your ass over there, and tell the woman you love how happy you are to see her."

Madison was about to argue some more when her eyes met Gabrielle's from across the room. Gabrielle's mouth pulled into a slow smile. Madison found herself grinning back like an idiot.

"See?" Cyndra gave her a none-too-gentle shove. "Now, go."

Madison walked toward Gabrielle. As patrons moved in front of her and obstructed her line of sight, she craned her neck to seek out Gabrielle again.

"What has you smiling so much?" Eva asked. She turned in the direction Gabrielle was facing. "Ah."

Gabrielle watched while Madison maneuvered around the crowd. She didn't think Madison would ever reach them. But then there she was, standing in front of her and looking so much better than she remembered.

"Hey," Madison said in a shy voice.

"Hey."

They stared at each other for a long time, both seemingly content at being in the other's presence.

"I think I'll go talk to a friend of mine I spotted when we walked in," Eva said. "Madison, wonderful show." She gave Gabrielle's arm a pat before walking away.

Gabrielle studied Madison's face. Gone were the dark circles under her eyes and the tight lines around her mouth.

"You look great, Madison."

Madison blushed, which made Gabrielle smile even more.

"So do you." Madison's eyes darted around the room and settled back on Gabrielle. "Listen, would you mind if we went somewhere afterward? Like I told you on the phone, I want to talk."

"Of course. We can go to my apartment." Gabrielle searched the crowd for Eva. "Hold on. I'll be right back." Gabrielle moved toward Eva who was chatting up a pretty blonde in the corner. "Eva, Madison will be coming to the apartment with me. Do you have a ride to get to your place?"

Eva raked her eyes over the blonde. "I believe I do."

The blonde hooked her arm in Eva's. "I'll take care of her."

"Thanks." As Gabrielle headed back over to Madison, she almost laughed out loud. She'd just thanked a woman who would soon be in bed with her ex. *And I don't care.*

"All set. Eva has a ride with someone else. We can go in my limo."

"As soon as the show winds down, we can head out." Madison peered over Gabrielle's shoulder. "Noah's waving for me." She leaned in to place a soft kiss on her lips. "Hopefully, this won't last too much longer."

Gabrielle ran her fingers over her tingling lips. She took in every inch of Madison's body as she walked away. As far as she was concerned, the show couldn't end fast enough.

* * *

Madison settled in the backseat of the limo next to Gabrielle. Their thighs pressed together, and Madison's muscles twitched with the contact. Sitting this close to Gabrielle for the first time in weeks made Madison's insides quiver and her palms sweat. She wondered if Gabrielle picked up on her nervousness. Then Gabrielle slid her hand over Madison's that rested on her knee. Madison turned her palm face up to lace their fingers together. In that one move, a calm returned to Madison's life that had been missing since Gabrielle had left.

"Your show was a smash, Madison. I'm so proud of you."

"Thank you, but you didn't need to buy a painting."

Gabrielle tilted Madison's face toward hers. "Here we go again. It seems we're always having this conversation about needs and wants. No, I didn't *need* to. I *wanted* to. There's a difference. I love your work and that painting in particular."

The painting Gabrielle had purchased was a smaller piece entitled *Joy*. She'd captured Free in mid-jump, his body contorted in the shape of a *U*.

"I asked Noah to deliver it tomorrow, and I know right where I'll hang it."

Madison waited for her to finish her thought, afraid that if she were hanging the painting in the apartment, it would mean she didn't plan to return to Florida anytime soon. But Gabrielle didn't offer more.

The limo pulled up to the curb in front of Gabrielle's high-rise apartment building. They continued holding hands as they rode the elevator up to Gabrielle's floor. Madison released Gabrielle's hand only when she rummaged for her key and opened the door.

"Would you like something to drink?" Gabrielle flipped on the lights.

"Water, if you don't mind."

"Not at all. Make yourself at home." Gabrielle walked toward the kitchen area of the open concept apartment.

"Wow." Madison approached the floor-to-ceiling windows overlooking Manhattan. "This is an amazing view."

"It should be, considering how much this place is costing me." Gabrielle returned with two opened bottles of Perrier. She handed one to Madison who sat down on the leather couch. Gabrielle kicked off her shoes and settled in next to her.

They drank in silence until Madison set her bottle on the glass coffee table. She turned sideways to face Gabrielle who set her bottle next to Madison's. Madison took hold of Gabrielle's hands.

"I love you, Gabrielle. I wanted to tell you that first before I share with you the rest of what I have to say." She felt Gabrielle's hands tense. "No, it's all good," Madison said.

"Oh, thank God," Gabrielle whispered.

"I want to thank you for your patience this past month in

allowing me to work through everything."

"And did you... work through everything?"

"Yes. I read the article in *Glam & Fashion* and what you had to say about your cancer and recovery. I thought here you are, ready to embrace life, even after facing death. You're taking each day at a time, but you're moving forward. I've been frozen in the past. I couldn't see beyond the cancer and your recent scare. The only thing I could see was that you might be taken away from me, just like Callie." Madison stopped to compose herself. Gabrielle squeezed her hands in silent encouragement. "But with the help of a friend of ours..." She smiled. "I think you know who."

"Free?"

"Who else? With his help, I realized I had to go on living and not simply exist from day to day."

"What did he do?"

"I would say, 'You're not going to believe this,' but since you know him, I don't need to."

Gabrielle smiled. "No, you don't."

"He showed up in the cove last week for the first time since you'd left for New York. When he looked at me, images from Callie's last Christmas flashed through my mind. He wanted me to watch the video. I didn't think I could. But he kept staring at me and then he left. I went back inside the house and pulled the DVD out that we'd recorded from the camcorder tape. It was hard, but I sat through the video. I was thinking, 'Is Free trying to torture me?' because I was back to where I was before I read the magazine article. Then Callie appeared on the screen from her hospital bed."

"Oh, honey."

"I wasn't ready for that obviously. She told me I never listened to her every time she tried to talk about me moving on and finding love again after she passed. She actually laughed and said I couldn't stop her now." Madison smiled again, remembering Callie's light laughter. "Here was my wife telling me to allow myself to love another woman after she was gone. This time, I listened." She reached out and touched Gabrielle's cheek. "I do love you, and if you'll still have me, I want to spend the rest of my life with you." She held her breath as she awaited Gabrielle's answer.

Gabrielle took Madison's hand, gently kissed her palm, and held it to her cheek again. "I love you, too, Madison. And I'm crazy about your daughter."

"I'm glad because we're a package deal." She brushed her thumb over Gabrielle's lips. "Will you come back home to Florida with me?"

Gabrielle kissed the tip of Madison's thumb. "Oh, yes, sweetheart. I'll come home."

"What about the apartment?"

Gabrielle rose to her feet and pulled Madison up with her. "I don't want to talk about the apartment, but I'd love to show you my bedroom."

Madison allowed Gabrielle to lead her down the hall. She watched the subtle, graceful movement of Gabrielle's hips with each step she took. Gabrielle turned on the lights in the bedroom but muted them with the dimmer. It was then that Madison saw the painting on the wall.

Gabrielle stood beside her as Madison recalled each brush stroke, each teardrop she shed as she painted this piece. It truly had been *A Good Day*. Callie was between chemo treatments at the time and had regained her strength, even though they both knew it was only temporary. It was enough to share a day out on the beach with their daughter, and it was a time for Madison to forget for just one day that her wife was dying.

Gabrielle put her arm around Madison's waist and rested her head on her shoulder. "I think I told you before that it's my favorite. Because you poured your soul into this one, didn't you?"

"Yes," Madison whispered. As she stared at Callie's image in the painting, she swore Callie turned her head toward her, tipped up the brim of her hat, and greeted her with that blazing smile of hers. Madison blinked, and the canvas was back to how she painted it.

"What is it, sweetheart? I'm sorry if it's made you uncomfortable."

In answer, Madison said, "Turn around. Please." When Gabrielle complied, Madison slowly unzipped her dress. "I've imagined doing this since I saw you across the gallery." She shivered when she saw Gabrielle wasn't wearing a bra and her panties were black lace bikinis. As she slipped the dress off Gabrielle's shoulders, she kissed her neck and brushed her fingertips down Gabrielle's back until she reached her panties. She hooked both thumbs in the delicate waistband and pushed them down until Gabrielle stepped out of them. Gabrielle was about to turn around, but Madison stopped her. "No. Stay."

Madison began stripping off her clothes.

"God, Madison. Let me see you."

"No, baby." When Madison had finished undressing, she pressed against Gabrielle and reached around to cup Gabrielle's breasts. As she rubbed Gabrielle's nipples until they hardened, Gabrielle leaned back into her and whimpered.

"You're making me so wet," Gabrielle whispered.

Madison pressed her lips against Gabrielle's neck. She kept tweaking Gabrielle's left nipple while she lowered her right hand to Gabrielle's quivering abdomen and past the soft hair below. She slid her fingers into Gabrielle's slick folds.

Gabrielle gasped. "I can't stand any longer. Please."

With that plea, Madison pushed her toward the bed. Gabrielle twisted around and grasped Madison's hair in both her hands, yanking her forward. She crushed her mouth to Madison's, and they battled for dominance with their tongues. Gabrielle moved backward onto the mattress and pulled Madison on top of her.

"God, how I've missed you," Gabrielle said with a gasp as Madison took her right nipple into her mouth. "Love me, Madison. Love me."

Madison licked her way over to Gabrielle's left nipple and sucked it as she palmed and kneaded Gabrielle's right breast.

"Feels so good. Everything you do. It feels... oh God!" Gabrielle cried out when Madison shifted down the bed and settled between her legs.

Madison slid her tongue through Gabrielle's wetness. She wanted to take her time. Wanted to savor every moment, but Gabrielle's hips squirmed in her hands.

"Please, please," Gabrielle begged, her voice barely above a whisper.

Madison gave in to her wishes and took Gabrielle's clit between her lips. She gently sucked as she entered Gabrielle with two fingers. Gabrielle's hips bucked up off the bed, but Madison held firm, pushing in and out while she worked Gabrielle with her mouth. She felt the beginning of Gabrielle's orgasm as her walls fluttered against her fingers. She pulled her mouth away and moved up the bed to use her thigh to thrust against her hand.

"That's it, Gabi. I'll catch you when you fall."

Gabrielle cried out Madison's name as she climaxed. Madison kept pushing into her until Gabrielle weakly tugged on her hand. Madison stayed still inside until Gabrielle's throbs dwindled down and stopped. Then she slowly pulled out and shifted up in the bed until she was next to Gabrielle and holding her. She felt Gabrielle's shoulders shake.

"Hey." Madison raised her hand to Gabrielle's cheek and found it wet. Her stomach lurched with fear. "I didn't hurt you, did I?"

Gabrielle let out a soft laugh. "No, sweetheart. You definitely didn't hurt me." She leaned on her elbow and brushed Madison's hair back. "What you did was love me."

Madison lifted her hand and wiped Gabrielle's cheek with her thumb. "I do love you."

"And I love you." Gabrielle pressed her hand between Madison's legs. "Let me show you just how much."

They made love deep into the night before falling asleep in each other's arms in the early morning hours. Madison woke up once, pressed into Gabrielle's back with her arm draped around her waist. She nuzzled the nape of Gabrielle's neck. Gabrielle stirred in her sleep, reached down, and tugged Madison's arm tighter against her waist. Madison drifted off to sleep again with a smile on her lips.

Chapter 30

They'd been back from New York for a couple of weeks. Gabrielle had moved her clothes and personal items over to Madison's house. She'd started the process of shipping what she wanted from her apartment to Islamorada, including the painting above her bed. Along with *A Good Day*, Gabrielle carried over Madison's other paintings to Madison's house. Madison took down the prints on one wall in her living room so Gabrielle could create what she dubbed "The Madison Lorraine Wall." But Madison only agreed to the arrangement if Gabrielle would also hang her own first painting there. Gabrielle at first balked, but when Mo chimed in about how much she loved it, she finally gave in.

Gabrielle couldn't part with the family vacation home her father had loved so much, though. Cyndra had been looking for a home to rent in the area but had been unsuccessful in finding anything in her price range. Without any encouragement from Madison, Gabrielle offered to rent her house to Cyndra at a rate much lower than what other homes and condos were renting for in the area.

Madison was out on the deck prepping the grill for their cookout when she caught movement in the water below. She grinned. She'd hoped Free would show up and see that Gabrielle had returned.

Gabrielle opened the sliding glass door and carried out a plate of raw hamburger patties. "Do you want me to set these down over here?" she asked as she held the plate above the picnic table.

"Our friend's back." Madison tipped her head toward the cove.

Gabrielle quickly set the plate down and rushed to the railing. "Yes, he is!" She hurried to the opened sliding glass doors and poked her head in the house. "Free's here, Mo!"

Madison laughed when she heard Mo scream, "Free!" Mo ran out of the house and down the stairs. Madison and Gabrielle followed close behind. They made it to the end of the dock just as Free surfaced in front of them. He stayed stationary and quiet with none of his usual chattering.

"Hi, Free," Mo said.

He nodded at her. Then he dipped below the water and swam toward the ladder. He circled the area, not making any move to swim away from them and perform his usual acrobatics in the middle of the cove.

"I think he wants us to come to the ladder," Gabrielle said.

Mo shucked off her sandals and started to climb down. Before she even got to the second rung, Madison grabbed her arm.

"Let me go down first so I can hold your waist, Mo." Madison slipped out of her sandals. They were all wearing tank tops and shorts in the thick summer heat. Madison stepped down the rungs until she was in the water up to her waist. "Okay, come down now and be careful."

Mo edged her way down until she was between Madison's arms. Madison wrapped her arm around Mo's waist and held onto the ladder with the other hand. Mo leaned over the water as Free swam close enough so Mo could pet his back. She stroked him a few times. Then he dipped below the water to again circle the area.

"Okay. You go on up, Mo." Madison waited until Mo had stepped back up on the dock. Free swam closer and blew air out of his blowhole, stilling his body in the water. She leaned forward and petted him. "You're saying goodbye, aren't you, boy," she said in a low voice so only he could hear her. She stroked his back a few more times before climbing back up the ladder. "Your turn, Gabrielle."

Like Madison, Gabrielle stepped down until she was up to her waist in the water. Free let her pet him for a few minutes. Then he submerged his nose and playfully flipped water on her. She laughed. It wasn't a complete dousing. Just enough to dampen the front of her tank top. Eventually, he dove below and swam out of view. Gabrielle climbed the ladder to join Madison and Mo.

Free jumped high, flopped on his side, and splashed hard against the surface. The ripples spread out from the middle of the cove until they reached the dock and faded away. Madison thought maybe he'd left them for open waters until he reappeared in front of them.

Free turned his head to look first at Mo. His blue eye then shifted over to Gabrielle before it settled on Madison. She remembered how she'd felt the first time he'd locked gazes with her. Like he was challenging her. At the time, she didn't know why. Now, she realized it was a challenge to move on in her life, and by moving on, to find love again.

"Thank you, Free," Madison said around the lump in her throat. "You can go now."

Mo jerked her head toward her. "What do you mean? No! I don't want him to leave."

Madison moved in front of Mo and placed her hands on her shoulders. "Do you remember what I told you when he first came here? That he was free? Then you named him Free. It's time to let him go, honey."

Montanna started crying. Madison closed her eyes to her own tears and pulled Mo into her arms.

"But won't he be lonely?"

"I don't think so." Madison wiped the moisture off Mo's cheeks. "He has his friends and family."

"Really?"

"Absolutely. He won't be alone."

"Okay."

Madison looked at Gabrielle who was swiping at her own tears. "I know, I know," Gabrielle said with a sniff. "He has to leave."

Madison stood between Gabrielle and Mo. She slipped one arm around Gabrielle's waist and draped her other arm around Mo's shoulders.

Free gave them one last look and dove below. He popped out of the water at the far end of the cove and rode his tail backward until he reached the other side. Then he submerged before leaping high and curling his body just as Madison had captured him in Gabrielle's painting. When he dove into the water this time, he didn't reappear until he jumped once more and swam toward the Gulf. Madison had thought they'd seen the last of him, but he jumped again as he reached open water. Only this time, other dolphins joined him in his acrobatic leaps.

"Mom, you're right! There are his friends."

Madison stroked Mo's hair. "I told you he wouldn't be alone."

Gabrielle leaned into Madison and whispered, "Free really won't be back, will he?"

Madison answered from a place once dark and without hope until Free entered their world, filling that place again with light and love... she answered from her heart.

"No, baby. His work here is done."

Chris Paynter with wife, Phyllis Manfredi

About the Author

Chris Paynter is the author of six novels, including the *Playing for First* baseball series. Her *Survived by Her Longtime Companion* was a 2013 Lambda Literary Award Finalist and winner of the 2013 Ann Bannon Popular Choice Award. Her short stories have appeared in two anthologies: Regal Crest's *Women in Uniform: Medics and Soldiers and Cops, Oh My!* (2010) and Cleis Press's *Love Burns Bright: A Lifetime of Lesbian Romance* (2013). After earning a Bachelor's degree in journalism, Chris worked as a general assignment reporter and sportswriter until accepting her current position as the editorial specialist to a law journal. A sports junkie, you can find her screaming at the TV during a Colts game or living vicariously through her Cincinnati Reds. She resides in Indianapolis with her wife, Phyllis, and their beagle, Buddy the Wonder Dog, also fondly known as "He who must be obeyed." When not writing or editing books, Chris loves to get lost in a good romance.

Visit her website: www.ckpaynter.com

Email her at: ckpaynter@ckpaynter.com

Visit her Author Page on Facebook:

www.facebook.com/ChrisPaynterAuthor

Find her on Twitter: @ckpaynter

If you enjoyed this book, be sure to look out for Chris Paynter's next book in the *Playing for First* series,

FROM THIRD TO HOME

Available Spring 2015, only from

COMPANION PUBLICATIONS

www.ckpaynter.com

"Ohmygodohmygodohmygod! I can't believe I'm standing here getting Amy Perry's autograph again. It's like it's not real, you know? Me and my best friend decided at the last minute to make a trip to Arizona for spring training because we just love you."

Amy waited for the petite blonde with the butch haircut to take a breath, but she wasn't finished yet.

"We, like, traveled to Phoenix two years ago to watch you play in the Arizona Fall League when the Reds signed you with the Mesa Solar Sox. Does that help your memory? We had you autograph the back of our T-shirts."

"No, I'm sor—"

"You're sure you don't remember us?" The woman, probably in her early twenties, motioned to her dark-haired companion. "What about when you were in Double-A Chattanooga? We drove down to a couple of your games. But we're not, like, stalkers or anything. Right, Cheryl?"

"Naw. We just like watching you play."

"Then last year, when you came up in May from Triple-A Indianapolis and were with the Reds for the season, how many games did we go to?" the blonde asked her friend.

"Wow. I dunno. Twenty?"

"That's a lot of games—" Amy started to say.

The blonde cut Amy off again. "We wanted to go to a lot more, but we have to work. Sorry about that loss at the end of the season. I bet that double play you hit into at the end of the tiebreaker game against the Rockies still haunts you, huh?"

By now, Amy wanted to smack the woman over the head. She'd had nightmares in the off-season over the play that had ended the Reds year and any chance to make the playoffs.

"Amy! Amy! Can I have your autograph?" a little boy yelled, hopping up and down beside the blonde.

Thank God, Amy thought. A reprieve. "I need to sign some more," she told the two women. "Thanks for your support." She managed to give them a tight smile before signing the boy's baseball and two more that kids thrust in her face. She took the program someone offered to her, not looking up.

"Could you make that out to 'the love of my life'?"

Amy's mouth pulled into a grin before gazing into the dark eyes of her partner, Stacy.

"I don't think so, ma'am. I'm taken," Amy said.

Stacy's face lit up and her dimples became more pronounced. She leaned over the railing and kissed Amy on the cheek. "Right answer, babe. Frankie asked if we wanted to go out to dinner tonight with her and Lisa. Is that okay?"

Amy spotted the reporters who hung out on the field at the Reds Goodyear, Arizona, spring training camp. Lisa Collins was talking with another sportswriter, Sarah Swift. Amy caught Lisa's eye and waved. Lisa waved back.

"Sure. The guys told me about a great Mexican restaurant. Would that be okay?" she asked Stacy.

"Sounds good."

"Come on, Perry, quit talking to your wife. We've got work to do."

Amy turned at the sound of her friend, third baseman Nick Sanders's voice.

"Keep your uni on, Sandy. I'm almost done."

"The next voice you hear won't be mine, you know," he said as he trotted off into the outfield to begin loosening up.

Max Murphy, her manager, stared at her from the infield grass with his hands on his hips. He jabbed a thumb toward the outfield.

"Guess I'd better let you go, huh?" Stacy said with a teasing lilt. "Don't want to get your boss upset on your first day in camp."

Amy squeezed her hand and jogged out to right field to join Nick in loosening up.

CPSIA information can be obtained at www.ICGtesting.com
Printed in the USA
LVOW06s0342050115

421509LV00001B/37/P